FOLLOW ME HOME

Other Fiction
by William Hoffman

FOLLOW ME HOME

Short stories by
WILLIAM HOFFMAN

LOUISIANA STATE UNIVERSITY PRESS   Baton Rouge
1994

*For
Nancy & Rick Fritz
Wm Hoffman
9/8/94*

03 02 01 00 99 98 97 96 95 94   5 4 3 2 1
Designer: *Glynnis Phoebe*
Typeface: *Galliard*
Typesetter: *G&S Typesetters, Inc.*
Printer and binder: *Thomson-Shore, Inc.*

Library of Congress Cataloging-in-Publication Data
Hoffman, William, 1925–
   Follow me home : short stories / by William Hoffman.
      p.   cm.
   Contents: Dancer — Tides — Coals — Sweet armageddon — Boy up a
tree — Abide with me — Night sport — Points — Business trip —
The secret garden — Expiation.
   ISBN 0-8071-1835-4 (alk. paper)
   I. Title.
PS3558.034638F65   1994
813'.54—dc20   94-13251
                                                CIP

The stories in this book were published previously as follows: "Dancer," "Abide with Me," "Points,"
and "Expiation," in the *Sewanee Review*; "Tides," in the *Southern Review*; "Coals," "Boy up a Tree,"
and "Business Trip," in *Shenandoah*; "Sweet Armageddon" and "The Secret Garden," in the *Virginia
Quarterly Review*; "Night Sport," in the *Atlantic*.

Publication of this book has been supported by a grant from the National Endowment for the Arts
in Washington, D.C., a federal agency.

FOR
Kaye and Henry

Contents

FOLLOW ME HOME

DANCER

Lizzie heard the music again while fixing dinner on a raw January evening—a slice of fried country ham, navy beans, two beaten biscuits, peanut butter, and a can of Budweiser. Wind blew hard from the northeast, causing the bottle-blue steel-shingle roof of the house to rise and clatter. The chimneys fluted, and her fire drew strongly, flames licking the damper of her Franklin stove.

The whole house creaked in the wind, as did Lizzie's bones most of the time—wind or not—as had Waif's. She didn't like to think about Waif. Instead she stood from the kitchen table, washed her few dishes at the sink, dried and fitted them into the wooden cabinet above the counter.

The wind subsided and returned. It rattled windows. She walked quickly through the darkened front hall to make certain rugs remained rolled tight against the bottoms of entranceways. The house had been a family place for five generations—sun-kilned brick, two chimneys at each end, rooms measuring twenty-five by twenty-five feet on both floors, a veranda across the front, a screened porch off the kitchen.

Radiators shut down to conserve furnace oil, those rooms were closed now. Life, she thought, had pretty well bled from them, leaving darkness and cold emptiness, at least during winter. She'd been living in the big kitchen, had set up her cot near the stove and carried a reading lamp and chair from the parlor. The kitchen stayed warm enough, and she'd also hooked up her radio and TV.

She kept things neat even in the unused rooms. She'd been born neat. On days when the pale Virginia sun gave out a little warmth, she dusted tables, windowsills, the photographs in their frames. She did it for herself, not others. Few village people came visiting now. She didn't want them if they believed they were helping by being sorry. She wouldn't answer the door for the Reverend Jericho Potter, the Methodist preacher, whose face was more mournful than an egg-sucking, chicken-stealing hound kicked in his south end slinking north.

As she was fixing to listen to the news, she heard the music a second time that night. Despite the wind, the music sounded just beyond the door. All right, she said, and danced a little, a fox-trot, her arms held to Oliver. When the music faltered, she hesitated, but then it came loudly. Wearing her long johns, sweat shirt, and bedroom slippers, she walked out the back door.

Cold hit her like a club. She'd once fallen from a canoe into the Staunton River while duck hunting, broken through a skim of ice, and that's how she felt now. Had the music stopped, she would've hurried inside, but the tempo changed to a teasing waltz, and she'd always loved waltzes. She stepped from the porch to the frozen grass. Sleet and snow lashed her. She shriveled and bent, yet felt gladness at the center of herself. She lifted shaky arms.

She danced over brittle grass that glowed in light from the kitchen window. Limbs of the red oak were the wind's harp. A few last leaves clacked. No tree held them through winter like an oak. A gust roared across the pasture. The barn roof slammed and clanged. "The Blue Danube" was stronger.

She twirled into wind, trembled, stumbled, yet held her head high. Her carriage had always been erect. Her mother taught her good posture was the foundation of grace. Lizzie's teeth clicked, and she made *Uh*-uh-uh noises to the three-quarter beat. She threw back her head and laughed flirtatiously, the peal half strangled before it passed over her fluttering lips.

Because her eyes were closed, she failed to see the car's splayed headlights. Wind music masked the engine. Her eyelids reddened, and she believed it the color wheel down at the Tantilla Gardens. When she blinked, the light shot directly at her. She paused and staggered. Had it not been for the oak, she might have fallen. Worst of all, the music ceased.

"But what do you think you were doing?" Mary Belle wailed—Lizzie's sister, who'd driven over from Richmond to see about her. Mary Belle was seven years younger, a wiry redheaded woman who'd married a man that owned a chain of automotive supply stores in Virginia, Tennessee, and the Carolinas.

Nearly hysterical, Mary Belle helped Lizzie into the house, undressed her before the fire, and bathed her by dipping a washrag in a pan of warm water. She made Lizzie lie on the cot and heaped blankets upon her. She heated a can of tomato soup and spooned it to Lizzie's mouth. The violent shaking ebbed.

"I'm calling a doctor," Sister said.

"You can't, I had the phone taken out," Lizzie said. "What I need's a drink."

"You don't give a person suffering hypothermia liquor!" Mary Belle said. "Will you please tell me what in the world you thought you were doing!"

"Part of my fitness program," Lizzie lied. Warmth hurt as it filled her body.

"Your what?" Mary Belle asked. She'd become stylish in the city—a sable coat, jewelry, leather boots that had black fur around the tops, slanty lavender glasses. She drove a small red Caddy, her husband Chester a big one. She'd also been to Europe and the Holy Land. "You were running around in the yard near naked and almost froze to death, and that's part of your fitness program?"

"The Finns do it," Lizzie said, her teeth hardly tapping now. She was able to take the cup of soup in her fingers. "Roll skinny in the snow to toughen themselves. Live longer than anybody."

"You can't really believe you are improving your health by jumping about in the sleet and snow wearing bedroom slippers. If you do, you shouldn't be allowed to walk around alone. Which is what I been hearing anyhow."

"Hearing?" Lizzie asked, pushing up straight from the cot and setting her feet on the hot metal hearth of the stove. She wiggled her toes. The nails wanted trimming. Grew faster than hoof.

"Nothing," Mary Belle said, draping blankets around Lizzie. Sister kept sniffing, peeking, and poking into things not her business. Maybe somebody had written or called about the dance at the Moose lodge. Lizzie had dressed up, but the ticket taker at the door told her couples only. She got in because he—a pulpwood cutter named Dwight Vassour—finally held his own arm to her. She was last to leave, and that prompted talk.

The dancing had been grand, though, she wearing her rose chiffon gown and silver heels. The gown smelled of mothballs, yet still fit after all these years. She'd always taken pride in her figure. Not a scrap of fat on her to this day.

"Woman my age just can't let herself go," she said, which was exactly what she'd been doing most of late.

"I'm not leaving you here all winter acting like you run out of track!" Mary Belle said. "You coming back with me."

"Not either."

"You are if I have to call the rescue squad to tie you down on a stretcher. I'll pack you a bag."

"You're one tough bitch, Sister, and I'll drive myself."

"No you won't!"

"Listen, you expect me to leave this house without a fight, you let me drive. Otherwise I'm pitching you out and locking the door."

They'd been after Lizzie's license. She hadn't had an accident, but there was the close call with the school bus. She'd not been speeding, merely looking ahead and seeing instead of the road the golden floor of the Tantilla Gardens ballroom, where she and Oliver used to dance weekends. Suddenly the yellowness of the school bus flared before her whole windshield. She'd managed to brake and swerve, but the experience had been hair-raising, the frightened children staring at her from the windows. The bus driver reported her to the superintendent of schools, and he phoned the sheriff.

"Miss Lizzie, why'n't you just turn in your license," he said. Most of his face lay around his jowls and chin, and it was questionable whether his Sam Browne belt held his pants up or him together. "They not going to renew your insurance anyhow."

"My policy's got eight months to run, and I'm holding onto my ticket till you come after me with a gun," she said.

"Never do that, " he said, embarrassed because she'd helped his daddy, Edgar, build a new tobacco barn when a fire burned down the old one. She'd loaned Edgar enough to get his family through the winter too.

"I'm driving right behind you," Mary Belle said. "Don't try any of your craziness."

But then Mary Belle decided to stay the night. She hated to but wasn't about to journey out into the sleet. Lizzie switched on the TV to keep from hearing her yap. Mary Belle opened cabinets, picked up cans, peered into boxes.

"Not enough food around here to feed even a tight tick," she complained. She intended to snooze on the blue divan Lizzie had brought from the parlor. Mary Belle kicked off her boots and settled her fur coat over herself. She wouldn't use Lizzie's toothbrush but had rubbed baking soda against her gums at the kitchen sink.

"You'll need somebody to feed Waif," she said.

"No I won't," Lizzie said. Waif had been her barn dog. "He's gone."

"Gone where?" Mary Belle asked, sitting upright. She was a dark blocky shape against the stove's glow.

"The place they serve T-bone steaks all day long and he can chase cats between meals. Dog heaven."

"What's happened to him?" Mary Belle asked. One thing about Sister—she did have feelings for animals. Long ago she'd kept a pet crow named Blacky who when she hollered would fly from the pines and light on her shoulder.

"Shot him," Lizzie said.

"Did what?" Mary Belle cried and flung the sable coat aside.

"He was suffering, dragging that hind leg, arthritis I guess, or something worse. Fed him half a pound of raw hamburger, and while he was curled up sleeping, I knelt, rubbed his neck, and shot him through the ear with Oliver's .22 pistol. He never opened his eyes, just jerked, shuddered, and gave up the ghost. About the hardest thing I ever did in my life."

Mary Belle got teary, the firelight glinting in her wetness. She wasn't a bad woman, just bossy, and had never heard much music, though in her big house she owned a baby grand she couldn't play.

"I'm real sorry," she said. "You had to bury him and all?"

"In the family plot," Lizzie said. "Built him a little coffin out of an old orange crate."

"That was nice," Sister said. She lay back on the divan and again drew her fur coat over herself. "Won't Midnight have to be grained?"

"Midnight's left too," Lizzie said.

"What you telling me!" Mary Belle hollered, this time rolling off the divan to her feet.

"Been gone since November. Remember how he liked that hackberry tree beside the hay barn? Ambled over, lay down, and snorted. It was a warm afternoon, Indian summer, and I thought he was just lazing around, but when I whistled and he didn't raise his head, I walked over, and he'd left."

Midnight—a foal dropped on the place thirty-three years earlier, at a time when Lizzie rode almost daily, saddled up early on hot summer days and cantered to the Staunton River to let her horses drink. Sometimes she skinny-dipped. Fishermen running a trotline across the river hooted at her one June morning, and she just waved and swam in the cooling water till ready to climb out and pull on her Levi's.

"Buried him too," Lizzie said. "Sunrise Funeral Home sent over their backhoe and dug his grave next to the family plot. I covered Midnight with a clean sheet before I let them drop in soil. I also set a stone over the spot."

"You might tell a body," Mary Belle said and sniffled.

She got settled a third time and cried herself to sleep. Bugs of firelight skittered on the ceiling. Sister had always been teary-eyed. Lizzie listened to wind working the roof. She heard faint music but held herself to the cot.

They locked up the house. Mary Belle in the small Caddy did follow Lizzie all the way to Richmond. Lizzie's car was a 1978 green Chevy, still in fair running order, yet not fit for the white gravel driveway of Sister's house any more than a junkyard mutt would be at a New York dog show. Chester, Mary Belle's husband, hurried out to help carry in Lizzie's suitcase.

"Day I can't tote my own, just plant me in the ground," she said.

Chester didn't insist. He was a big man but soft. Top of his head had more scalp than hair. He wore his Saturday loafing clothes—gray suede shoes, checkered wool slacks, and a black turtleneck sweater.

"I'd offer you a shooter, but she's cut me off," Chester whispered soon as Mary Belle was beyond hearing. "Tried hiding a bottle in the garage, but she sniffed it out. If you got to drink under the gun, might as well guzzle orange juice."

Chester was all right. Lizzie couldn't've found a better brother-in-law. He knew money, scented it like a bird dog winding. His automotive shops had expanded into hydraulic presses and driveshaft repairs. His trouble was he'd allowed Sister to kick him ass-over-end so often it'd become a habit. She kept the liquor locked in the sideboard. Chester acted like a visitor in his own house.

Sister put Lizzie in a guest room painted piggy pink. On walls hung silhouette pictures of southern belles and hat-doffing cavaliers. Cute. Though the house was large for the city, these rooms couldn't compare in size to the farm. Lizzie was accustomed to space and air. At Sister's she felt cornered, and the air blew from a machine through louvered panels.

Mary Belle wanted her to see a doctor, but Lizzie dug in. She didn't even catch cold from the dancing Sister had caught her at. The thing to do was get back to the farm first chance. Trouble was Mary Belle not only watched her, but also snatched the keys to the Chevy.

Lizzie didn't demand them. She bided time till Sister left for her bridge club on Thursday afternoon. Lizzie slipped into the master bedroom. It was baby blue with white flounces everywhere. She found her keys beside the jewelry box in a dressing-table drawer. Carrying her suitcase, she tiptoed downstairs so the maid, a white-haired uniformed black woman named Dorcus, wouldn't hear, then slipped out the front and around to the Chevy. As Lizzie started the engine and backed, Dorcus rushed waving from the kitchen.

Lizzie waved too and drove off so fast her tires hurled gravel. She sped through the city, hoping to break free before Dorcus got hold of Mary Belle or Chester. The police might put it on the radio. When at last she left buildings and houses behind, she relaxed, slowed, and breathed deeply of the warmth from the rattling heater.

She looked across a picked cornfield and saw a gaunt oak seeming in full foliage. She realized they weren't leaves but hundreds of blackbirds along the limb. Suddenly they flew and became quarter notes against power lines stretched across the pale winter sky. She heard the music, sweet and gliding, a slow dance.

She ran the Chevy off the road. It rocked down a bank, slammed into a drainage ditch, and tumbled over the field. She'd never installed seat belts and was tossed about inside. The car came to rest on its top. For a time she lay dazed and tangled across the steering column. She worked herself upright, cranked open a window, and crawled partway out. People were running toward her.

She was bloodied and skinned, her dress half tore off, but not bad hurt. Men of the emergency squad lifted her into an ambulance, which ran siren howling to the hospital. A young doctor laid gentle fingers on her before sending her by wheelchair to X-ray.

"You going to keep scaring us half to death!" Mary Belle sniffled, balling her handkerchief. "And how dare you go into my dressing-table drawers!"

The doctor made Lizzie stay a night in the hospital. The next afternoon Sister and Chester drove her to the house. When Mary Belle was talking to Dorcus in the kitchen, Chester sneaked a half-pint of vodka into the bedroom.

"Thought you might need a little sip of the old snakebite medicine," he said. Lizzie swallowed two long swigs, and Chester one. Then the bottle appeared so used up, they finished it off.

"I'll smuggle the empty to the office," he said. "Mary Belle checks the trash out back."

Chester wanted her to stay in bed, but Lizzie walked downstairs to the long dinner table under the Williamsburg chandelier. Sister wouldn't look at Lizzie directly and hadn't spoken a word since grace. Chester tried to take up slack by talking about an investment he was considering making in restoring old houses of Richmond's historic district. He'd receive a special tax break.

"All right, let's have it," Lizzie said finally to Mary Belle, who seemed to be taking ten minutes to chew each dainty bite of her chicken croquette.

"You could've killed yourself!" Mary Belle cried and threw up her arms as if awaiting the embrace of the Holy Ghost.

"Could've don't count when I'm sitting right here," Lizzie said.

"No thanks to you," Sister said.

"Thanks to whoever then," Lizzie said.

"I want you to see Dr. Dunaway," Sister said.

"I've already seen more doctors the last twenty-four hours than my five-year quota," Lizzie said.

"I insist!" Sister said and slapped the table so hard the silver jingled and water quivered in the crystal goblets.

"Who gave you the right to insist me?" Lizzie asked.

"I'm the last family you have, and I mean to help whether you want it or not."

To keep the peace Lizzie let Sister drive her to the clinic. Dr. Dunaway was tall, courtly, his black hair invaded by gray. Lizzie had seen pictures of him in the Richmond paper attending balls where men wore hunt colors on their collars and lapels. For a society doctor he didn't act snooty. His clinic had tropical fish and plants growing all over the waiting room. When the test results were collected, he stopped by the house and sat with Lizzie in what Sister called the music room because of the baby grand she couldn't play.

"Wish I had more like you," Dr. Dunaway said. "A few calcified joints, but no cataracts, glaucoma, or other visual or hearing impairments. Your heart's strong and regular, your blood pressure within a reasonable range, and you don't have diabetes or any illness detectable in blood or urine. Actually you're in better shape than many much younger women."

"What I told Sister," Lizzie said.

"There's one thing," Dr. Dunaway said, removing his glasses with fine clean white fingers. He looked solemn. "Mary Belle suspects you wrecked your car on purpose."

"Not a word of truth to it," Lizzie said.

"The police report states it was a single-car accident," the doctor said.

"I was listening to music," Lizzie said, thinking of the blackbirds lifting off the oak and becoming quarter notes against the power lines.

"Ah, lulled by the radio," Dr. Dunaway said.

No use attempting to explain how the music came and went, the sound nothing like violins or saxophones but chiefly a feeling, if you could mix into melody the smell of hay curing, the whisper of the river dragging under willow branches, the taste of a freshly picked tomato still warm from the sun, the sense of a good horse under you, the sight of a spiraling hawk in a fresh summer sky, the touch of a loving man.

"As we age, we tend to become single-minded," Dr. Dunaway said, standing by pushing his palms against knees of his tailored bluish gray suit. "Lately I've been leaving my hat places. My nurse calls around to find where. Now I concentrate on remembering. It might be best if you forsook driving altogether, but if you won't, try to give it your fullest concentration."

"Hope you're not charging Mary Belle and Chester for giving me advice like that," Lizzie said. "Be darn near highway robbery."

"Of course I'll stick it to them," Dr. Dunaway said and laughed. "Otherwise they might not believe I've helped you."

Sister had more money than mind anyhow. Let her waste Chester's pile if that settled her feathers. What worried Lizzie was how she could make it back to the farm, the home where she'd stayed even after marrying Oliver. He'd had to agree to move in before she'd march to the altar. Every day of his married working life he'd driven fifty miles and back to his job at Hill City Savings & Loan in Lynchburg.

He was a city-bred man who took to farming. She taught him how to split wood, sharpen a chain saw, and drive a tractor. Together they put in fencing—locust posts and chestnut rails trucked down from the mountains. They had a child, a boy named Jimmy John, who lived a life of health and happiness till the Christmas afternoon he slipped away to the pond. They found him under the ice, his face and hands pressed up against it as if peering through a frosted window. Dissolved in his pants pockets were candy canes off the tree. He lay buried beside his father.

Oliver wasn't able to plow a straight furrow but could dance like a god. Nobody ever called him handsome, yet he knew how to make a lady feel she floated on air. He taught her the fox-trot, the Big Apple, the Lindy hop, the Lambeth Walk, the conga. They two-stepped, waltzed, and jitterbugged across half the state. Before Jimmy John was born, they'd drive two or three hundred miles to hear Glenn Miller, Tommy Dorsey, and Woody Herman. They shagged barefooted in the Atlantic surf to the music of Glen Gray outside Virginia Beach's Casa Loma. They entered and won a ballroom contest at Tantilla Gardens. For a time she'd kept the silver-plated trophy polished, and it still rested on a corner of the parlor mantel.

After Jimmy John went under the ice, they stopped dancing awhile. Those had been terrible days. They could hardly find words to speak. In the house they might as well have been strangers who passed on a city street. Their pain flashed into argument, and they said too much. She slapped and clawed Oliver. He hit her. They were horrified, grabbed one another, and held on as they toppled about the kitchen weeping. When they began to heal, they whittled at the pain till they subdued it to a dark, ever-throbbing nub.

"You intend to keep me prisoner?" Lizzie asked Mary Belle. They watched TV before the fire in the wainscoted den.

"I'm not allowing you to go back to that drafty house and catch your death," Sister answered. She'd had a permanent, and her reddish hair fit tight around her head and shone like metal. She'd never been pretty but could've appeared attractive if only she'd eased up a little.

"I been staying warm through winters many a year," Lizzie said. The TV had blurred before her eyes.

"I know you been staying warm," Mary Belle said and sniffed. "You and the Finns."

"Now, ladies," Chester said, rousing from his La-Z-Boy recliner and resettling.

Lizzie had to get out of the house now and again even when wind whipped the boxwoods and ornamental grasses. Mary Belle didn't want to turn her loose a minute. Sister insisted on coming along. Lizzie walked fast and soon had Mary Belle—dolled up in her sable coat, gloves, and hat—puffing. Wind took care of that tight permanent.

"I know what you're trying," Mary Belle said. "You think if you wear me out, I'll let you go on alone and you can sneak off somewhere."

"I could get away anyhow," Lizzie said. "All I need do is call the police and ask them to make you let me go."

"Don't be too certain just what it is the police would make me do," Mary Belle said.

That sounded like a threat. Sister might be hinting about seeking a court order. Lawyers could cause Lizzie to look pretty bad living alone, drinking, shooting her dog, and flinging about in long johns during a winter storm.

She'd bide her time. Chester tried to help. He drove her to Virginia

Commonwealth University basketball games. He bought season tickets and loved hollering at officials. During the half they sneaked tips of the vodka bottle into their Dr. Pepper cups. She liked listening to the bands and watching light reflect off the golden horns. Chester would've been a blue ribbon winner if the proper kind of woman had got hold of him and left him his spine intact.

Another snowstorm, from the northeast, the flakes horizontal on the wind. TV announcers enjoyed talking about the record lows. Lizzie thought of the farm. Nothing left to bother her except the pipes—no animals, no stock, not a single Rhode Island Red or guinea, no life. She pictured her furniture, the four-poster that had belonged to her mother and father, nothing fashionable, heavy white oak ruggedly put together by a local craftsman in another century. She thought of the trophy atop the mantel and framed photographs on her chiffonnier and night table.

One was of Jimmy John holding a bass he'd caught, the lunker near as big as him. Another of Oliver wearing his tuxedo. He'd been city puny when he came to the farm, but chores had muscled and hardened his body. He sported a field tan at the S & L and by the third summer of their marriage could pitch hay bales into the barn as good as the young blacks hired to help. Nights he'd shower down and come to her smelling of soap and man.

After Jimmy John left them, they occasionally danced. They attended the Fall Ball at the Moose lodge, drove home at two in the morning, and she fried up eggs and link sausage. Oliver looked at her from the kitchen table as if he was hearing a strange noise and would speak. He tilted from his chair to the floor. They'd had drinks, and she knelt to him laughing. She tickled his ribs. When he didn't stir, fear gushed through her. She laid her ear to his lips. No breath. She tore open his shirt and pressed an ear over his heart. No beat. She pounded the heart and blew her breath into his mouth.

She grabbed the telephone to call the county ambulance. She just couldn't wait for the medics. She lifted Oliver, a man sixty pounds heavier than she, and carried him out the lane. The ambulance, siren shrilling, turned in just as she reached the road.

She never cried. There was hurt past crying. She watched them lower Oliver into the red soil beside Jimmy John, walked back to the house, and washed her face. She greeted people who brought casseroles, pies, loaves of bread. The next day she worked in her garden, picking tomatoes before the first frost and wrapping them in newspaper to last into the winter. Villagers waited for her to break, not understanding she wasn't even alive but like a piece of machinery that had been gassed up and let go.

She'd lived without music a number of years. The first time it returned she was sitting on the side porch snapping beans, and a thunderstorm blew in from the southwest. She watched darkness scythe the sunny tobacco plants, smelled the freshness of rain, and heard drops beat the coarse leaf. Wind swept over her, and for an instant she believed she must've left the radio on or some kid had his car stereo booming out on the highway.

The music lasted only a few seconds and stopped just as suddenly as it began. She hurried inside to bang down windows and looked out to see whether Midnight had reached his stall. She let Waif in the basement because though he was ordinarily a brave dog and would've fought to the death for her, thunder slunk him under the Chevy.

Well, the house would stand, and if the pipes froze, she'd have them replaced. Oliver had left enough insurance money to keep things up halfway. She saw to it plaster was mended, steps fixed, the roof patched. Repairing fences was beyond her now, yet it made no difference since she raised no livestock. She went halves on her tobacco with Lester Daniel, a neighbor down that road. She could still drive a tractor, though, and the men liked that.

As she lay on her bed at Mary Belle's, she yearned for spring. She'd never failed to put in a garden and would again this year: English peas, kale, beets, carrots, snaps, butter beans, tomatoes, okra, sweet corn, and melons. She'd taught Oliver to garden, and nothing had pleased her more than to see him working among the rows.

Sister invited people in to play cards, drink cocktails, and eat dinner. She unfailingly asked Lizzie to come down and join the party, but she never called her Lizzie in front of company, always Louise. Lizzie didn't care for cards or society and mostly stayed in her room. Chester would sneak her up a highball, and she had her own small TV and table radio. She studied the seed catalogs.

On the first warm day in March, she asked Mary Belle to let her go.

"Too early," Sister said, doing her nails purplish to match her glossy lipstick. "There's a pile of winter left."

A snow blew in that looked as if it would end the world. Flakes coated the trees, buds that had swollen, and the uncurling crocuses. Just as quickly the snow melted, leaving puddles, softening the ground, allowing grass to right itself. Birds nested and sang in the boxwoods. Still Mary Belle put her off.

Lizzie slipped out the door while Mary Belle was taking her afternoon nap. She had no money. Sister had got that from her too. Lizzie meant to reach Route 360 South and catch a ride. When she was half a block short of the ramp, Chester in his big Caddy caught up with her.

"You got to come back," he said. "She's having a fit and will call the authorities. I'm sorry, but if you don't get in the car, they'll chase after you."

She rode back with him to the house. Sister didn't fuss. She acted betrayed and hurt. Chester tried to pour oil on the waters.

"You can put in a garden," he said. "Plenty of yard. I'll get Henry to plow you up a little plot."

Henry was the black man who tended the yard.

"It's too shady," Lizzie said. "And the soil's acid. Besides Mary Belle don't want me messing up her flowers and box bushes."

"You can tear things up if you want," Mary Belle said, her expression long-suffering. "'Course by the time you pay for seed, fertilizer, and insect spray, you're better off buying vegetables at Winn-Dixie. Japanese beetles taking over the countryside. But go ahead if you so desire."

"I don't so desire," Lizzie said.

Because Dorcus didn't work Sundays and they didn't want to leave Lizzie alone, they took her to worship. It was a stone church with twin bell towers, fluted columns inside, stained-glass windows, and an organ that upreared at least fifty golden pipes. St. Luke's was nothing like Mount Olivet Presbyterian she attended at home—a small white frame building that had a red tin roof and a lopsided belfry pigeons and starlings nested in. Winters the men set a stove among bare pews of the nave, and each member brought two sticks of wood to lay on the fire— one for Sunday school, the second for preaching.

Summers the deacons left the windows open. There were no people wearing vestments, parading gold crosses, no kneeling and carrying on, no grand organ, just an upright piano and a plain-talking reverend who might pastor three or four churches. If you didn't care for the sermon, you could listen to the flies and dirt daubers buzzing, cattle lowing, the pulsating chirr of locusts in mossy elms, and the happy cries of children romping among headstones of the graveyard. At Christian Endeavor bats flew to the light, and the ladies hollered and covered their heads to protect their hair.

After the snow, spring sprung—doves calling, daffodils blooming, black women on street corners selling bouquets of fresh cut flowers wrapped in sheets of newspaper. Mockingbirds trilled a silver sound, and Lizzie smelled the earth renewing, the scent stronger even than the odors of barbecue smoke from neighborhood charcoal grills. Pollen dropped so heavily from tulip poplars it pattered the roof like a gentle rain.

As Lizzie went downstairs from her room, she overheard Sister talking to Chester in the den speak the work *Meadowbrook*. Questioned, Mary Belle said Meadowbrook was a nursery where she'd ordered red azaleas to line the front walk. She could never lie. Lizzie looked up the name in the phone book. It listed no nursery, but there was a convalescent and retirement home advertised in big letters. Lizzie knew Sister had been after Chester to take her to Spain.

Mary Belle wanted the house repainted. Men arrived in a pickup truck hauling ladders, buckets, and drop cloths. They wore white caps and coveralls. Lizzie got to know their names—Basil, Wayne, and Wayne's son Otis, just a youth learning the job from his elders, who were jokingly patient with him. When Lizzie volunteered to help mix paint, Sister didn't like it.

"I'm paying them to do the work," Mary Belle said.

"What's it hurting?" Chester asked, for once showing a sliver of backbone. "It don't matter whether she's ladylike or not."

"Never wanted to be a lady anyhow," Lizzie said. "Keeps you from spitting in public."

Toward the end of the week, music drifted in on the smell of mowed grass, the breeze from the river, the sight of peonies blooming so heavily they bowed to the ground. She picked a wild strawberry along the backyard fence and squeezed its bittersweet juice against her tongue. The day was music everywhere.

After her nap she rose to look out the window and saw the men cleaning their brushes. They hadn't finished and would return Monday. She washed her face, went downstairs, and walked out into the backyard. As she looked up into the limbs of a tulip poplar, she held out a palm to catch the slowly spiraling pollen. She glimpsed new green against the cloudless lemony sky. The grass, the peonies, the sunny pollen formed a sea of music around her, beating against her ears like rhythmic combers.

The men had been painting eaves at the rear of the house and left a ladder standing. She didn't seem to be climbing as much as growing lighter. By the time Sister and Dorcus discovered her and ran out, she had reached the second floor.

"Louise, come down this very instant, you hear!" Mary Belle squawked.

Lizzie continued to the top of the ladder, which leaned against a copper gutter. She'd never minded heights. She breathed fragrances filtered through a green veil of trees, lifted her chin to sunshine, and watched a flight of swifts sweep around the chimney. The silver glint of an airplane left a white trail across the sky. She felt weightless and as if drifting among treetops.

They shouted at her to come down—Mary Belle, Chester, Dorcus. Chester climbed a few rungs but stopped, frightened by the ladder's sway. Police and firemen arrived. Chester pleaded. Sister wailed. Each time a fireman started up, Lizzie pushed away from the ladder.

She heard noises on the other side of the house. A fireman appeared, climbing to the roof's crown. He was a young good-looking boy, tanned, helmeted, strong.

"Lady, why don't you let me take you by the hand?" he asked.

Firemen hurried about unfolding a net they meant to open beneath her. Music sounded very loud—strains of corn silk, the feel of eggs still holding heat from the hen's breast, the strong good smell of seasoned tobacco, morning light spreading across a soybean field, a canter through the pine woods, whispers of the river, the loveliness of lips upon her nipples.

Below, boxwoods of the garden reminded her of hoop skirts and the shimmering line of a quadrille. She wore her rose chiffon gown and silver heels.

"Why yes," she said to the handsome young man and feeling lighter than air lifted her arms and stepped into the swirl of a flowing waltz.

TIDES

Wilford watched his son shinny up the aluminum mast to retape a white plastic boot over the spreader so it wouldn't snag the main. Dave, lean and tan, was now twenty-one, having finished at Duke, a B.A., and the two of them were on the water for August. When their cruise ended, the boy would begin work for Carolina National in Raleigh as a management trainee. News of the job had been the lifting of a load from Wilford and his wife, Nancy.

He and the boy sailed Albemarle Sound to Currituck and through the ditch to the Elizabeth River, Norfolk, and the Chesapeake Bay. A ten-to-twelve-knot southwesterly allowed a northward reach. Dave trailed a line fixed to a Cisco Kid and caught an eight-pound bluefish he filleted on the cutting board and cooked over the grill after they anchored in a quiet, shadowed cove near the mouth of the Ware River off Mobjack Bay.

"I guess this trip's a ritual celebrating the official end of fun in my life," Dave said when he eased down the mast. His long brown hair was sun-bleached, and he resembled Wilford, though lighter of bone. Wilford had played ball for UNC. Dave had never cared much for any sport except swimming and not bothered to go out for that team. He'd have to get his hair cut.

"Life's not quite over for you," Wilford said. Laughing gulls circled a crabber motoring in from checking his pots. The white deadrise rode above its own reflection across the calm bluish water.

"Like the curtain coming down," Dave said. "End of play."

That night the breeze changed to an easterly, welcome because it brought cooler air and pushed skeeters inland. Wilford and the boy spread cockpit cushions on the cabin top. Drained from sun, beer, and food, they lay identifying stars. Dave slept before Wilford realized he was talking only to himself.

During the night *Wayfarer* dragged a bit. Wilford had taken bearings on a seine shack and dead pine in which ospreys nested. He lengthened the anchor line's scope. Dave didn't waken. As an immense sun reddened the pines, Wilford heated coffee on the alcohol stove. Red in the morning. He listened to the weather broadcast from NOAA but heard no warnings. In any case, he and Dave were in no hurry. This anchorage was pleasant. They could read, swim, and fish.

They swam ashore at midafternoon, diving from the stern, grateful the stinging nettles were few. The water felt like warm soup. Jagged stumps of pines, which had died from erosion and salt, lined the sandy beach. They found the seine shack fallen in and empty except for a broken oar. They walked the beach and discovered a wooden skiff half sunk and rotted, as well as a white crab-pot float a storm had blown among reeds.

"We should plan to do this every summer," Wilford said. He hoped it would be so for at least a time but realized their sailing together had to end. Thank God Dave was finally attracted to a girl, a commercial artist in Winston-Salem, her name Margaret. They'd talked marriage, and if plans worked out, life would take them over, wrap them up with responsibilities and children, the pattern sad and good at the same time.

Wilford meant this cruise to be a celebration. He'd never been a person to speak his emotions openly. He'd always assumed the intensity of his feelings for the boy would beam out, radiate, make themselves known. Perhaps before they headed south again, he could summon words to make the appreciation of his son official.

The air stilled, the heat heavy, scratchy like moist wool. They had a dip and lay on sand in flimsy pine shade to snooze. Gulls wheeled and rocked above them. Terns dived, mullet thrashed in shallows. So far the biting flies, the greenies, hadn't discovered them. Despite the shade the sun was so intense it bloodied the eyelids.

Wilford raised to an elbow to watch his son sleep. Dave was handsome, almost pretty, and that had worried Wilford mightily. As a child the boy had been frail, allergic to foods, plants, insects. During college he'd become interested in theater and talked of becoming an actor-playwright. Friends Dave brought home had been definitely faggy. Wilford struggled to prevent certain pictures from forming in his mind, though prepared to stand by his son come what might. The filling satisfaction to have him as he was now. Bless Margaret too, Wilford thought, and lowered his head to the sand.

He dozed till the osprey's shrill cry woke him. Sitting up, he saw a small, wiry man watching him. The man wore a Panama hat, a tightly fitted khaki suit, and a maroon tie over a purple shirt. His full black mustache seemed much too large for his face. His skin was sweat shiny, particularly scar tissue curved across a cheek. His sideburns were long and curly. He held a strapped leather briefcase.

"Your boat?" he asked, indicating *Wayfarer* at anchor. She was a Pearson 33, rigged tall, her hull white with a blue boot. "Maybe you'd hire it out for a buck?"

"For what?" Wilford asked. Dave was rousing.

"Short trip. Take me across to Cape Charles."

"We're not commercial," Wilford said.

The man squinted over blackish eyes. Except for the smooth scar tissue, his face was pitted. He half turned to listen landward, looking back toward the pines and possibly a road, though Wilford had heard no sounds of traffic.

"A hundred GWs cash," the man said. He had a slight accent, perhaps Hispanic.

"Wish we could accommodate you," Wilford said, standing and pulling at his canvas swimming shorts. "For a hundred you can find somebody inland who'll drive you by way of the bridge."

The man stared at *Wayfarer*. The anchor line was slack, the water so undisturbed she seemed fused to it. "You got a radio," he said. He'd spotted the mast antenna. "I'll pay to use it."

"You'd have to swim over," Dave said. He stood, brushed sand from his rump, and pushed back his hair.

"I see a rubber boat, don't I?" the man asked. "You could come get me."

Wilford's eyes met Dave's. There was something about the man's voice. He seemed removed, dreamy, as if unconcerned whether they heard or not. Sand clung to his black kilties, and his wine-colored socks had snagged briars. Beggar's-lice clung to his pants. He'd been running.

"Like to help, but your best bet is find a phone," Wilford said.

The man pulled the gun casually from beneath his jacket at the back of his waist—a blue-black automatic. His fingers appeared bony against the checkered pearl grip. The pistol seemed much too large for the thin, small hand.

"The boy stays, you go for the rubber boat," he said to Wilford. "Keep in sight. Come back and get us, and we trip to Cape Charles. Okay?"

Wilford hesitated, trying to think of something quick, but the gun lifted toward his chest, the muzzle dark and deadly.

"It's all right, Dad," Dave said. Yet he stood so exposed, so fragile before the gun.

Wilford waded hip deep into the water, dove under, and swam his racing crawl to the boat. He pulled himself up on the chrome transom ladder and sidestepped along the port scupper to the cabin top, where the rubber dinghy was strapped. He unfastened it, turned it upright, and slid it over the side, all the while holding the nylon painter. He

fitted together the collapsible aluminum oars. He stepped into the dinghy and sat quickly to keep his balance on the unstable bottom. Maybe
he could use an oar as a weapon. Doubtful. They were too lightly
constructed.

Dave waited at the water's edge, the man a few paces behind. The
dinghy scraped to a stop short of shore. The man indicated with the
gun that Dave should precede him. He did not remove his fancy black
slippers or roll up his pants but walked right into the water. Loaded,
the dinghy was grounded. Dave had to drop off the bow, tug them
free, and hop back in.

The man rested the gun on his briefcase. He gazed from those dark
dreamy eyes at Wilford, who fought fear. Christ, he thought, don't start
shaking. Don't let Dave see that.

They reached *Wayfarer* and pulled to the ladder. Try it, Wilford
thought. He laid down one oar and gripped the other like a bat. The
man might become unbalanced an instant as he climbed aboard. But if
Wilford failed to do enough damage, rage and bloodshed could result.
After seeing into those eyes, Wilford had no doubt the man would use
the automatic. He laid the second oar on the dinghy's bottom and made
the painter fast to a stern cleat. The man stepped into the cockpit.

Wilford hoped Dave would dive and swim away underwater. He'd
need to surface only to snatch air, but chances were the man couldn't
hit him at any distance using a pistol. The boy, however, would think
of Wilford and not desert him.

"Your ass up front," the man said to Dave. "Stay in eyeballing
territory."

Dave obeyed, moving as far as the forestay. He held to it. As yet
no sign of fright or weakness.

"We do the radio," the man said to Wilford.

Wilford stepped below and lifted fingers to the VHF bolted
through the bulkhead. The red light indicating power flashed as he

switched on channel 16. They heard the jabber of boats and ships communicating.

"How do I talk to Baltimore?" the man asked, leaning down into the cabin.

"If you mean telephone, you'll need the marine operator," Wilford said.

"Reach me this number," the man said as from his hip pocket he drew a wallet. Using the gun to wedge the wallet against his stomach, he pinched out a slip of paper. The number looked as if it'd been penciled by a child. Wilford complied. The sensible thing was to go along, get the man to Cape Charles and off the boat as soon as possible. He gave the marine operator the phone number and his own credit card's before stretching the coiled cord to hand the man the mike.

"You come up here," the man said. He'd never let go of the briefcase. When Wilford climbed back into the cockpit, the man stepped halfway down the ladder. Wilford glanced forward to Dave. The boy lifted his hands as if to say, What now? Wilford was unsure. Maybe they should both make a running dive over the side and strike out for shore. But the man bobbed his head topside to watch.

"Lie face down, your hands on your head," he ordered.

Wilford lowered himself to the cockpit decking. The man rose to look aft. From the VHF came the sound of a woman's voice, not the operator's.

"You where?" she asked.

"Slight change of fucking agenda," the man said, gun ready. "Sydney failed to connect."

"But you got it?"

"Cat have an ass?" the man asked.

"When?" she asked.

"How long to Baltimore?" the man called to Wilford.

"Under sail?"

"Fastest way."

"We've only a small engine and currents to buck. Eighteen, twenty hours if everything works right."

"Tomorrow some fucking time," the man said into the mike.

"Sonofabitch," the woman said.

"Ain't it?" the man asked.

Wilford raised his head to see the man hang the mike on the hook and switch off the VHF. The man climbed into the cockpit. Water squeezed from his black slippers onto the deck. He motioned Wilford to stand.

"You ever been to Baltimore?" he asked. "You'll love that whore of a city."

Wilford calculated. They carried less than half a tank of fuel, enough to proceed a distance up the bay, but not as far as Baltimore. Somewhere they'd need to pull into a marina.

"I'll start the engine," Wilford said and faced forward. "Catch the anchor, Dave!"

Wilford lifted the ignition toggle. The Perkins caught and sounded richly good, the result of a winter overhaul. He eased *Wayfarer* forward so Dave could take in line. When the bow was directly over the anchor, Dave snubbed the line around a cleat and allowed the natural rise and fall of the boat to free her from mud. Dave dunked the anchor half a dozen times to wash it before hauling it aboard and stowing it in its mount.

"Stay put!" the man called when Dave started aft.

Wilford steered 120 degrees, a course that would carry them from Mobjack to the Chesapeake Bay and Baltimore Channel. He'd then follow a line of markers northward. There would be boat traffic, and perhaps he or Dave could sneak out a distress signal. His fingers sweated on the stainless-steel helm.

"What's to drink?" the man asked. He pushed back his hat and loosened his tie. He still held the briefcase.

"In the cooler," Wilford answered and pointed below.

Before stepping down, the man ordered Dave to sit. The boy obliged, fitting his back to the bow pulpit. The man located the Styrofoam cooler under the companionway ladder, lifted a beer from chunk ice, and climbed quickly topside. He popped the can and drank, those eyes all the while on Wilford. He sighed and wiped his mouth. He looked worn. That was the thing, he had to be so tired he'd need rest. There'd be opportunity for overcoming him or escape.

The sun lowered, laying an orange cast on the bay. An uneven formation of cormorants flew past, the flapping of their wings audible. The man toed off his wet slippers. He peeled away his wine-colored socks and hung them over a lifeline. His feet were narrow, the dark, bluish skin puckered. Wilford set the wheel on autopilot and moved toward the cabin.

"One fucking minute!" the man said, shifting the briefcase to raise the pistol.

Wilford explained he and Dave needed shirts. They still wore only their swimming shorts.

"Be a smart daddy," the man said and spat over the side.

Wilford tossed a shirt forward. It fluttered to the cabin's top. Dave had to stretch to reach it. The man watched, ready with the gun. For an instant Wilford looked into his son's green eyes and tried to transmit hope and courage. The boy winked.

The sun's rays slanted, and water darkened. Wilford asked permission to switch on their running lights. The man replied with a slow exaggerated nod. Wilford stepped below to the master panel. He thought of blinking on SOS on the bow light, but the man leaned forward to observe. As Wilford returned to the cockpit, it occurred to him he shouldn't have mentioned lights at all. People on other boats might notice, approach to investigate, or report the infraction to the Coast Guard.

He returned to the wheel. The man straightened and gradually let down. He was sleepy, his chin lowered, and he jerked himself upright to stare wildly. He rubbed the back of a hand against his mouth.

"Food," he said.

"You can check the galley," Wilford said. Dave pushed up to look aft.

"You make me one goddamn good sandwich," the man said and waggled the pistol.

Wilford set the pilot and went below. He and Dave usually cooked on the grill, which had a clamp and hinge allowing it to be swung overboard, reducing the danger of fire. Before they left home, Nancy had baked them half a dozen casseroles she wrapped in aluminum foil. They'd also stocked hot dogs, hamburger, cold cuts, margarine, and milk in the ice locker.

As Wilford fixed a cheese-and-baloney sandwich on whole wheat, he eyed the VHF. The man peered down from the cockpit. No chance of transmitting a Mayday. He thought of poisons, something to spread on the sandwich like iodine from the first-aid kit. Stupid. At the first nibble the man would taste the bitterness.

Wilford laid the sandwich on a paper towel and carried it topside. The man took the sandwich in one hand and motioned Wilford away before lifting a slice of bread to examine what was between. He bit into the sandwich and chewed so hard his jawbone ridged flesh of his face. He kept the briefcase close at this side.

"'Nother beer if you fucking please," he said.

That suited Wilford. The more the man drank, the sleepier he'd become. Wilford popped the beer for the man, sat behind the wheel, and looked across the water. The night sky was partly cloudy. An airplane blinking red lights flew over high. Running lights of other boats glimmered in darkness. He spotted the fifteen-second flash of Wolf Trap.

"I need to change course," Wilford said.

"How do I know this to be?" the man asked.

"If we hold this heading, we'll run into shallows off the Eastern Shore."

The man stood holding the briefcase. He stared forward, tossed the beer can overboard, and again gave the big nod. Wilford brought the boat up to compass north and again set the pilot. The man granted permission to check the chart. They should next pick up Stingray Point light.

"My son and I are hungry too," Wilford said.

"So have yourself a fucking feast," the man said.

Wilford switched on the galley light and fixed tuna sandwiches. The man squatted at the top of the companionway to watch.

"Give me the sandwich," he said. "I'll put it on the cabin for the pretty boy. You don't come up."

Wilford sat at the chart table to eat, bread dry in his mouth. He heard Dave move a few steps aft and return to the bow. The man lounged behind the wheel, the briefcase with him. Rosy light from the binnacle tinted his small, narrow face. He leaned back, adjusted a flotation cushion to become comfortable, but wouldn't give way to exhaustion. I've got to rush him, Wilford thought. If I'm able to hold him a moment, Dave can come running. But would he?

"What you looking up here for?" the man asked, flapping the gun above his thigh.

"Checking weather," Wilford said.

"Weather's all right. Don't watch me."

Wilford backed deeper into the cabin and sat on a berth. He'd chewed only the one bite of the sandwich. If they had a blow, the man would need them. The wind, however, was ten knots or less, and the bay continued to roll in long benign swells from the south. Water languidly slapped the hull.

The forward hatch over the V berths was close. Maybe Wilford could slip forward, tap softly on the hatch, and raise it enough to whisper Dave a message.

"Permission to use the head?" he called.

"Leave the door open," the man ordered.

Leaving the head door open was fine. It swung aft and blocked a view from the cockpit. Wilford hurriedly relieved himself, pumped the john, and kneed himself onto the V berths. His fingers drummed the hatch cover and pushed gently. He glimpsed a slash of night sky.

"Don't speak!" he whispered, "When we rush, I'll shout!"

"Hey, Dad, what you doing?" the man called.

"Finished!" Wilford called back, stepped into the head, and again pumped the john.

Trembling, he closed the head door and sat at the chart table. Their course was only general. Tides and current as well as shifting wind might nudge them a significant number of degrees. The question was whether or not to tell the man. Difficulty could be opportunity. If they rushed, a vicious, deadly struggle might result. Would the boy be up to it?

"Need to use the head," Dave called. Wilford couldn't be sure his son had heard him through the hatch.

"Use the fucking bay," the man ordered. "It is free to all."

Wilford heard them both relieve themselves over the side. In the distance a bell buoy gonged. Dave again settled on the bow. He'd never really been strong.

"Fucking boat!" the man shouted.

Wilford climbed into the cockpit. She was a ship of the menhaden fleet—lighted, stinking of alewives, engines pumping and discharging waste water. They were on a closing course of 45 degrees. Somebody might be signaled.

"Hey, Dad, do something!" the man said.

"We'll miss her," Wilford said.

"I don't like it. Turn this mothering tub!"

Wilford released the autopilot and veered off. Dave started back from the bow. The man whipped the pistol against Wilford's elbow. Pain seared the arm. They fell away from the menhaden boat.

"You were trying something cute," the man said.

"We'd have avoided her all right," Wilford said, a hand cupped over his crazy bone, it still shooting fire.

"Listen, I'm no fucking moron, but you are if you think different. Now set the thing again and be like a sweetheart to me."

Wilford angled *Wayfarer* northward, but on a course that would carry them closer to the Eastern Shore and its many navigable creeks. Dave had come partway aft.

"Back, pretty boy!" the man shouted. To Wilford: "You, down in the cabin."

This time Wilford lay on the berth feeling the pulse of the engine and hearing the wash of water past the hull. He estimated they'd covered seventy or eighty miles. I should, he thought, have done something by now.

He peeked up the companionway and saw only the man's bare feet. Wilford pulled back quickly. Any action might incite fury. He bit the edge of his left hand. The goddamn fear! Not for himself, but for Dave. He rubbed his elbow.

The wind picked up, the boat rose and fell, yet no storm. From a bronze porthole he glimpsed stars. He remembered how the night before he and Dave had lain on the cabin top and identified the Pleiades, Orion, and Andromeda. The sky had then seemed benevolent.

Wilford leaned from the berth and squinted into the cockpit's darkness. No response. The man was resting. Otherwise he'd have reacted. The autopilot made its slight corrections with a quiet whirring precision. The man could well be asleep. Now, Wilford thought, charge topside and shout for Dave. He searched for a weapon and grasped a winch handle. It was heavy enough to do damage. Help me, Lord, he prayed.

As he gathered himself, the man's feet moved, and the plastic cushions squeaked. The man said something, not a word, a sound. Wilford drew back. He was shaking so hard his shoulder thumped the bulkhead. Sweat rolled from beneath his armpits.

He lowered himself to the berth, the winch handle at his side. His unfinished sandwich lay on the chart table. Again he lifted himself to peer into the cockpit. The man had drawn up his feet, and only the pedestal's base showed. Do something! Wilford told himself. Yet he waited.

"Lights!" the man called.

The lights were distantly blinking red and green markers, probably the entrance to Pungoteague Creek. If allowed to take *Wayfarer* in, Wilford might suddenly hard over the helm and ram a dock or vessel—anything to distract the man long enough to dive into dark water. Wilford would shout to Dave to do the same. The man couldn't shoot what he was unable to see.

"We need fuel," Wilford said.

"Show me the fucking gauge," the man said.

The gauge was set into the aft locker bulkhead along with the ammeter, the log, and the knot meter. Wilford switched on the instrument lights. The man knelt, at the same time pointing the gun at Wilford.

"Quarter tank," he said.

"We ought to top up," Wilford said. "It's a long way yet."

The man looked over the water toward the blinking markers. He adjusted his hat. He pulled on his socks and slippers. He tightened his tie.

"Get pretty boy," he said.

Wilford called Dave. The man uncleated a nylon mooring line and motioned Dave below.

"Stay behind the wheel," the man ordered Wilford. To Dave: "Face down on the bunk."

He tied Dave's hands behind him, looped the line around Dave's ankles, and knotted it at the wrists. Wilford tasted vomit.

The man climbed into the cockpit. He jerked his head toward the blinkers. Wilford changed course. The man held the briefcase to his chest. He eyed the channel as they entered. Among pines, windows of houses were lighted.

"How's it done?" the man asked.

"We make fast at the dock, and an attendant will bring a hose."

"You pay cash?"

"Credit card."

"Where's the tank?"

Wilford pointed to the cap on the port scupper. He maneuvered *Wayfarer* up the winding, narrowing channel. Water birds flapped into the night. Ahead, more lights flickered on the creek—an Exxon sign and pier. Darkened clam boats were moored along the shore. Nothing resembled what Wilford remembered of Pungoteague Creek.

He brought *Wayfarer* alongside the two pumps. Beyond was the combination dockmaster's office and small store, its shingled siding decorated with floats, nets, and toss rings. A stout woman wearing black rubber boots, coveralls, and a yellow long-billed cap came out.

"Gas or diesel?" she called.

"Not a fucking word more than you have to," the man whispered to Wilford. The gun jabbed his lower back.

The marina had lines hanging from pilings, and as Wilford cleated them the woman dragged the diesel hose to the dock's edge. While Wilford filled the tank, the man stood close. Wilford handed the woman his credit card. She carried it to the store and brought back the slip for him to sign. He saw they were at Little Red's Marina on Onancock Creek. He thought of writing *Help!* but felt the man's presence at his back.

"You all laying over?" the woman asked.

"Headed up to Baltimore," Wilford answered. He blinked out an SOS using his right eyelid. The woman laughed and hauled the hose back to the pump.

"Good thing my husband ain't here," she said.

"Scratch fucking out!" the man ordered and again jabbed the gun into Wilford's spine.

Wilford cast off, brought the boat around, and steered a return course down channel to the bay. Their luminous wake splashed the shore.

"School time 'cause you don't learn so good," the man said and slapped Wilford, knocking his head aside. Wilford righted himself on the wheel. He expected a second blow, but the man glanced into the cabin and sat on flotation cushions. He tightened an arm against the briefcase as if to reassure himself.

The moon waned, yet shone brightly on the water till thin ragged clouds slid over it from the southwest. The clouds contained no weather.

"Untie my son," Wilford said. "Please."

"After what you done back there?"

"It was me, not him. Tie me and let him handle the boat."

The man stared toward the diminishing marker lights. Wilford saw only the portion of Dave's legs hinged back. The boy had to be in pain. Seated, the man was again nodding off.

"Please!" Wilford said a second time.

"Just fucking cool it," the man said but stood holding the pistol and briefcase. He climbed into the cabin and loosened knots. "Get your royal red ass up front again," he said to Dave. The boy rubbed his wrists and stumbled slightly. One leg was asleep. The man watched till Dave reached the bow before settling. "You used up all your luck," he said to Wilford. "Understand? Now set the thing and get in the cabin."

Wilford backed down the companionway steps and sat on the berth. The line that had bound Dave lay across the winch handle. He thought of slipping forward again and whispering through the hatch. What was there to say?

He heard the man relieve himself. He had to be standing on the stern pulpit. If Wilford rushed, he might be able to shove him overboard. But the man would be ready, perhaps have the pistol aimed behind him.

Wilford thought of the flare gun in the storage area beneath the berth. He'd never used it, but the red shells were large and shot balls of fire. Suppose he fumbled the gun or the flare failed. They'd been aboard *Wayfarer* a number of years and should've been replaced. He was second-guessing himself into immobility.

He peeked at the man, who rested propped among cushions behind the wheel. His body rocked slightly with the boat's motion. Now, Wilford thought. He'd alert Dave. He moved forward. The man did not react. Another two slow steps. If challenged, Wilford would claim he needed the head. He reached the V berths and tapped softly on the hatch. No reply. Dave too could be sleeping.

The man shouted. Wilford stumbled aft through the cabin and onto deck. He heard and sensed the massive power of the ship before he saw her—a cargo carrier looming black as a mountain over them, running lights high, the bow white from water pushed ahead of it. He released the autopilot and spun the wheel to port, but for a moment the rusted side of the ship and *Wayfarer* rasped. A suction between the hulls bonded and carried *Wayfarer* along.

Wilford feared the ship might drive them under. He gunned the

Perkins, the bond broke, and they rocked free. As the ship passed, her great propeller thrashed and swirled out a turbulence that pitched *Wayfarer* violently and doused water into the cockpit.

"Bastard sonofabitch!" the man shouted, slinging water off himself. "You stay with me!" he ordered Wilford. He picked up his hat, which had been knocked off. "Get back!" he yelled at Dave.

The ship's lights drew away. Too late now for Wilford to sound *Wayfarer's* horn. He returned her to course, following the foaming wake of the cargo carrier. The man continued to curse, brush at himself, and peer around angrily. He held the pistol and briefcase close.

They motored the rest of the night, Wilford behind the wheel, the man sitting and eyeing him. If they sighted another craft, Wilford had to steer off. A school of porpoises arched alongside. Their blowing scared the man. He jumped up and aimed his pistol at the water.

The morning dawned clean, cirrus clouds catching the sunrise and spreading a golden veil over calm waters on which gulls rested. Boats angled out from tidal creeks to check crab pots and pound nets. Wilford didn't need to be told to avoid them. The man's narrow face seemed more threatening because of dark beard stubble. He'd kept on his hat during the night. His eyes were reddened, the lids heavy.

Wilford first heard the chopper. The man crouched and used the pistol to shield his eyes. The other hand clutched the briefcase. The chopper sped low across the water. The man ducked into the cabin and backed among shadows. He aimed the pistol at Wilford.

"Wave friendly-like and show your goddamn teeth!" he shouted. "The boy too."

The chopper swopped at *Wayfarer* and hovered. It tipped to their starboard quarter. The helicopter bore the red-and-white crest of the Coast Guard. A seaman wearing denims and a yellow helmet stood at an open bay and studied them through binoculars. Dave rose to his knees at the bow. Wilford waved and smiled. The chopper circled, its wind wash smashing the water, dipped, and canted away toward other boats.

The man remained crouched below till the chopper became distant. Cautiously he climbed through the companionway, watched the helicopter, and dragged the back of the hand holding the pistol across his mouth.

"Set the fucking thing," he said, indicating the autopilot. Still hugging the briefcase, he let himself down to the cushions. The chopper was definitely gone. He pushed at his hat with the pistol, checked his watch, and sighed. "Little food," he said.

When Wilford stepped down into the galley, the man relieved himself over the side. Wilford poured Grape Nuts into bowls and added sugar and milk. He should've fried bacon and thrown hot grease into the man's face. Maybe at lunch if he could gather the courage. God, let me be brave this once, he thought, and handed a bowl to the man before starting forward with one for Dave.

"Leave it on the cabin!" the man ordered. He sniffed the cereal before eating. Dave carried his back to the bow. Wilford wondered whether the woman at Little Red's Marina had figured out his blinking signal. Maybe the chopper's inspecting them had been simply routine or had something to do with dope.

The morning grew still and hot. They passed Smith Island and came abeam of Fishing Creek. Dave stretched out on the bow and seemed to have himself under control. Few seabirds flew. The sun burned down, causing wavy air to surround them. The man removed his jacket, loosened his tie, checked his watch, and yawned. He again kicked off his slippers. He wiggled his toes. He adjusted his hat to shade his eyes and touched the briefcase. His head hung forward as he fought sleep. Finally he dozed.

The pistol lay limp-wristed across a thigh, and his body wobbled slightly from the boat's motion. Now! Wilford told himself, yet did not move. Maybe this could work out. After they reached Baltimore, the man might allow them to go. Was that likely, when they were able to identify him? Wilford rose to look forward but couldn't see Dave, who probably slept. Wilford thought of bullets, pain, blood, and death. God, don't let me be a coward in front of my son.

Something moved in the cabin. Wilford glanced at the man and into shadows. Dave! He'd snaked down through the hatch and made his way aft. He held the flare gun. Wilford almost shouted, No!

Dave set himself to rush but tripped over the companionway's high sill. The sound brought the man out of sleep. Flailing, he struck Dave across the face with the pistol. A flare popped, fizzed, and sizzled into the water, trailing the nitric odor of powder. Dave sprawled onto Wilford's feet. Blood dripped from his chin. He'd dropped the flare gun. The man seized and hurled it over the side. He pushed the pistol into the boy's ear.

"Don't!" Dave said and started crying. He held one hand to his bleeding face and raised the other in supplication. "Please, please don't!" he said and wept. Tears mixed with blood.

"Not him!" Wilford pleaded. "Me!"

"Why the hell not him?" the man asked, his dark eyes roving furiously. To Dave: "Stand and get your pretty ass off this boat!"

Dave, blubbering, lowered his bloody face and shook his head.

"He's too far from shore," Wilford said. "Let him use the dinghy."

"His ass can walk on water," the man said.

"I didn't mean anything!" Dave begged.

"Oh shit no," the man said. "Off, fish food!"

"I'll go over!" Wilford said and climbed onto the cockpit seat. He'd not be able to survive the tidal strength sweeping toward the ocean. He thought of himself tiring and sinking into lightless depths, his body spiraling slowly, like seaweed.

To Wilford's horror, Dave wailed and did a shameful thing. As he begged, he reached to the man's foot and kissed it. He kept kissing the foot. Cursing, the man stepped back off balance. On his belly Dave thrust after him and shouted, "Grab him, Dad!"

The automatic fired beside Wilford's ear. He felt heat, and concussion knocked his vision out of focus. Still he held the man, bear-hugged and lifted him from deck. The pistol fired a second time, and Wilford feared Dave had been hit, but then his son fought beside him. They wrestled the man, who cursed, kicked, and shot the pistol over their backs as they threw him to the deck.

Wilford felt a blow across his mouth, tasted blood, and wondered whether he'd been hit by a bullet. He pounded the man's head against the steering pedestal. Blood seeped from the kinky hair. He lay still. Dave had the pistol first pinned under a knee and then in his fingers. He would've thrown it over, but Wilford reached to his arm. The police would want the gun.

"Watch him while I get a line," Wilford said, so winded he could just form words. He was panting and dribbled blood and vomit.

The man needed no guard. He lay unresisting, his mouth gaping, as they tied him. Wilford radioed the Coast Guard, giving *Wayfarer*'s position and intent to put in at Cambridge.

He and Dave were battered. Wilford brought out the first-aid kit, and they ministered to each other. They looked into each other's eyes and hugged hard.

"Hey, I'm all right," Dave said. "It was an act. I used to be an actor, remember?"

The boy reached into his mouth and pinched out a tooth. The bloody incisor shone brightly on his tan palm. Dave shrugged and started to toss the tooth overboard, but Wilford took it from him and held it. The man stirred and cursed, but his words lacked power. He lay staring at the sky. Blood splotched his khaki suit.

Dave lifted the briefcase and opened it. Fat neat bundles of greenbacks lay packed inside.

"Mere money," the boy said, restrapped the briefcase, and pitched it underhanded down onto a berth.

Wilford went below to check his charts and call a compass course to Dave. The boy stepped over the man to the wheel. Weak and shaky, Wilford climbed topside and sat beside his son. Dave's bleeding had stopped as had his own.

Wilford started to correct course slightly, a father's habit, by laying his hand on the wheel. He pulled back and dropped the hand to the throttle, which he pushed full forward. *Wayfarer* had plenty of water under her and a good man at the helm.

"You take her in," he said to his son and sat back against cushions, lifting his chin to allow the breeze from their speed to reach the sweat on his dry and aching throat. Only then did he realize he still clutched in his other hand the tooth he intended never to release.

COALS

"Ce-leste!" she holler while I doing my best to fix her supper, and she know I busy, know I got my hands in the vegetables. Mean she gotten, rich, wears a red wig like she a pleasure woman, though her arms and legs I fit a thumb and finger 'round—if she allow me to fit anything at all.

Celeste! Day and night! When I sleeping I hear her screechy voice even when she not calling, though I never sure when she do and don't, so sometimes I answer when she ain't called and sometimes I don't and she do.

"I'm waiting my tonic!" she calling, her voice enough to cause dogs to tuck tail and hide under the henhouse. They use her voice down to the fire company, take the si-reen off the courthouse and save electricity.

"Whyn't you up and quit?" my Jim say, he a big man, still strong, though his leg gone, lost when that Oliver tractor crush it flat as a frog on the highway. Jim so black you see him in darkness. He can still lift a mule if he get set right. He work now down at the shoe factory in Danville where he sit on a stool and stitch soles. He an all right man except when he get to drinking, even then not mean, but trifling, giggling, and hollering out in the night, "Bring me my leg!" They took it at the hospital, never give it back, and he believe they fasten it on somebody else, like he see on the TV. He eye everybody's legs he pass, women's too, 'cept for different reason.

"I promise Mr. Ben Ranson I'd look after her," I say. "And I promise the children too."

"They children no longer and could look after her theyselves," Jim say. "What they got to do but hit balls around country clubs?"

"Mr. Ben Ranson favor me in his will," I say.

"He didn't favor you that much. Thirty-five dollar a week. Get a lot more at the shoe factory."

"I give him my word," I say. "Besides, she the prettiest thing I ever see once. Threw me a rose."

It'd be a lot easier down at the shoe factory. Just work eight hours and time off for lunch. Lots of gal gossip on the line. But Mr. Ben Ranson help my daughter Winona get in business school. He saw to my Billy when he in trouble with the man and took care of Jim too and pay the hospital. My Billy hang dry-wall down in Richmond town, married, has him a long-legged boy, and Winona bosses the perfume counter at the fanciest department store in Baltimore. Everybody there smell good.

Jim not disappoint Mr. Ben Ranson either. He just talking, 'specially when he sitting on the back porch looking out to the garden and dusty pines edging the bean field. 'Specially if he hold a Bud bottle in his hand.

Our house got two rooms and a kitchen, but Miss Alice Louella's is brick three stories, two balconies, two baths for the upstairs people, two for the down, and one in the basement for the help. I is the help. Even if I upstairs working and need to go, she make me climb all the way to the basement. She can tell by the water running where I go. Sometimes I fool her and don't flush till she sleeping after her tonic.

"I'm waiting!" she call, though I got my hands in the biscuit dough. "You know it's time for my tonic!"

Huh, her kind of tonic make birds fall out the trees. Raincoat bring it. Raincoat wear a brown raincoat summer or winter, rain or shine. Raincoat got extra pockets in his raincoat. Sometime he carry so many tonics for ladies in Tobaccoton he clink like a China cabinet during thunder. They 'fraid preacher see them in the tonic store. He come to Miss Alice Louella's every Tuesday, Thursday, and Saturday, and when he leaving he clink not as much as he coming. He grin at me.

I carry ice up in a crystal bowl that got handles shaped like pea-fowls. She sit at the window of her bedroom where she look over the lawn to the street and watch people with her 'noculars. She keep the 'noculars on the marble-top table by her chair. That table got bowlegs. That chair does. Half the furniture in the house got bowlegs. Her bed got a white canopy and white tassels on the pillows. She don't let me open windows. I clean the panes so she can look through the 'noculars at people on the way to Mosley's Market. I set the bowl on the table.

"You ever hurry in your life?" she say. She once some woman, tall, lots of meat, big milkers, but she shrunk. She like her room shaded, and her skin got whiter than the powder she powder with. She keep on her red wig, though she wear a blue negligee most times, and little satin slippers that is embroidered with yellow butterflies. She don't come downstairs no more. She could. She just like to see me work. "You deliberately make me wait," she say. "You continually try my patience."

"What patience?" I ask.

"No sass, you hear?" she say. "Trouble is you're not organized." She reach with spidery fingers to claw ice for her tonic. She still paint her nails ruby red. She wear rings even when she sleep. Maybe she think I steal them. "My Mr. Ben believed an organized life was a satis-fied life."

Her man Mr. Ben Ranson made a mountain of money raising dark-fired tobacco. Before he die, he own and rent more government allot-ments than they people in Howell County. At pulling time he drive field to field in his black Cadillac car, and when he go down to Rich-mond to sit in the General Assembly, the governor shake his hand and come to lunch.

"Easy to organize when you rich," I say, starting downstairs to finish fixing her meal.

"Are you sassing me?" she asked. "If you're sassing me, I shall notify the bank."

"People does the organizing for you when you has money," I say. "Fact of life."

"I will not tolerate sass," she say and rattle the ice cubes in her tonic glass at me. It already half empty.

I start to tell her I do the tolerating, but it lead to more fuss. I go to the kitchen and fill her plate. For a shrinking woman, she eat—she like fruit in hot weather, country ham, potato salad, butter beans, lime sherbet, and mint iced tea. Course she got to have two glasses of tonic first.

Banker John come to see me. He a big man, not like Jim, but round big. If he get any rounder, he gonna roll not walk downhill. He a banker 'cause his daddy was a banker. He wear a Panama hat and seersucker suit, polka-dot bow tie, black shoes, and white socks.

"She claims you sassing her," he say to me. He sit on my porch. I never sit on his. He fan his face with his hat. "I wish you all could get along better, be nicer to one another."

"Nicing and getting along take two," I say.

"I know Mrs. Ranson can be hard to please," he say. "She misses her husband and tends to be high-strung."

"All women who got dead husbands missing them," I say. "I buried two 'fore Jim. Enough to string anybody."

"If the situation don't improve, changes might be necessary," he say. "You realize by terms of the trust agreement the bank can no longer pay you if you're not working at the house."

"I get me a job anytime at the shoe factory," I say. "Make a mess more money."

"Perhaps that would be wisest," he say.

I work till the end of the week, gather my things from the basement room, and tell good-bye to Miss Alice Louella, who in her bed.

"I try to keep my promise to Mr. Ben," I tell her.

"I will not tolerate sass," she say, that all, though I been at her house full-time four years come winter, working all day and sleeping six nights a week in that basement that smell of earth and mildewed old harness from Mr. Ben Ranson's trotting team. I put on my hat and leave out the front door. I don't look back. She probably seeing me through her 'noculars. I waggle my hips in case she watching me go down the walk.

I work at the shoe factory that winter. Jim ride me to Danville in his Ford pickup. We on the same shift. It good work, nobody yelling, time off to smoke, and at night we go home and watch the TV. Jim put his arm around me on the sofa. Losing his leg don't have nothing to do with that.

It spring, dogwood blooming, pine pollen blowing like rain, and Saturday I planting 'taters, snaps, sweet corn, and okra. Banker John drive up in his white Lincoln. He wearing his seersucker and polka-dot bow tie. He stand in the shade of a hackberry tree.

"By terms of the trust we have authority to increase your pay at Miss Alice Louella's," he said. "To sixty dollars."

"She want me back?" I ask. I know the answer to that and other things too. Working at the shoe factory you hear what happening round and about.

"The bank has found it difficult to secure competent help," Banker John say. "Our hope is you'll return. I'm sure Miss Alice Louella learned to appreciate how much you did for her."

What I know is they been three different women working for

her, one white. The white woman last two days. Patricia, Miss Alice Louella's daughter, come back from Winston-Salem and stay with her mother not only weekends but the rest of the time too.

"One hundred dollars," I say. "And I got to have me an understanding."

"What sort of understanding?" he ask, and his hat still. We talking money now, and he like a bird dog on point in patch of lespedeza.

"I go back, I get paid if she run me out again," I say.

"Paid how long?" Banker John ask and his coon-grape eyes don't blink. Talk money, he quit breathing.

"A year be enough," I say.

"I cannot recommend that arrangement and suggest you reconsider," he say.

"I have just done reconsidered reconsidering," I say.

Banker John leaving almost run over my Rhode Island rooster. Feathers flying. Jim been listening inside the house. He stick his head out the screen door.

"You told it right," he say and giggle. "Come in here and let's rub your feet."

"You feet rubbing turns out to be rubbing something else too," I say. Course I like it.

Miss Alice Louella's son and daughter, Ben Lee and Patricia, come see me. Patricia a tall gal, strawberry hair, green eyes, resemble what Miss Alice Louella look like once, except less milkers. Ben Lee so white you never see him in snow. His hair white too, just a tinge of lemon, though he hardly forty.

"We want you to change your mind about Mamma," he say. They sit on my porch. I never sit on theirs. They careful of dirt. My house clean, and they mamma's house clean while I kept it. Clean my middle name.

"I believe it's a misunderstanding," Patricia say. I never call her Patricia. Always Miss. "Mamma misses you. She is sorry you left."

"What you two had was a communication problem," Ben Lee say. He wear a white suit and vest. He a lawyer in Richmond town and like his daddy eat lunch with the governor.

"If you'd reconsider, we'd supplement your pay somewhat," Patricia say. She chew at a corner of her mouth. She a nervous woman and hold her hands to keep them from flying off. She been married to a pretty man who turned out to have a wife in two other places. He in jail.

"An additional ten dollars a week," Ben Lee say. He never marry. He grow fuzz on his face like corn silking instead of beard. His vest got shiny black buttons.

"I need it be written down," I say. "Her name be on it and motorized."

"Motorized?" Ben Lee ask.

"Notarized," Patricia said. She smarter than Ben Lee.

"We'll see what we can do," he say.

He write up a paper which tell how much I get paid and guarantee it six months. It say I be fired only for dereliction of duty and disregard of the law. I tell them I never derelicted anybody, I a churchwoman, and in regard to the law I always been regarding. Miss Alice Louella sign the paper. Patricia and Ben Lee sign it. I sign. It motorized.

"Notarized," Jim say after he read it and giggle.

"They like it when I dumb," I say. "Make them feel smarter. Feel smarter, they treat me better. Everybody happy."

"Me too," he say, keep giggling. "You about as dumb as a cat in the cream."

I go back to Alice Louella's on Monday afternoon in July. It hot and dry, tobacco drooping in the fields, the crows too lazy to fly off the road where they pecking on a runover dead blacksnake shiny in the sun. They just walk into the Queen Anne's lace and beggar-lice lining the ditch to wait for me to go by. I not wear a uniform. I still got them, green dresses with white collars like waitresses at the Kitty Kat Kafe, but in the bottom of my chiffonnier drawer. They going to stay there.

Patricia glad to see me. She already pack her bag. She on the porch waiting. She chew the corner of her mouth so much it pull her face crooked.

"Mamma's taking her nap," she whisper. "I have your first week's pay. I told Mamma she shouldn't knock her cane on the floor. I bought her a little bell. You phone if you have trouble. I had a long talk with Mamma and am sure you won't."

Then she gone. She leave so fast it ten minutes 'fore the dust settle on the grass. I look around the kitchen. Dirty dishes high in the sink. Patricia leave them piled for me.

I soaping dishes, the bell ring. It a tinkly bell, like Reverend Jubal J. Bottom use in Sunday school at Mercy Seat Church. I climb the stairs. They steeper.

Miss Alice Louella in bed. She have on her blue negligee, rings, and red wig. She propped up by pillows. She smile till she see I not wearing a uniform.

"Celeste, I'm so happy you're back," she say. "I'm certain we'll get along better. I expect you outgrew those old uniforms. We'll order new ones."

"Waste of money," I say. "We'll not wear 'em."

"On the contrary, you have always worn uniforms in this house. It will save you money and your everyday clothes."

"It not in the understanding I have to wear uniforms," I say. I see she been taking her tonic.

"Nevertheless, I would prefer you to do so."

"No'm, I give up uniforms. I got my own dresses. They cooler on my back."

"Now look here, Celeste, you haven't been in this house ten minutes and you're sassing me," she say.

"You want me to leave?" I say. "I don't mind. I get paid if I do or don't."

"You wouldn't!" Her rings jingle on her fingers.

"I just go on home, sit on the porch, and get paid. All up to you, Miss Alice Louella."

Her mouth squeeze, her eyes blink, and she raise her chin. It tremble.

"We'll talk about the issue later," she say. "We'll now discuss dinner."

"Chipped beef on toast," I say.

"It is much too hot for chipped beef," she say. "A nice fruit salad I think. Yes. A nice melon salad."

"No melons in the icebox," I say. "Chipped beef on toast all Miss Patricia leave. Too hot to walk to market."

"You are sassing me again and I won't have it! Nor will I eat chipped beef on toast. You understand plain English?"

"Yes'm I do, I plain," I say and go back down the steps to the kitchen. I fix myself a glass of mint tea. Patricia leave newspapers on the table. I read about the diving horse at the Howell County Fair. He dive off a fifty-foot platform into a tank of water. A yellow-haired girl in a red bathing suit ride him. I think it be nice to ride out of hotness on a white horse into a tank of water. Some splash.

The bell tinkle. It five o'clock, tonic time. I sit in the chair, turn pages, and read 'bout Chinese chickens that lay square eggs. Fit on toast. The bell ring again. I turn page and read "Blondie." Her husband Dagwood hide in closet to get out of cutting grass. Bad as Jim. The bell ring a third time.

"Ice!" she holler. "You know I can't take my tonic without ice."

I stand, go to the steps, and say, "Pretty please."

"What?" she suck air and call back.

"I just like to hear you say please one time."

She silent. She so silent I hear it. That silence so thick you put it in a box and mail it to Mississippi.

"I am telling you one more time to bring ice for my tonic," she say.

I say nothing. I hear that silence moving around up there. I go back to the kitchen. She taking her tonic without the ice. She also dialing the phone, maybe calling Patricia, Ben Lee, or Banker John. I read about a goat that is nursing eight puppies. Cocker spaniards.

She eat at six. I wait for the bell. It ring at seven. I go to the steps.

"I am ready for my dinner," she holler from her room.

"Coming up," I say and heat the chipped beef. I carry it on a tray along with a peeled pear and iced tea. She still in the bed. She stare at the tray.

"I told you I would not!" she say.

"I sit it right here by the bed and maybe you change your mind," I say.

"I am not about to change my mind," she say and reach for the phone.

I go back down the steps, eat her plate of chipped beef, pear, drink tea, and read the paper. I read about a man who live eight years in the furnace room of the Norfolk city hall before anybody discover him. Got caught when his snoring heard through new heating ducks. Miss Alice Louella still dialing the phone. Maybe she having hard time raising people. She taking more tonic. No ice.

When I carry up milk before she sleep, I ask if anything she need.

"You will not be here tomorrow," she say.

"That case, don't expect no breakfast," I say.

I sleep good. The basement quiet. Jim sneak around back, and I let him in. I slip him out before sunup.

I fix myself scrambled eggs, bacon, and hot biscuits spread with blackberry jam. She bound to smell the coffee, but she don't ring the bell. More tonic I think.

This a day Raincoat come. I ready for him. He bring her tonic in a brown paper sack. He tie a miller's knot using baler twine. He leave the tonic in the pie safe on the back porch. He never been in the house. Ben Lee see he get money. Not this time.

"She don't want it no more," I say. "You stay away from this place."

"You have Miss Louella tell me," Raincoat say and grin. He a scarecrow hanging on sticks. A clinking scarecrow.

"I going have Jim do the telling," I say. "You come around here again, and I going to have Jim tell you all kinds of new news."

Raincoat, he stop grinning. He then settle the brown sack back in his raincoat and walk off down the drive, his fast feet raising slow dust. I hear her moving around upstairs. She see him too.

She ring the bell. She standing at the head of the steps. She has on her negligee and is poking her cane. It black with a brass knob. Once belong to Mr. Ben Ranson.

"Was that Raincoat I saw walking away?" she ask. "Did he leave anything for me?"

"No'm, we just pass the time of day," I say.

She push a hand to the neck of her negligee, and the cane tap the floor.

"I am out of my tonic," she say.

"I fix you a soft egg and strip of bacon," I say.

"I do not want a soft egg and strip of bacon," she say. "I want what I need, which is my daily tonic as Dr. Throckmorton prescribed and ordered."

"Well Raincoat he gone," I say. Old Dr. Throckmorton prescribe and order anything to be shut of her.

"I will see that he returns," she say.

She again on the phone. She on the phone most of the afternoon. I hear her dialing. She wear that phone out. Using an umbrella to carry my shade with me, I walk down to Mr. Mosley's market near the courthouse. I buy groceries, which he tote up on his palm and arm. He send the bill to the bank. Mr. Mosley he win the watermelon-seed-spitting contest every year at the Howell County Fair. Got a trophy on the counter. When I come back, she still phoning. I cut up, flour, and fry a pullet.

"You hungry yet?" I holler up the steps. She don't answer. She dial. She keep dialing. Nobody much to home. I eat a chicken leg and read about a woman who fat 'cause she walk in her sleep. Years she don't know she eat but wake up fat. She think her man raiding the icebox. He now fasten it with a combination lock.

"You hate me, don't you?" Miss Alice Louella holler. "You have always hated me."

I go to the foot of the steps. "I don't hate nobody," I say. "Hate is sin. Down here is some hot-peppered chicken if you want to eat."

"I cannot come down those stairs," she say.

"You put one foot after the other," I say. "Easy as pie."

"All you black people hate us whites now," she say. "We didn't make you black. It is not our fault."

"That sure right," I say. "But these old feet tired. I don't believe they make it up the steps. I put some chicken on the plate here. You come down and get it when you ready."

"Hate!" she shout. "You're full of hate!"

I leave the chicken on the steps. It getting toward dark, and I peek from the kitchen. She still not come down. She on the phone again. Guess everybody out of town. She bang the cane. I read about an alligator who eat dog food off porches down in Florida. Gator like Gravy Train.

At dark I go get plate of chicken. Jim come around. I feed and run him off. No time to be messing around. I don't go to the basement to sleep. I sit in the kitchen, lights out.

She sneak down late. I hear her in the dark. She stop on the steps. She search for her chicken. She stand on the steps. Then she come on down to the hall. I tiptoe to the pantry. She shuffle into the kitchen and switch on the lights. She go to the icebox. I slip out the pantry and surprise her.

"See, you walking fine," I say. "Exercise good for you legs."

"You are black vileness!" she say. "I'll have the law on you. I'll call the sheriff."

"The sheriff he might be busy," I say. "You hungry, I fix a sandwich. Got monkey meat."

"I'm not eating monkey meat or anything else from your spiteful hand!" she say and go back up the steps. She dial. She dial through the night.

In the morning I cook a big breakfast—biscuits, fried ham, eggs, apples, grits, redeye gravy, all the good smells rising up. I fix a nice tray, linen napkin, silver, coffee, glass of ice water, and carry it to her. She lie face down on the bed crying. She got the bed shaking she cry so hard. Canopy and tassels quivering. Black streaking her cheeks from eyes running over.

"Why is everybody treating me this way?" she wail. "I was beautiful once. I was loved!"

I remember her from the Moose Parade, she young, wearing a white shining gown, bare shoulders, and a big white hat with a red band, and she stand on a float shaped like a swan to throw flowers. Her red hair long. I never seen anybody so pretty. She throw me a rose.

"You was," I say. "I pretty once too. Not like you, but I not always fat, and Jim think I fine. Why you reckon he do?"

"I am not well," she say. "For a long time I've not been well." She push at her wig, which has got crooked on her head, and almost fall off. She got white tufts of hair, like blobs of cotton pasted on patches of pink scalp. She again wail. "I am horrible and ugly. I wish I could die! I want to be dead!"

I sit on the bed and lift her. She a little girl, a baby doll, and I hold her. I fix her negligee, set her wig on, and thumb dark tears off her cheeks. She cry against me like she my own Winona, spoilt rotten once, now boss the perfume counter in the Baltimore department store.

"I remember you," I say. "I wait and watch you leave the church on your wedding day, and I think you the prettiest woman I ever see. You brush past, and I think I burn my fingers just to touch you. I comb rice from my hair for a week and save it in a dish. You still got pretty in you. Pretty don't die. It just hide. It there now behind your green eyes."

She sniffle, sit up from me, wipe her nose. I set out food on her marble table. She real hungry. She eat faster than she want in front of me. I pretend I don't watch. When she finish she lean back and touch her throat.

"Do you think perhaps Raincoat might come today?" she ask.

"Might be," I say. "He likely pay us a visit. Maybe I have a little tonic with you to help my feet. You know my feet need a little medicine sometime."

She lie on the bed and sleep. I walk to Mosley's Market, and when I see Raincoat sitting under the sycamore, I tell him to stop by the house. Miss Alice Louella rest most of the afternoon, and when she stir I carry up her tonic and ice. She too ladylike to reach after it quick. I been to the garden and find a pink cornflower out near the old carriage house where Mr. Ben Ranson kept his buggies. They cobwebbed now and covered with dust. I put cornflower on the tray too.

"Celeste," she say as she sip her tonic and eye me, "how can you be so nice when I've been so horrible to you?"

"I nice not for what you has been but what you was and can be," I say.

I believe she almost say thank you. Hard for her to do. That night after I clean up in the kitchen and snap out the lights, she call to me from the head of the steps.

"I might come down tomorrow," she say. "Take a walk through the boxwood garden if you'll help. And you'll perhaps want to use the bedroom on the first floor, the rear. It'd be cooler for you there, the night breeze if you open a window."

Next morning when I carry up her breakfast, she got my cornflower in a little silver vase sitting in sunlight on her marble-top table. Spot of tarnish. 'Fore the day over I think I probably polish that vase. Good chance.

SWEET ARMAGEDDON

A quiet winter thunder during the blowing night caused Amos to turn his head on the pillow and lift his thin aching body to stare toward the nailed window. Skeletal branches of a leafless Judas tree jerked as if suffering. His breathing slowed. Martha sighed beside him, a gentle wheeze. Fingers of her right hand drifted across the sheet in search of him.

. . . a great earthquake . . . the moon became as blood. . . .

The thunder a CSX coal drag passing through Richmond's freight yard on a journey to Newport News and the Chesapeake Bay. The coal would be dumped into a ship's hold, blackness showering down, and if a man lay under it, could he know a deeper darkness? Yes. At the end would come the perfection of everything, even blackness itself.

He lowered himself to the bed so as not to disturb Martha. He no longer minded his body's pain. Pain was honest and spoke the truth. When an arm, a shoulder, a spinal disc hurt, the message signaled a malfunctioning of parts. Pain too would be perfected. Was not that the message given mankind these last days?

. . . thrust in thy sickle and reap . . . for the time is come . . . the harvest of the earth is ripe. . . .

Signs were incessant, their velocity increasing like a whirlwind. Everywhere his eyes fell upon destruction. INFANT BABY FOUND IN DUMPSTER. He'd wakened during the chilled night and pictured a newborn child among eggshells, melon rinds, and moist coffee grounds. Images of wickedness no longer sickened him. They confirmed.

. . . I will turn thee back and put hooks in thy jaws. . . .

He listened to sounds from the street: a pickup starting, dogs barking, shoes slapping cracked pavement. In this neighborhood somebody
was always running, flight in their feet, rapacity in their stride. Wind
gusted, causing a limb of the Judas to scrape the gutter. Noise easily
penetrated flimsy siding of the tiny house.

Despite the constant scouring of limb against gutter, he slipped
back into a dusky sleep for thirty minutes, brought fully awake by
squealing tires and the gunning of an engine in front of the house, a
residence lived in dozens of times before he rented it from a dark man
who knocked late Friday nights to collect his money. Floors were covered with cracked and buckled linoleum, windows needed caulking, and
the water heater leaked, about it the faint smell of gas. Down at the
corner the neighborhood became black. Numberless raucous children
spun frantically or climbed misshapen apple trees to throw hard, shriveled fruit at one another.

He and Martha had never owned a house, not in forty-two years
of marriage. They possessed only a few sticks of furniture. All their
lives together they had been sojourners. How many decrepit residences
filled with cast-off sofas, chairs whose legs were not substantial, dishes
stained yellow, knives never sharp? If either of them wished to discard
an item, the hullabaloo from the congregations.

How long, O Lord? How long?

He dressed slowly, careful of his balance, or lack of it, steadying
himself on the antique chest of drawers, a single possession from Martha's family, as he pulled at his long johns and wool trousers. He also
wore a plaid shirt, a sweater, and a felt cap. He'd once been tall, had
run the distances at Davidson and established a North Carolina colle-
giate record for the mile which remained on the books nearly a decade.
Age, the relentless wear of the ministry, had honed him down.

. . . even to hoar hairs will I carry you. . . .

For a time a black-and-white photograph of him hung in the gym passageway, framed behind glass, and during years he returned to homecomings, he walked past that picture, not eyeing it openly, rather glancing sidelong shyly. The October afternoon he passed and it was gone, he broke stride and felt lightheaded—as if robbed of his body.

    . . . *God will not hear vanity.* . . .

He walked softly down through the cold house to the kitchen, so small and dismal in spite of paintings—flaming mums, pink roses, blue iris—Martha had hung, none new, most done years before she gave herself entirely to him, her life, her dreams, in the old way of women to men. He clenched his eyes as if standing in a storm and thought of what he'd given her in return.

Her hair had once been thickly dark, and she'd been gladdened by all sights before her violet eyes, a child at a feast till he took her to the mountains where they lived in little more than a shack, the wind a skinning knife, howling like the damned, the manse's water frozen, she wearing a mink stole at the neck of her bathrobe as she chipped ice from their sink and tried not to weep. He held her shivering body against his own, trying to keep her from knowing winter.

    . . . *they seemed unto him but a few days, for the love he*
    had to her. . . .

He stopped before the scarred sink, blackened where dripping had worn away enamel. The faucets he'd fixed countless times ate washers. He bent to look out the window at the narrow backyard and unpainted plank fence. His patching hadn't prevented children from using his yard as a shortcut to an alley which in turn led to a street and middle-school playground. They left a trail that ruined his meager grass. Children climbed over, dogs dug under despite brickbats and rocks he'd stomped into holes. A brown mongrel turned on him snarling, backing Amos into his own house.

    . . . *then shall be great tribulation . . . one stone not left*
    upon another. . . .

He peered at the sky. For an instant a growing redness thrilled him, a celestial conflagration, yet even as his knees gave, he saw it was only the sun's first scarlet rays striking disjoining clouds. He pictured the cataclysm, the rolling thunder and horrible lightning streaking down black corridors of the earth, the dazzling rapture in the heavens.

He heated a pan of water for his tea. He did not drink coffee or other, stronger stimulants. His freshman year in college he'd become tipsy when an upperclassman fed him grapefruit juice spiked with tasteless vodka. Amos climbed an ancient sycamore beside the river and alarmed others, who called for him to come down from the white branches. Like a tightrope walker he made his way along the limb, not realizing what he'd drunk, believing his feeling simply the joy of life on a languid June afternoon, the goodness of God's world. He spread his arms and dived into the fast tawny water. They thought him broken, drowned, dead, but he was merely knocked windless, his face and chest lacerated on rocks beneath the surface. They cheered him that afternoon, girls too, and he received a bid to a fraternity, which he declined not only from lack of funds but also the suspicion he was already promised.

. . . wine . . . at the last it biteth like a serpent and stingeth like an adder. . . .

So many doors had been open to him, hallways of marble and power. A recruiter offered a position with the trust department of the largest bank in Virginia; yet Amos made his irrevocable choice, which came not on a mountaintop or even a scene of great peace and beauty, but along a busy Richmond street when he, while wrestling with decision, looked upward among shadows of tomblike white buildings to a simple cross touched by resplendent sunlight atop the belfry of a colonial church as out of place in the business district as milk in oil. That cross sparkled in his eyes, seemed to detach itself and float down like a shimmering blossom and settle burning on his forehead, a divine kiss.

At the same time over the din of traffic, under it, from within, from everywhere he heard a still small voice say, "Take my hand and walk with me."

    . . . choose you this day whom you will serve. . . .

His water was ready, the boiling rattling the nearly empty pan. He sat at the small, round table he himself had built. He was no handyman, no person with a gift for tools, but he'd been forced through necessity to adapt his fingers to hammer and saw. He could repair minor leaks, mend furniture, and had wired the extra telephone to the upstairs bedroom.

As if his thinking caused it, those phones rang now. He hurried to the set at the foot of the steps so Martha would not be disturbed.

"Shiner," the voice said. "Blind my eyes!"

Laughter before the connection broke. Neighborhood children who made fun of his baldness, the sunlight reflecting from it. They would never believe he'd once had fine hair, auburn locks that fell across his brow when he preached. He hardly remembered losing it, as if waking one winter morning, gazing into the mirror, and seeing for the first time the deterioration wrought by age and devoted service.

    . . . Thou shalt come to thy grave in a full age, like as a
    shock of corn cometh in in his season. . . .

A rumbling, a vibration reached his feet through the floor. He stood from the table, rushed to the front door, and opened it. Only more heavy trucks. Sounds of traffic, night or day. Wet clotted leaves lay plastered flat against broken pavement. A flight of pigeons flew over so close he heard the wash of wings. Then sonic boom, the plane unseen, perhaps an aircraft to be used by God for the last clenching of His angry hand. The plane flew on.

He knelt for the newspaper on the stoop. During the summer glossy blue lizards had crept from crumbled mortar to sun themselves and made him think of Brazil and his years among Indians at the jungle's edge—quiet, dark-eyed people whose aroused savagery was like the wrath of terrible children. Now he lived in the American jungle proclaimed by the *Times-Dispatch* he held: MAN KNIFES TWO DAUGH-TERS, WIFE, NEIGHBOR.

He stopped reading and would allow his subscription to lapse. Did he not know what appeared in the papers and periodicals before they lay at his door?

> . . . *nation shall rise against nation* . . . *earthquakes* . . .
> *famine* . . . *pestilences* . . . *fearful sights.* . . .

Fearful sights: LONG VIOLATED CHILDREN CLAIM THEY LOVE THEIR FATHER. God's omnipotent hand was lifted against the world's culminating evil.

> . . . *she shall be burned with fire; for strong is the Lord*
> *God who judgeth her.* . . .

As he returned to the kitchen, he heard Martha rise from their bed and scuff her way to the house's single bathroom. He listened to her cough and the noisy gurgling of the old plumbing. She washed herself. He knew every sound of her. Long ago they reached the point when nothing lay hidden. Dissected each was before the other's eye, but tenderly.

> . . . *better a dinner of herbs where love is.* . . .

She came down the steps, a brittle woman now, her skin old linen, her arms crossed against cold, her posture pulled forward by the arms. She'd wrapped herself in a mended lilac housecoat. She wore white wool socks pulled high on her shrinking calves and the rose-colored slippers he'd bought for her last birthday. The luster of her dark hair, now sparsely white and carefully brushed, had been what first attracted him as he walked behind her from a Grace Street market—long, bouncy, alive with a sunlit vibrancy.

"I'll do your tea," he said, again haunted by her face, time's leaching of it. Her smile was automatic, her brave banner. She could've come from some grave misfortune, a ghastly hurt or death, and her reddish brown eyes darted at him as if surprised he was present.

. . . *bring down my gray hairs with sorrow to the grave. . . .*

"Will you be going to the post office?" she asked, her voice a slight tremolo. With a ladylike sweep of hands beneath her housecoat, she sat at the table and prayed. Her bluish fingers curved to her cup. He felt he could've reached to her hair and plucked it from her head like cotton. I never, he thought, wanted this to happen to you. I meant to bring you treasure.

Yes, he said, he would go to the post office, but first he fixed her a slice of toast, buttered it, and spread it with orange marmalade. He didn't realize the hot water had again failed till he rinsed his cup at the sink. She'd washed herself in cold and not complained.

He crossed to the utility closet at the rear of the kitchen where the heater was enclosed, pipes rusty and corroded around the joints. As he sniffed, he adjusted the burner, yet no matter how he fooled with the controls, the yellow flame burned feebly and as if about to expire. He'd telephoned the gas people and been told it was not their responsibility, since the heater was inside the house. That meant asking a plumber to come, and the last insolent bloodsucker had charged forty-five dollars just for walking in the door.

On his knees Amos shut off the gas, cleaned the burner nozzle with a snip of stove wire, and again lit the flame. He looked for Martha and found her in the parlor dusting—parlor too grand a word for the shadowy room hardly large enough to hold the love seat, the black upright piano, and two chairs. He'd taped the rosebud wallpaper at the top to keep it from peeling farther. A mildew dampness prevailed even in the fullness of summer's heat.

At times she played the piano, leaning to the hymnal open upon it, her stiff delicate fingers arched to the keys as if touching flesh. From walls hung more of her flower paintings and sunny landscapes as well as the enlargement of her and Amos standing young, tanned, and happy on a Brazil beach, between them Mary, their daughter, a bright, grinning four-year-old holding a seashell toward the camera while beyond lay the ocean, not blue, but a shimmering undisturbed green, like a pasture, solid enough to walk across.

. . . the flocks of my pasture are men. . . .

"Let me," he said, drawing the dustrag, a piece of old flannel nightgown, from her hand. She'd been running it over the coffee table, which held theological pamphlets, his leather-covered Bible, and the one book he'd authored, *The Ever Perfect God,* published not by any notable press but a private Memphis house with the last money Martha had held onto from her inheritance. The volume received one review, that in a conservative Presbyterian journal, and sold less than two hundred copies over a decade. Cardboard boxes containing the remainder of the limited printing were stored in the cramped, dirt-dauber-infested attic.

"I'm stronger today," she told him, not wishing to give up the cloth.

"Better to rest," he said.

What was wrong with her? Nothing specific, no ailment the doctors could positively identify and say do this, take that. She had simply broken down physically, her body called on too long to bear weight and to function. At times a leg would wobble or a hand not obey. In lifting her cup, she might bump her chin. She stumbled when no obstruction existed to tangle her feet.

He accompanied her up to their bed, the room displaying pots of geraniums on a bench before the window. All windows were nailed against thieves. She kept plants growing no matter where they traveled over the earth. The view was to the east and brown frame houses nearly identical to the one they lived in, dwellings built for employees of the Philip Morris stemmery, from which the coarse odor of tobacco seeped through the neighborhood.

A middle-aged man who worked for the city lived directly across the street, and Amos had seen him beat his wife—on a Saturday night, a silent, flat drama during which the woman simply hunched against a wall and held fingers curved over her face. She was passive, sullen, and never raised her eyes. Her flaxen hair flung about with the blows.

. . . *woman is the glory of man.* . . .

Martha turned on her side toward the flowers. He drew a blanket over her, went back downstairs, buttoned on his overcoat, and reset his cap. When he left the house, he relocked the door behind, though anyone half determined could easily force entry.

Break-ins around the neighborhood were almost as common as the arrogant quarreling starlings, and during late summer he'd wakened with the certainty somebody stood outside touching the house. He switched on the bedside lamp, hoping to scare off whoever was there, but pretended to Martha he wished only to rearrange the coverlet.

. . . *I come as a thief.* . . .

Wind gusted, punching him, gathering street grit to throw against his face, stirring trash of the gutters. A bristling yellowish cur barked at him, the rigidly moving dog a member of a gang that dug in his yard. He walked wide to pass, careful to keep his gaze from meeting the animal's bulging flickering eyes—a contact, he'd read, which often prompted attack.

He needed gloves. He turned up his coat collar and again adjusted the cap blown loose on his head. Or was he actually shrinking? He felt smaller, lighter, as if his bones were twigs and his skin a paperish fabric over them. If he knocked against an object, he might tear.

He glanced at the sky, a silverish blue, cumulus clouds bunching, steeds of the heavens.

. . . behold a pale horse . . . his name that sat on him was Death. . . .

Two young blacks ran down the sidewalk toward him, causing fear to squeeze up through his chest to his throat. As they flew past, he whirled. They sped across a lot where a house had burned to cinders. At the rear they leaped through a fence gap. No one gave chase. His heart beat wildly.

At the corner he walked toward Hull Street and his post office. He allowed no mail delivery to the house. Too much was stolen on the block, including a check that had required months to straighten out with the Board of Missions. For an entire week he and Martha had lived mostly on breakfast food, peanut butter, and A & P pancake mix.

Sirens startled him, and he winced as fire engines swept by, red lights flaring and reflecting in the truck's yellow sheen. Their power pushed him like a flow of water, and he reached both hands to hold his cap in place. The roar caused his ears to ache. Great tires beat the pavement, and the tromboning exhausts left behind an oily blue pall.

. . . power was given unto him to scorch men with fire. . . .

Again he walked, on the fringe of commerce now: a beauty parlor, a music store displaying trumpets in its dusty window, a doughnut shop, a launderette where women slouched smoking and waiting in orange plastic chairs, sidewalk street vendors selling used furniture, pots and pans, motorcycles, some disemboweled. Across a cinder-block wall an obscene word had been sprayed with red paint.

Then the gantlet of youths, loitering, both black and white, a few older, yet not men either, people in society's limbo, only dangerous. They leaned against storefronts and power poles, hands in gleaming colorful jackets, their eyes weighing passersby. Amos believed they sensed when he carried money, that those feral eyes invaded his pockets and thus it was only a matter of time and opportunity till he was seized and shaken to be emptied.

"Give us the word, Shiner," one said, though Amos saw no lips move. The laughter contained no mirth, and he willed himself not to hurry or show fright. Blood pounded his ears.

. . . *in the last days scoffers, walking after their own lusts.* . . .

The post office was a substation where clerks worked behind caged windows. Tarnished combination boxes were no longer used, their glass insets shattered. A trash bin overflowed. The spray-painter had been here too, the same filthy word written this time over a spotless young sailor proclaiming Go with the Best!

Amos stood in line. Ahead were two black women, one holding a baby that peered over its mother's shoulder at him, the ebony eyes unblinking and seemingly worldly. The other woman bought a money order and stamped envelope, acts which required shifts of a shopping bag and pocketbook. Suddenly the baby squalled, still staring at Amos, and the mother faced him threateningly as if he'd done something to cause it.

When Amos reached the window, the clerk recognized him and turned to ranks of wooden alphabetized pigeonholes. Apprehension gripped Amos when he failed to see the grayish envelope sent by Ministerial Retirement, but then it appeared, lodged between unsolicited catalogs. He kept all catalogs, not that he ordered from them, but it pleased Martha to leaf through the advertisements.

A fourth piece of mail was a letter from the development office at Davidson. He no longer sent money, yet the college continued to carry him on its roll. Once he'd welcomed the magazine, eager to learn what classmates were doing. Now he felt he knew those men in another century. At least the hurt was gone, his sense of failure caused by turning page after page listing accomplishments and awards. The year his book came out, Davidson mentioned it—not with a review or recommendation, but merely a sentence in the alumni notes.

   . . . *envy is the rottenness of the bones.* . . .

He began the second leg of his journey, the walk from the post office to the bank. He fitted the check into the breast pocket of his shirt and pulled his sweater down tight against it. As he crossed Hull with the light, a city bus rolled by so close he felt its diesel exhaust against his legs. Passengers stared at him from the superiority of elevation. The rear of the bus displayed a poster of a beautiful black girl wearing a skimpy pink bathing suit and drinking diet cola. Beneath, the caption read, Your Soul Refreshment!

He passed the tattoo parlor, relieved that this time of morning no gangs loitered at the entrance, and averted his eyes from the coiled green dragon with its yellow fiery mouth and split red tongue. There were carmine hearts, entwined serpents, and a voluptuous Asiatic woman who grew from petals of a blue tulip. The whore, he thought, of Babylon.

Then a series of empty stores, one displaying headless unclothed manikins in the window. He heard a moan, perhaps human, or the wind, and thought of hideous perversions taking place in darkness. He was glad to see in the distance a city policeman mounted on a plodding sorrel.

   . . . *Behold a red horse.* . . .

He pressed his inner arm against the check, so little for what he'd given the church. It, his social security, and the pittance from the Board of Missions was all he had in this world. For a time he held services in the abandoned bakery, preaching the word to men whose drink- and life-ravaged faces were glazed with doom and despair.

He passed an alley, careful to curve out from it in case anyone lay in wait, and saw two grown men fighting—hitting each other with quiet deadliness, both bloody, clothes torn, their bodies bunched in violence. He hurried past.

. . . every man's sword shall be against his brother. . . .

Even the paltry check had to be cashed at a bank. For that he crossed Lee Bridge and the James River, which was like the passage over a border to a more prosperous country. White buildings rose in sunshine, concrete gleamed, and tinted glass shone as if the purplish eyes of insects. A fountain splashed above a scalloped pond before the temple of money.

. . . I will rain upon him an overflowing rain. . . .

Swift doors hissed open before him, and he walked among potted shrubs, tubular furniture, and sculptured birds on pedestals. Vultures, he thought. He endorsed the back of the check before a teller's eyes, a young woman painted and doll-like who always asked whether he had an account, though certain he did not. She'd seen him a hundred times, yet required identification, which she studied before accepting the check and subtracting the bank's five-dollar fee. He and Martha could eat an entire day on that fee.

Cash in hand, he feared the return to the house. He thought of himself as an unarmed ship making its way among mines and submarines. His routine was to travel extra blocks to avoid the route used to reach the bank. Often he wove a path through a Safeway store to throw off anyone who might be following.

He used another trick. He sat in a chrome-and-plastic chair near the bank's entrance and when nobody watched bent quickly to shape the twenty-dollar bills around his skinny ankles. He jerked his white cotton socks up over the money. Elastic bound it tight. A surprised woman customer glanced down at him. He pretended to be retying his shoelaces.

A large man walked laughing from the branch manager's office beside the radiant vault. He wore a gray homburg and a gray overcoat with black piping at the collar. Despite his size, he moved easily, and his skin shone under the gilded lighting. His dark trousers were sharply creased, his black shoes polished. He pulled on bronze-colored pigskin gloves as he talked over his shoulder to the manager, who followed with an air of subservience. The large man's green eyes moved past Amos and swept back.

"Speed, is it you?" he asked.

"Whale?" Amos replied, and they stepped to each other and embraced. Whale buffeted Amos, pounded his back, danced him while the branch manager, tellers, and customers watched and smiled.

"Look at him, will you!" Whale cried, holding Amos at arm's length and turning him for all to see. Whale's complexion was rosy, his teeth outsized. Swept-back silverish hair had been precisely barbered, the flesh of his jowls shaved to a gloss. He smelled of cologne. Those heavy jowls quivered with delight.

"Thinking about you just this morning, telling Pam how you and I stole the class bell and hid it in the cemetery!" Whale said, still manhandling Amos. "Listen, you're eating breakfast with me."

Denying Whale was like standing up to a force of nature. He became all encompassing arms and pressing body. Amos explained he had to get back to Martha, and Whale offered to pick her up too. Amos didn't want him to see the shabby little house, the decaying neighborhood, his diminished wife.

"She can't," he said. "She's under a doctor's care."

A bent truth, and Amos hated lying. All his life in the big things he'd told the truth, but he would protect Martha from the shock and humiliation of having Whale appear at the door when she'd had no time to prepare herself, mask her frailty, induce color into her cheeks, lift from the closet some last sheer garment.

"Well, let's take her flowers," Whale said, and Amos dissuaded him from that too. The easiest out was to go to breakfast and escape as soon as possible. The manager invited Amos into the spongy-carpeted office and handed him a modish ivory phone. His fingers shaky, Amos touched the lighted buttons while Whale and the manager stood in the doorway talking of new accounts. The manager, a fair young man, wore a charcoal suit with vest.

The phone rang seven times before Martha answered, and Amos almost panicked. He pictured her lying on the floor of the cold house, her robe loose, her feet bare. He envisioned her violated and bloody. Then her voice—well bred, friendly, despite the tremolo expressing no alarm.

"Why I'm fine," she said. "I was playing the piano. Whale? You mean Thomas Ferguson? How very nice. You were such friends. Don't worry about me. I'm warm. Thomas used to ask me out. Always breaking things. Tell him I send love."

"If you smell gas—"

"Amos, I'm not helpless."

Then Whale had the phone from Amos' hand, talking to Martha, his voice loud and hearty, speaking so everybody in the bank could hear, calling her beautiful, telling her she'd always been his favorite girl, promising that his Pam would get them together for dinner. Though dinner was never likely—Amos had learned to come up with quick excuses—he knew how pleased and flattered Martha must feel. He imagined her lifting fingers to her hair in the immemorial primping of women.

Amos received the phone back, yet was hardly able to hang up before Whale had hold of him again, crowding him out through the lobby and glass doorway. They crossed to the lot at the side of the bank and a bluish black limousine parked in a reserved space. The seats were liver-colored leather, and the dash controls had the stainless-steel complexity of a laboratory. It is, Amos thought, the kind of car I've ridden in only at funerals. The smiling manager opened the door for Whale and waved as they backed off.

> . . . *all the chariots of Egypt, and captains over every one of them.* . . .

"I no longer need to work," Whale told Amos. "They kicked my butt upstairs, use me mostly on consulting stuff. But I love the life."

He drove aggressively, pushing the car's nose into the street so boldly the other traffic had to swerve, honk, make room. Whale grinned and winked as he sped them uptown.

"Where you carrying us?" Amos asked.

"Got to fatten you up, buddy. Now give me a playback on your life these past years."

Amos wouldn't even attempt to explain he'd been to the mountains, runty towns, the muddied Amazon, to Philistines everywhere, that he'd been mocked and rejected and was not only awaiting the end but praying for it. Each morning he opened his eyes hoping the dawn the last the heavens were denied to the faithful. Whale wouldn't understand. Amos had as well speak in a dead language. He said merely that he'd been occupied with duties of the ministry till his retirement of the last eighteen months.

"I noticed you limping," Whale said.

"The gnawings of arthritis."

"Thought maybe a witch doctor got you. You were down in the jungle, weren't you? Poisoned spear or arrow. Makes a better story."

They'd roomed together at Davidson, both athletes, Whale center on the football team, yet they were never alike. Whale worshiped in chapel with no more change of spirit than when snapping his wet towel through the locker room or lying beside a girl in the grass. Amos loved him, however, and helped him graduate, while Whale in turn wished to share every joy he came upon with Amos.

They moved along stately Monument Avenue now, before the granite mansions artfully restored under the gaze of Confederate heroes on horses forever noble. Stylish citizens walked past decorative gates, iron fences, and gaily painted jockeys. Brass lamps and nameplates glinted on elegant porches. Cars parked at the curbs had the European flair.

. . . riches profit not in the days of wrath. . . .

"You swiped Martha away, you know that," Whale said. "Why she picked a brain like you instead of a warm lovable human being like me I can't figure. And you dragged her to the jungle."

Whale drove too fast and waved at a policeman beyond Lee's statue. Amos had indeed taken Martha down to the jungle and remembered the pain in her violet eyes when she first saw children with open sores. She'd kept the clinic running even as funds were withdrawn till in her weakness and despair at the death of their daughter, Mary, she'd also fallen prey to meningitis and lain burning with fever on a straw mattress for twenty days. He would lift her mosquito netting and sponge her parchment-like face. During the evening of the twentieth day she raised fingers to his wrist, making no words with her trembling lips but a sound like the rasping of sandpaper.

. . . beauty is vain: but a woman that feareth the Lord,
she shall be praised. . . .

"Me, I've tied the knot again," Whale said, slowing at a light, yet impatient, the signal a personal affront for changing against him. They stopped beside a church built of hewn stone in the Gothic manner, a soaring structure whose arched stained-glass windows portrayed the feeding of the multitude, Christ's walking on water, and the dolorous procession of the cross. It was a society church, the sort of pulpit Amos had never been offered. His largest congregation was less than two hundred souls, and in the end he lost even that because of stands he'd taken.

"What happened to your first wife?" he asked.

"Becky left me for a Winston-Salem horse breeder. Parting was friendly, unlike Tess, who was looking for a fancy man—which God knows I'm not—and tried to empty my pockets."

"Tess?" Amos asked, turning to him. "You've been married three times?"

"I believe in family," Whale said and laughed uproariously as he punched at Amos with gloved knuckles.

Whale apparently traded women in like used cars for newer, sleeker models. During Amos' life it never occurred to him his helpmate could be other than Martha. She was more than anything he believed he would ever possess or deserve. When in Cumberland Gap the pretty redheaded organist entered his study and bared her breasts for him, he'd bowed his head and covered his eyes, causing her to pull furiously at her blouse, leave the church, and not come back.

... *thy wife shall be as a fruitful vine by the sides of thine houses.* ...

Whale swerved to the curb before one of the grander brownstones. A green canopy with white initials in English script covered the entranceway. Amos glimpsed an empty terrace, balconies, turrets, and a uniformed doorman. The place was a private men's club.

"I'm not dressed!" Amos protested.

"Saturday mornings make no difference," Whale said. "Members come any way they want. I've been in Bermudas."

A coveralled young black parked the car. The uniformed white doorman opened the club's brass-appointed door and bowed them past. They walked through an amber foyer to the elevator, which carried them up from street level to the second floor with its wine carpets and gilded portraits of Lee, Stuart, and Jackson. Wooden columns and wainscoting reflected a somber light. They hung their coats on numbered brass-capped pegs.

Amos, aware of his seediness, felt a surge of inferiority. He seemed insubstantial and as if he cast no shadow in these opulent rooms hung

with hunting tapestries and glittering teardrop chandeliers. Whale, laying an arm around Amos' shoulder, forced him along the corridor.

They passed through double doors into a vaulted chamber where
three rows of banquet tables had been set and men were already drinking, eating, calling to one another. Whale had been correct about dress.
Some were properly turned out, but others wore jeans, boots, and a
few who'd been playing squash or paddle tennis had on sweat suits.
The room was too warm, logs burning in a stone fireplace large enough
to enclose an entire cow on an iron spit. Above the fireplace another
portrait, this one of a stern, periwigged George Washington. Whale
hauled Amos around to make introductions.

"This character got me through college," Whale said. "I'd have
flunked everything except women without him."

Big men, beefy, important, who shook hands strongly, and Amos
felt the emanations of power from their fingers. Casual dress or not,
there were fine watches, diamonds, and tables covered with heavy linen,
silver, and goblets. Shiny white-jacketed black waiters carried trays
steaming with meats, eggs, pastries, and pewter pots of jams, coffee,
cream.

The world's victors, Amos thought, and stiffened his back. He held
their eyes. These men possessed the sureness and strength of those dedi-
cated to money. He sat and ate at the urging of Whale, who heaped
Amos' plate, but the hotly spiced abundance became dust in his mouth.
He felt small, old, and angry he'd devoted his life to God's work for so
little while these men reveled in vulgar abundance.

Immediately he was shamed at himself and silently asked forgive-
ness. Their time would come. It was written:

> . . . *the merchants of the earth shall weep and mourn . . .*
> *for no man buyeth their merchandise any longer . . . the*
> *gold and silver, the precious stones . . . purple and silk . . .*
> *ivory . . . chariots . . . and souls of men. . . .*

"He was better than the rest of us," Whale said, talking loud enough to be heard down the table. "He made us feel we'd spit on the floor. One hell of a guy."

Let him talk, Amos thought, not attempting to explain his life now, for it would be inconceivable to Whale and those gathered here to feast that before the church court he'd charged his denomination had become too liberal and worldly. He argued men of the cloth no longer believed fully in the sacred inviolability of Scripture, that pastors stood in the pulpit who denied the Virgin Birth and the very deity of Jesus Himself, calling Him merely a window on the nature of God. Christ a window! What blasphemy!

So he'd written his book, *The Ever Perfect God,* the volume he'd spent the last of Martha's inheritance on, and named names, called lords of the church Pharisees whose interests were their own ambitions and not the spread of the pure and holy Word.

. . . they shall lay hands on you and persecute you. . . .

He wasn't banished. The church no longer did that, believing itself too civilized. He received a softly worded warning by the Committee on Ministers, yet afterward had slight chance of finding a congregation. The story spread he was a belligerent fundamentalist and troublemaker. He would've accepted even a country pulpit, but no delegation arrived to hear him preach or question his theology. In a sick, facile society that had forgotten its roots, he carried spiritual contagion.

Finally it had been left to him to nail up a sign, painted by Martha, over the doorway of the closed neighborhood bakery. Daily he preached to those off the street, who sat in secondhand chairs and sang from tattered hymnals while Martha played a piano the keys of which stuck. The lost, the drunks, the derelicts, men and women who hoped for a little warmth, coffee, a doughnut, a kind word. Yet he taught them. Truth isn't partial, he said. The absolute cannot be modified.

The pitiful collection of battered coins and grimy dollars wasn't enough for him and Martha to live on. He worked part-time as an orderly in a nursing home, while she clerked in a florist shop, arriving home nights so weary she dropped onto the love seat and sighed as if giving up the ghost. It was a question of their persevering and keeping the faith till he reached the age to qualify for his pensions, including the Board of Missions pittance he'd had to battle for.

"What are you if not denominational?" a jut-jawed attorney down the table asked. He held a speared link of sausage dripping egg yolk before his yearning lips.

"I'm a believer in God's sovereignty and the sole efficacy of Christ's blood," Amos answered and raised his own chin as if challenged.

"Well, okay then," the attorney said. He cut his eyes and raised his brows at others along the table.

Amos wanted out, to be away from this pagan gathering, this heated temple of excess, to return to his loving wife and his Bible. He stood and made excuses. Men raised their glasses to him. Whale, his mouth flashing gobs of food, rose to go to the door with him. Others called farewell.

"I mean we got to get together," Whale said, helping Amos on with his coat. "I intend to plant a big wet kiss right smack on Martha. Give me your phone number."

Whale drew a silver pencil and a small leather-covered notebook from the jacket of his banker's suite. The leather had his initials embossed on it in gold. Amos spoke the number, one digit purposely incorrect. Still, Whale might be able to track them down. Refusals would have to be constructed.

The doorman saluted Amos as he moved quickly through the entrance flanked by stone horses. Under the blowing canopy, Whale caught and again hugged him, laying his cheek alongside Amos', and for an instant Amos fought tears. He felt if he didn't hurry away, he might weep. What kind of tears would they be? For the loss of the world and dear ones left behind.

"Let me drive you," Whale called after him.

"I've business to attend to," Amos answered and walked rapidly in the direction of downtown, but as soon as he reached the corner, he doubled back to the rear of the club, where a clanging fan exhausted odors of the indulgent repast inside.

> *. . . and the great men, and the rich men, and the chief captains, and all the mighty men . . . hid themselves in the dens of the rocks of the mountains and said, Fall on us and hide us from the face of him that sitteth on the throne. . . .*

Worried about Martha, he waited for a city bus that seemed would never arrive. He sat near the driver and door so he could be off fast, yet still had four blocks to cover. He half ran, his breath came in gasps, and the stitch in his side caused him to bow. Keep her well, he prayed. Keep her well.

At the house he fitted the trembling key to the lock. He thought he smelled gas, but Martha was all right. She had put on her gray wool dress, brown sweater, and cotton stockings. She sat at the kitchen table dealing out a hand of solitaire, using cards she'd carried all these years, white fleurs-de-lis on a royal blue background, perhaps from a sorority or bridge club, a deck from another life.

> *O thou whom my soul loveth. . . .*

Her fingers were so fragile, made for the holding of roses and fine porcelain. He checked the gas heater. The pilot flame burned feebly. He laid money on the table, and they made small piles of the bills and coins, each dollar allotted to its purpose. He answered questions about Whale and pretended to have enjoyed the breakfast.

During the afternoon they napped side by side, prayed, and he read to her, not another volume from the free library, but his own book, the passage they both loved:

> "Whom the Lord loveth, he chasteneth." How the words shock till one understands that what appears to be misfortune is merely correction arising from the

loving concern of a father preparing his child for a feast at his gorgeous table. The pagan is lost. The Father will not waste Himself but allow them to have what they wish in this world because at the end they will be wisped away like smoke in a whirlwind; but when at last God collects His loving family, He will minister unto them through the golden corridors of a joyous eternity.

Amos believed it with all his being.

For supper he served them lettuce, applesauce, a portion of chicken, and a glass of low-fat milk. By nightfall they had prayed and lay again in bed. They sang the old hymns to one another as fingers touched.

Dogs barked. A plane flew over. Amos believed he heard a shout, perhaps a scream, but his ears were no longer trustworthy, and the sound might have been wind or the skeletal Judas branch scraping the gutter. A police car raced up the street, its siren shrilling, the flashing blue lights penetrating the darkness of the bedroom's cold ceiling.

. . . *Blessed is he that watcheth.* . . .

He woke fully, not knowing the time, but at the nailed window he saw a crimson glow and simultaneously felt a tremor pass through the earth. Was that a trumpet he heard? Stretching upward, his heart drumming, he pushed a hand to Martha and lifted the other toward the rattling panes as if offering her and himself skyward on his own agitated palm.

BOY UP A TREE

I discovered the boy up our leafless sassafras tree. I spotted him during a quiet snow the Saturday morning in January my parents made their annual trip to Florida. I licked snow palmed off our sundial, walked the frozen fishpond, and broke icicles from eaves of our garden house. I pulled a Flexible Flyer along the bottom slope of our wooded West Virginia hillside, but the snow wasn't packed tightly enough to support the runners, so I lay on my back and squinted into falling flakes. They sped twirling into my eyes.

The boy stared down at me. He gripped an upper limb and didn't blink. Snow lined sassafras branches and him. His face was dark-complected and his eyes gleamed black. They could've belonged to a lynx.

"What you doing on our property?" I asked, standing quickly and backing off.

He didn't answer. Those wild shiny eyes watched. I ran down the slope and jerked the sled after me.

"My father won't like you up his tree!" I shouted.

My pink-and-white room faced the hillside. Even from that distance the boy could've looked into my second-story window and seen me undressed.

"Doing what?" my brother Clifford asked when I told him. He peered from our dining room toward the tree. He was fair, blond, and two years older than me. Carrying his .22 rifle, he rushed from the house. Aunt Minnie, the colored woman who kept us while our parents were away, would never have allowed that, but she'd gone to market in Beaver Creek. I didn't want Clifford shooting anybody, not even coal-camp trash, and I ran after him. He stopped under the sassafras and aimed at the boy.

"Come down or it's bullets up the ass!" he threatened.

The boy clutched a lower limb, and his knees clamped it. He had straggly hair and wore a railroader's cap, a black vinyl jacket, brown corduroy pants, and laced rubber boots. Against the snow he didn't appear altogether clean.

"Last chance!" Clifford shouted and clicked off the safety.

"Let's go to the house and wait for Aunt Minnie," I said. "She'll call the sheriff."

"No sir!" Clifford said. "He's coming down!"

Clifford fired, and snow scattered. The bullet splintered a limb near the boy's wet boots, yet he didn't flinch. Clifford fired a second time. His rifle was a Winchester repeater, and he pulled the trigger rapidly till the limb gave way, dipped, and the boy fell, bringing down bark, dead branches, and more snow.

He flailed and tried to grab snags but bounced off limbs. He hit the ground hard. He grunted, rolled to his feet, and ran. He was so small. He escaped among snow-shrouded white ash trees, his feet leaving zigzagging slewed prints. Clifford shot once over the boy's head and grinned.

"That little wop won't be coming back!" he said.

We never told Aunt Minnie or my parents. Poo turkey, Daddy would've thrown a fit. I watched that sassafras tree though, and always pulled my blinds.

During Easter vacation Clifford drove to a movie at the Alhambra

Theatre in Bluefield. After the show he walked through the dark parking lot behind the building. As he unlocked his Mustang, somebody landed across his back and not only beat on his head, but also bit his neck. When my brother reached home, teeth marks were sunk deep into his pretty skin.

"I couldn't see for sure, but it has to be," Clifford said. "That runt smelled bad and fought like they do in Cinder Hollow."

Our parents were away that night attending the Coal Convention in Beckley. Daddy, a mining engineer who'd graduated from Virginia Polytechnic Institute, would've phoned the law. Cinder Hollow was a settlement located in the lower end of Shawnee County. Daddy called the inhabitants ridge-running hillbillies, mostly unschooled people who'd drifted down from the high country to find work in the mines.

"Reckon I'll catch blood poison?" Clifford asked, bending around to see his neck in the bathroom mirror. I painted Mercurochrome on the bites. Around the house he wore his collar high.

Daddy, with me beside him, stopped the Buick to catch the last inning of a Beavers game on a Sunday afternoon in July. He'd played college ball back in Virginia. He never let anybody forget he was from Virginia, and before Clifford and I were hatched, Daddy drove Mom across the state line to a Roanoke hospital so we could claim that state's birth.

Beaver Creek had no regular team. Fans contributed each spring to the upkeep of the dilapidated little park near smoldering mine gob. Purple-berried pokeweed sprouted wanly. Pokeweed would grow on the moon. Chicken wire backed up the dirt diamond's home plate. Preceding the season's first game, the players held a fish fry, the money raised spent to buy bits of uniforms.

After wiping off peanut shells, we sat in the rickety stands. Men chewed tobacco and dribbled spit between their feet in long brown strings. Not even weeds grew beneath the bleachers. Wisps of yellowish smoke lifted the stinging odor of burning mine waste over the park when a breeze blew north off Black Mountain.

As players loped past, I saw the boy-up-a-tree. His uniform was so large and baggy his pants legs kept slipping down around his ankles. He also chewed tobacco, the cud producing a ridiculously large lustrous bulge in his jaw. Nobody sold programs, but I heard a comment from a bald, sweating fat man wearing a T-shirt. On the shirt a fierce beaver held a bat menacingly.

"Little clam don't hit so good, but no balls slips past."

I didn't understand till the boy scooped up a hot grounder and threw to first. People applauded, and again I heard the words "little clam." Little Clem! Where'd a name like that come from except up-hollow? He got a single, and a walked batter moved him to second base. A teammate looped a ball down the line near chicken wire guarding the Norfolk & Western tracks. Hoping to score, Little Clem took off, his sneakers pounding the dry ground and spuming red dust. His arms pumped madly. His tongue stuck out. People in the stand, including Daddy, rose to shout. The boy appeared so ferociously determined—as if the whole of his existence depended on reaching home plate. His pants flapped. His cap fell behind.

As he rounded third where I sat, he glimpsed me and faltered. For an instant he forgot what he was about. He missed a step, a split-second's hesitation before dashing on. The ball arched in, and by the time Little Clem slid to the plate the throw had overtaken him and socked into the extended mitt of the catcher.

Cheers from the Stony Gap Wildcats. Little Clem slouched away, knocked dust off his uniform. His manager, a section foreman for the railroad, kicked dirt and spat. The game was over.

"What a funny little fellow," Daddy said as we walked to the car. "Ever see anybody run so hard?" He turned to me. "He seemed to recognize you."

"I don't recognize him," I replied and hurried ahead before he could carry the conversation farther.

That same summer I became sixteen, and Douglas Duncan phoned. Daddy gave me permission to date if I followed his rules about getting home on time and staying away from roadhouses. Douglas' father owned the Yellow Eagle mines, and Douglas attended prep school in Virginia. Going to school in Virginia automatically made Doug a gentleman in Daddy's mind. It pleased and softened him.

Doug played on the tennis team. He was the first boy I knew who owned white tie and tails. He was also the first to push a hand under my dress. I liked it there but remembered my mother Molly's words. She was a mountain lady, West Virginia born in a coal camp near Bear Paw, where her father operated the Great Kanawha collieries.

"Makes not a speck of difference how tall and stylish they seem or whether they come from Beaver Creek or Boston. They all trying to sneak the same thing."

Which is why I always managed to capture Douglas' hands after a minute or two.

"You could furnish me some relief," Doug pleaded.

"What you'd furnish wouldn't relieve me," I said.

He drove us in his father's big Chrysler to a tea dance at Indian Lick honoring the daughter of Senator Lamar Bristow. The senator, who resembled a slit-eyed possum wearing a polka-dot bow tie, lived in a brick mansion on top a hill. From Daddy I had permission to stay out an hour later because of the thirty-mile drive. Seemed we couldn't do anything in Beaver Creek without driving.

Coming back at dark we passed Cinder Hollow. Doug slowed at a roadhouse named The Pit. He and the other boys had been drinking up at the senator's, stealing around behind the stable to do it. He wanted a six-pack.

"You're not old enough," I said as I tried to keep him from turning in.

"They don't care who they sell to in these places," he said and pulled onto the littered dirt apron in front of the honky-tonk, its lapped sides painted black like coal. Red neon tubes outlined round windows. The tubes buzzed like angry insects. Over the doorway hung an old-fashioned miner's pick.

When he entered, hillbilly music swirled out along with smoke and inflamed, agitated light. The light reflected off muddy puddles. As I sat waiting, I thought of what it must smell like inside, all those dirty, sweaty bodies, the drinking odors, the cheap orange-blossom perfume used by the kind of women who'd go into such a place. If Daddy saw me there, he'd have withdrawn my dating privileges the rest of my life.

Doug came out carrying a paper sack. Because of his polished black loafers, he walked carefully. He stopped. Three boys stepped from darkness at the side of The Pit. They wore sleeveless black T-shirts, jeans, and harness-strap boots. They positioned themselves between Doug and the Chrysler.

He tried to back off and reach the car. They sidled to block him. No matter which direction he moved, they shifted to stay in front of him. The honky-tonk's glow reddened their faces devilishly. Fear shaped Doug's face.

"Lost ain't you?" the largest boy asked, adjusting a beaded Indian headband.

"I'm not looking for trouble," Doug said.

"Thing about trouble is it can come looking for you," the boy said and lifted fingers to the sack Doug carried. "Kid like you shouldn't be fooling with no stuff like this."

"Sweet enough to be wearing a dress," a second boy said, thin and albinic, his pale hair stringing straight to his shoulders.

Doug tried to protect the sack, but the Indian-headband boy snatched it away. Bottles fell and rolled across cinders. Slowly I slid to the driver's seat.

"I paid for them," Doug said as if that would save the day.

"We're upholding the law," the third boy said. Short and greasily muscled, he wore a black bandanna around his neck. "Got proof of your age?"

The boys stooped to gather bottles. Doug brought out his wallet. I thought he meant to produce fake ID, but he offered money. He always had plenty.

"Take it and let me go," he said.

They took it as well as his wallet. They emptied the wallet and tossed it back at him. The greasily muscled boy opened a beer by biting off the cap and spitting it out. He licked at foaming suds. Doug again tried to approach the Chrysler. The boys grinned and blocked him. He made a wide circle to the driver's side of the car, but they still cut him off.

"Guess what's out here waiting," the albino said. He had a cocked pink eye.

"Maybe she'd like to give us a ride," the Indian-headband boy said.

Doug lunged toward the car. They tripped and jumped him. He struggled in dirt and cinders, but they held and hit down on him. It was horrible, the fists rising red and Doug struggling to escape the blows. I screamed. They pulled at his seersucker pants. I kept screaming. Because of the thumping music, nobody inside the roadhouse heard.

I tried to start the car. The Indian-headband boy sprang at me. He grabbed my hair and hooked an arm around my throat. I smelled coal and beer on him. I was choking. I couldn't scream or breathe. His fingers shoved down into my new linen dress, rasped my chest, and wrenched my brassiere.

He flung away. I heard shouts of pain. When I pushed up, I saw a fourth boy swinging a hoe handle. He whacked the Indian-headband boy and the others. They had Doug's pants off. They bent backwards cursing and howling, their arms raised. The albino fell and scampered away. They retreated to darkness.

The boy wielding the flailing hoe handle chased them. I hadn't seen him clearly in the reddish glow, yet recognized his shape—that small, intense wiriness, that fury.

I got the car started. Doug pulled at his clothes and tumbled in. Trembling, weeping, I burned rubber driving off. Doug sobbed and patted his handkerchief against his bleeding face. We stopped short of Beaver Creek to doctor him. I dipped my handkerchief in ditch water and wiped away blood. He drove then but wouldn't look at me. Flaring headlights of oncoming traffic shone from his eyes' wetness.

I couldn't console him, and he never again called, though I didn't breathe a word about the fight, particularly not to Daddy. From time to time at parties I saw Doug, and he greeted me politely, yet averted his eyes. I reminded him too much of that night.

In August our chimes sounded, and Daddy rose from the table to answer the door. We had not half finished dinner, and he tossed his napkin on his chair.

"Visitors ought to know when others dine," he said.

Mamma and I heard talking from the front. Daddy came back, his expression both annoyed and accusing.

"That runty baseball player name of L. C. Spraggs," Daddy said. "You told me you didn't know him."

For a second I couldn't place who he was talking about till I thought of Little Clem's face peering down from the sassafras tree.

"I don't know him like you really know somebody," I said and looked toward the front of the house.

"He wanted to linger, but I told him we were eating," Daddy said, sitting and spreading his napkin across his lap.

"You might've let him wait," Mamma said.

"Soon as he spoke I could tell he was from up-hollow," Daddy said. "Hair slicked down. Tried to make no mistakes in his English."

"Maybe I want to see him," I said.

"Whatever for?" Daddy asked, astonished.

"He was nice to Doug Duncan and me once," I said. "Helped with the car."

"Gratitude has limits," Daddy said. "You have to be kind, but don't encourage relationships."

L. C. phoned at one o'clock the next afternoon. I guess he knew Daddy would be away working. L. C. spoke slowly, his voice a kind of drone, yet no amount of care could mask the hillbilly. He asked permission to come to the house. Despite Daddy, I just wasn't able to say no.

L. C. rang our door chimes at exactly seven that evening. They joined the gonging of our grandfather clock on the staircase landing. Under the porch light he appeared almost presentable in a blue summer suit, white shirt, and red tie, except everything he wore was glazed as glass. He might've gone to a store that very day. He'd had his hair cut. You could've leveled bricks by the trim of his dark sideburns. His socks were white.

We shook hands. His clean fingers were fleeting as if fearful they'd stain or soil mine. His complexion could've passed as a suntan. I led him into our living room. I smelled no chewing tobacco on him.

He glanced sideways at the oil portrait over our fireplace of my great-great-grandfather Sneed, who'd been a genuine colonel in the Confederate army and served a term as a U.S. senator from Virginia. He wore a butternut uniform with a high collar, gold epaulets, and a silver saber sash. He had reddish brown hair and a sharp goatee. His eyes were amber—like kerosene lamps at dusk.

L. C. would have no portraits in his family. Perhaps a mantel held a color photo bright as intestines, snapped in a booth at the Shawnee County Fair—if there were any mantel at all. I seated him on our rose settee. Before him were an inlaid coffee table, fashionable magazines, and a silver candy dish. He held one hand tight on top the other as though fearing they might escape and fly up our chimney.

"I came hoping you'd allow me the pleasure of taking you to a movie Saturday," he said so woodenly I felt certain he'd memorized that little speech, perhaps written it down and labored over it.

"Uh huh," I said.

"I'd appreciate your company," he said, serious as a deacon.

I couldn't hardly keep from laughing, but L. C. wasn't so terrible except for his size, accent, and the sheen of his new clothes. My phone hadn't been ringing a lot lately. On impulse I told him I'd be ready at six-thirty. His hands broke apart and he stood quick, his arms stiff at his sides. When I showed him out, he tripped over one of the stone urns Daddy rooted his English boxwoods in. He had no car and walked down our drive as if marching to war.

"Wish you hadn't," Daddy said after I told him I'd agreed to go to the movie.

"He acted very polite," Mamma said. "You can tell he respects her."

"I've asked around," Daddy said. "Lives with his father, and they work a rathole mine. Never knew anything but a dirt floor till they came to town."

"Not everybody can be a Tidewater aristocrat," Mamma said. She sometimes turned peevish over Daddy's Virginia snobbery.

"It can lead only to hurt," he said.

Of course L. C. was on time. I wore a white blouse, khaki skirt, and leather sandals. He was overdressed in the same white shirt, red tie, and blue suit shiny as metal. Strike it, and it'd spark. Cleanliness shone from him like a light burning within.

"I dislike you all being on the road at night," Daddy said. "Saturday half the miners are drunk."

"More than half," L. C. said. "But I don't drink liquor."

"You don't go to school either," Daddy said.

"I quit to help in the business," L. C. said.

"I heard a man was shot near Cinder Hollow yesterday," Daddy said.

"Ran a picket line," L. C. said.

"Unions believe they're above the law," Daddy said.

I was relieved L. C. had a car. He opened the door of an old Chevy, black and bare, yet waxed and so spick-and-span inside you could've licked soup off the floor. The worn gray seats had been vacuumed, the dash dusted, the knobs polished. L. C. drove rigidly away, aware Daddy would be watching from a window of the house.

"Terrible about the man being shot," I said.

"Tried to reach the tipple with a load of coal," L. C. said.

"Do they know who did it?"

"They don't, I do," he said.

"You tell the police?"

He cut his dark eyes at me as if I'd spoken craziness.

"Up Cinder Hollow you don't tell police noth—anything. You settle it yourself."

We drove the shadowed valley to the Mountaineer Theatre but were early. Swallows flitted across a sky still blue and streaked yellow. He parked up front and reached for a speaker to hang on the door. We sat staring at bats diving at the silver screen. Country music played. I worked to get him talking.

"Your car?" I asked.

"Bought it from a friend," he said.

"I'd like to ask another question," I said. "Why'd you climb our tree?"

"To look at you."

"Couldn't you just have come right to the door?"

He stuck a finger inside his collar and didn't answer. Cars parked around us, some full of friends from Shawnee High. Each time I waved and called, L. C. scowled. Those boys wore shorts. One was tall, loose-limbed Dorsey Bobbit, a senior who'd be going to William and Mary to become a lawyer like his father. Dorsey ran the mile for Shawnee. He and Janice Peck went steady.

Night seeped down from wooded ridges around us, and the movie started—a story about children of an entire village who turned into vampires. The boys sucked blood from the girls, the girls from boys. They held midnight rock parties and appeared normal till they smiled and blood shone on their fangs. Kids in cars near us hooted and cheered whenever somebody got bit.

"I been looking at you more than that," L. C. said during a scene when all the young vampires rose from their caskets in moonlight. "My dad cut grass at your house a couple of times. I helped edge the walks."

I thought back. Occasionally coal sold poorly, and Cinder Hollow dwellers came to Beaver Creek to find work. Daddy might hire a person to trim trees, clean gutters, rake leaves. I remembered an angry, fiery-eyed little man who smelled of soured sweat and acted ready to fight anybody that looked at him crooked. He spat a lot, and Daddy, in front of ladies, corrected him for doing it on the concrete drive close to our house. The man never returned.

"Hid in laurel bushes and watched you," L. C. said, still facing the movie screen where smirking young vampires slipped into a high-school dance. They licked their lips. "Saw you in Bluefield too. Followed you one afternoon you was—you were Christmas shopping."

"I didn't see you."

"Nah, you looked right through me."

At intermission the drive-in's lights switched on, and as I'd hoped, L. C. offered to buy popcorn. He walked toward the concession stand, his shoulders squared. Janice Peck, perky and cute in an orangey sunback, stopped at the car on her way to the ladies' room.

"Where'd you find *him?*" she asked, making a face at the old Chevy.

"He's not so bad," I said.

"Looks like grit to me. Listen, after the show we're meeting down at the landing. You all come."

Janice hurried on and then back to Dorsey, who had his bare feet stuck from a red Corvette's window. L. C. came carrying one little box of popcorn and nothing to drink. Maybe he'd spent all his money for clothes and the car. I started to send him back to the concession stand with a dollar of my own but realized he'd probably be insulted and shamed.

I remembered what Daddy had said about L. C. and his father working a rathole mine. Many of those were illegal because of poor ventilation and safety conditions. You could hardly pick up a newspaper without reading about a roof fall. Often the independent and union miners fought.

"Care for a soda?" L. C. asked at the end of the movie.

"That'd be nice," I said. So he hadn't spent quite all his money.

He drove us not to the Pizza Palace but to a lonely valley Amoco station which had lighted drink machines outside. The station wasn't even open. He definitely counted his change before dropping coins in the slot. He brought back a single moist can of Dr. Pepper.

"I'm not thirsty," he said, presenting it to me.

The drive-in crowd passed. They'd been to the Pizza Palace. Boys were still hollering. Janice Peck leaned from a window. "Come on!" she called. Cars sped toward the landing.

"We could go awhile," I said, thinking anything would be better than sitting on concrete of a locked gas station in a dark valley. "It'll be cool by the water."

He nodded, cranked up, and shifted gears. To reach the river you drove to the lower end of the county where a secondary road wound from the highway down to the landing. That road was under repair, and construction equipment lay about. Warning lights blinked on top yellow metal drums. In my parents' time there'd been a pavilion and lanterns strung from sycamores. Now remnants of the collapsed pavilion rotted among weeds, though the asphalt dance area remained. Thistles grew from cracks.

Summers the Shawnee High crowd gathered at the landing. We parked along edges of the asphalt and left the headlights burning. We all turned our radios to the same Bluefield station. L. C. tried to avoid potholes. He didn't want to jolt that old Chevy apart. He wouldn't leave his lights on for fear of running down the battery. The Chevy had no radio.

Drinking beer, boys and girls sat on fenders and hoods or sprawled across car roofs. Couples danced, their shadows long among the sycamores. Frogs be-wonked. Maybe they enjoyed the music.

I didn't intend just to sit in the Chevy. We didn't have even a Dr. Pepper, and getting talk out of L. C. was like hauling logs. I knew he'd never have the nerve to kiss me. I asked whether he wanted to dance.

"Call it dancing?" he said.

I guess he meant it wasn't dancing Cinder Hollow style. Our crowd did a step brought back from the beach, the Carolina shag. I doubt L. C. had ever been to a beach or seen the ocean.

"We just sitting all night?" I asked. Bugs tapped the Chevy's windshield. "We at least ought to be sociable."

When I stepped from the car, he followed. I moved from group to group. I introduced him around, but he wouldn't hold out a hand or say anything. He could've been an overdressed fencepost.

Dorsey Bobbit asked me to dance. Nobody shagged better than Dorsey. He knew how to make himself and a girl look good. Tanned, his brown hair bleached, he wore white cotton shorts and a red shirt. He kept tossing his hair back from his brow. He held a beer, and when we came together, he lifted the can to my mouth. Music beat across the dark flowing river. L. C. stood in shadows slapping gnats and mosquitoes.

Shouts! Boys were pushing yellow drums down the slope from the road construction. The drums bounced among weeds. The boys climbed on the drums and used their feet to roll them across the dance area. Several hot dogs toppled off but held their cans without spilling beer.

Janice Peck organized races. Each boy on a drum became an entry in the Kentucky Derby. Dorsey was Secretariat. Janice pretended to be holding a starting pistol. When she raised her arm and hollered *bang,* the horses were off.

Riders fell. Dorsey barely kept his balance, as did Willie Walker and Dewey Amos. They footed those barrels toward the finish line, where Sis Lilly stood waving a green handkerchief. Dorsey crossed first. Janice kissed him and fed him beer. Dorsey shook his fists over his head.

More races. Bets made. We cheered and ran beside the horses. Dorsey won a second time. He thumped his chest and gave a Tarzan yell.

I'd forgotten L. C. till he climbed on a drum. He looked so out of place in his shiny suit and tight collar. He was more appropriately dressed for one of the board-and-batten Pentecostal churches up-hollow. "Count Fleet," Janice named him.

Dorsey took the lead. He had so much confidence he show-boated—reversing on the drum as well as jumping and landing after a spin like trick surfing. Two boys crashed, fell, and lay laughing, holding their beers high.

L. C. was serious. He crouched, leveled his arms, and kept his eyes on his feet. Those feet flew, his new shoes slapping metal and making the drum boom. He broke to the front, and by the time Dorsey realized he might be whipped, it was too late. L. C. crossed the line where Sis waved the handkerchief and declared Count Fleet the winner.

L. C. received acclaim, looked surprised, and then pleased. Dorsey, used to being first and a little tight, didn't like that a bit.

"Two out of three," he demanded.

"Got to get on home," L. C. said, turning to me.

"Cluck-cluck-cluck," Dorsey said.

That made L. C. so mad I thought he'd fight Dorsey, but Janice herded them back to the starting line. She raised her pistol finger and fired.

This time Dorsey too was serious. As did L. C., he hunched to the drum. It was like logrolling. We ran beside them shouting. Bettors encouraged their horses. I didn't call names, but I was for Count Fleet because I understood L. C. was giving his best for me, trying to be my champion. The drums scraped and sparks sprayed. Neck and neck they ran. Lots of hollering. At the last instant Dorsey surged ahead, and Sis chopped her handkerchief after him.

Cheering, money changing hands. Janice presented a beer to Dorsey. She tried to award one to L. C., but he wouldn't accept it. He was breathing hard and had popped sweat. So had Dorsey, yet he also mugged and swaggered. L. C. followed him.

"Ready to go again?" he asked Dorsey.

"Some nags never learn," Dorsey said and neighed. He pawed the asphalt.

L. C. took off his jacket and tie and laid them in the old Chevy. He leaned against a fender to remove his shoes and socks. His feet were tiny, narrow, bony. Carefully he rolled his pants up around his calves. He unbuttoned his shirt collar.

"Probably first time he ever wore shoes," Garnet Porter whispered.

I frowned. More bets, with Clive Morris giving odds on Dorsey, who continued to prance and neigh. L. C. looked grim as death.

Janice fired her fingers, and they were off, L. C. surer now, faster, his feet better able to find purchase. He shot to the lead, but Dorsey closed the gap. He drew even. L. C.'s feet pounded so fast against his drum they blurred. Everybody kept hollering. Dorsey's style was more upright, yet his long legs jammed down and boomed the barrel. He didn't grin or showboat.

A second time L. C. moved ahead. Dorsey drove hard, but L. C. gave nothing back. He pulled farther in front. A hoot. Less yelling more laughter. Something was happening. A shriek, and Janice pointed. L. C.'s pants! As he charged toward the finish, the cheap shiny material was splitting along a seam. Flash of flesh. He had on no undershorts! He wore those pants over his bare bottom. It mooned in the headlights!

He crossed the finish first and stayed balanced on his drum. Count Fleet expected congratulations, yet received only more pointing and laughter. He kept turning, not understanding. The more confused he became, the greater the hilarity.

Finally he felt behind himself and twisted around to look. He gaped, clutched the rip, and jumped down. He sidestepped bent to his car. Everybody whistled, hollered, rocked forward and slapped at themselves. Some collapsed laughing to the asphalt. Shame distorted L. C.'s face into horror. I tried to reach him, but he drove that Chevy fast up the road, the red taillights wobbling and dimming in swirling dust his tires raised.

That September Daddy sent me off to St. Elizabeth's School in Warrenton. He was determined to make a Virginian of me. He helped carry things up to my room. The dormitory was a creepy old stone building

so hot and humid all curl drooped out of my hair. The basement probably held spider webs and dungeons.

"My mother graduated from St. Elizabeth's," Daddy said for about
the thousandth time. "You're perpetuating a tradition."

I felt lonely and homesick among the blue bloods. I missed my
cooling mountains. I yearned for Shawnee High. The snooty girls considered me a hick and teased about my accent, though they were the
ones who talked funny. The only boys we could date attended private
schools. Not many asked me out, most being airheads and interested
mainly in my social connections and how much money Daddy had.
Rollo, son of a plastic surgeon, puked on my rose chiffon gown. He
also dumped me.

I sniffled a little, and my roommate, a girl from Fairfax named
Vicky whose father worked in the State Department, called me a cry-
baby. I slapped her and got summoned to Mademoiselle's, the headmistress', office.

"We're ladies here," Mademoiselle said, ancient, painted, perfumed,
and as erect as an enthroned empress.

Mademoiselle placed me on restriction, which meant I couldn't go
home Thanksgiving. I did receive a package in the mail. I believed it'd
been sent by my mother, but when I tore off the brown wrapping I
found a cardboard box full of newspaper clippings from the Shawnee
Advance. They covered years and were all about me—my birthday parties, a sock hop, trips to summer camp, my booth at the Episcopal
bazaar, and photographs taken the spring I was a handmaiden to the
queen during the Coal Festival.

The box contained no note or explanation. It'd once held Mason
jars. My address was neatly printed in pencil, the postmark Cinderella,
W. Va. No clipping had even seemingly been fingered. They had to have
come from L. C. I didn't show them to Vicky and carried them home
Christmas, where I put them on my closet shelf.

I hoped he'd phone. I helped Mamma hang wreaths and decorate the blue spruce in the front yard of our house. While shopping in Beckley, I thought I glimpsed L. C. at the bus station. I was walking on the other side of Railroad Avenue. When I stopped to squint and wave, his small face disappeared in fuming exhaust smoke of a crowded bay.

If it was L. C. Perhaps he'd been following me. Still he didn't call. Finally near the end of my vacation I asked Daddy about him. Daddy, looking pained, said the talk around was L. C. had joined the army. For an instant I again saw his face—like looking back into a dark tunnel you're leaving and know you'll never return to.

I had lots of new clothes but hated thoughts of St. Elizabeth's. I was no longer sure I wanted to be a lady. My last day home it snowed. As I packed, I glanced from my bedroom window and caught my breath. Some living creature was up that sassafras tree! I blinked and rubbed the steamy glass. I ran out back without coat or boots and climbed the slope in the snow. When I lifted my face to the branch, I saw not a boy but a coon hugging his perch and peering down from masked dark wild eyes.

I did a crazy thing. I cupped snow in both palms and offered it up to him as if he would come and eat. Of course he didn't but simply continued to stare. I backed off slowly and walked to the house. I was cold, shivering, my penny loafers wet. I had to finish packing. I set the box of clippings in the farthest corner of my closet. Several times before nightfall I looked out to see that coon still up the tree.

ABIDE WITH ME

Using the last of black powder saved from his mining days, Harmon blasted rock from a slope of Kentucky's Ram's Horn Mountain—tawny soapstone he'd shape with hammer, chisel, and gouge. He set his charge, boring in by leaning on a chest auger from old times when men shot their coal. Hefting an iron pipe, he tamped his load. He patted moist soil from the banks of Bitter Creek around the dangling squib. The explosion was muffled, yet shook the ground all the way to the creek, causing fabric of its flow to quiver.

He levered stones down the slope to the stream, which snaked fast along the narrow shaded valley and ran full even during the hot fuming stillness of summer. Deer ghosted from wooded ridges to drink out of Bitter Creek, the taste not bad at all—clear cold water having just a little grit from its stirred-up sandy bottom. If you climbed high enough, brook trout swam in gravel pools, fish hardly larger than a man's thumb. You rolled them in cornmeal, fried them in deep fat, and ate them head and all, the tiny bones crunching sweetly in your mouth.

First thing was to scour the stones. He worked chunks into the creek and used Glenna Anne's scrub brush. Doing the job tired him mightily. He built to it, resting most of those first days, lying on scratchy wild grass as ragged crows flying over cawed. When an east wind blew, he heard faint sounds of traffic running the interstate as well as bleating Merinos on Ike MacDermott's highland farm.

Harmon's wife, Glenna Anne, wasn't happy but didn't shift into a first-gear fit either. She sniffed, clucked, and snorted when he hauled himself onto the porch so weary he could do nothing more than slump in his rocker. Still, she fetched iced tea, a glass pitcher which had yellow tulips painted on it. During this past July, the clink of ice cubes in that pitcher was prettier than stomping music at the Firehouse Fish Fry.

"I coulda married Joe Morgan, who owns three Tastee Freezes," she said, a graying, round-faced woman, large now, though once so light he lifted her as easily as a sheaf of cornstalks. He'd been big then, she small. These days everything was reversed. Weight had settled into her hips, legs, and ankles. His pounds had seemed to go out with his breath. Where did lost weight end up? Maybe somebody else inhaled it.

"You don't need no more Strawberry Delights," he answered. When he'd rested and washed, she fed him at the pink tubular kitchen table. She'd do that no matter how put out. Their aluminum-sided dwelling had two bedrooms and a screened porch. From his rocker he'd look out over Bitter Creek Valley to Mad Sheep Knob and the Ram's Horn beyond, highest elevation in Krogh County. Never in his life had he traveled more than seventy miles distant, that only a short spell while working in Letcher County for Panther Coal and Lumber. This was his land, its soil made personal by one hundred twenty years of kin lying beneath.

"Special this week's Marshmallow Heaven," Glenna Anne said. She wiped eggplant from an iron skillet hog-seasoned by generations of use. She could consider him a fool and still try to please. They'd reached that state in their long marriage they accepted the truth each was unable to change the other. She did fret he didn't help more with the vegetables in their hillside garden. But it was a only fourth-gear fret.

He was too busy, mornings rising at first light and flipping his own sausage patties and flapjacks. Glenna Anne slept till seven. By the time she cut on the TV, he was long gone. He carried half a dozen of her biscuits, sweetened by his own sourwood honey and wrapped in wax paper. Those and cooling water from Bitter Creek supplied his lunch.

He drove his Chevy pickup down into the valley and up again, following a sheep trail above the creek to the pasture, the place he worked his stone. He'd been at it since his release from the ward of the Big Coal Hospital where the vision unfolded. He'd wakened after the operation and sensed the doctors had whacked out a goodly portion of him. Or a bad one. He'd felt the hole in himself. He joked they'd cut near everything between his head and hind end. When he could eat, food dropped through him like a pebble down a cistern.

"I mean I seen!" he whispered to Glenna Anne as she sat beside his bed. "Standing right above me and smiling like we'd been having us a time. Spoke and said, 'You got that right, Harmon. Both of us is fishermen, sure enough.'"

Just before the vision, Harmon teetered over the black pit, staring the foul dog of death in his glinting yellow eyes, but each time he felt himself being dragged down to sulphur, the smiling Him appeared to kick that stinking mongrel howling. "Thank you kindly," Harmon said. "You right welcome," Him said.

Harmon felt himself floating to the light. Pretty young gals wearing stiff white uniforms pampered and helped him walk hospital corridors. Once home, he exercised slowly till he grew strong enough to lift a hand to work. He sweated, groaned, and rested beside Bitter Creek, splashing water on his face and neck. His skin again tanned in the Ram's Horn's healing sunlight.

He shaped the base stones roughly and needed a way to carry them up Mad Sheep Knob. He'd arranged with Ike MacDermott to use the land. No charge. He and Ike had bear-hunted together.

Harmon drove into Willow Springs and Thurston's Garage. Willow Springs was a settlement on either side of the post office–superette run by Thurston's wife, Mary Mobley. Harmon explained he wanted loan of their wrecker to lift the stones. Thurston, a bearded heavy-footed man who rarely spoke, would've charged, but Mary Mobley refused to allow her husband to accept money. She was a freckled redhead whose shrill voice could strip the hair off hide. When she spoke, Thurston grew smaller, that voice of hers whittling him down.

"You'd snatch money from dead in their grave," she said.

"So does undertakers," Thurston said, not loud enough for her to hear as he banged a salvaged driveshaft with a sledge as if meaning to demolish it.

He owned a Mack wrecker used occasionally for big rigs that broke down on the interstate. Grumbling, he winched and towed stones from the creek to the knob. Harmon had already leveled concrete. Thurston's boom, however, could lift a load only eight feet above the pad.

"Not nary!" Thurston said, backing off as if from a rattler when Harmon offered a ten-dollar bill. "Mary Mobley'd beat hell out of me in my sleep."

To set the top stones Harmon needed a lift. He borrowed Bartholomew Sharp's Little Cat. Bartholomew was the last independent still stripping coal in Krogh County. When young, he and Harmon had worked the Princess seam. Bartholomew sent over the Little Cat on a lowboy. Harmon directed the stacking of the stones, which when finished reached a height of fifteen feet. The only shaping other than squaring was the top block. He gave it a hint of shoulders and upper arms.

The head was special, and for it Harmon experimented in the shed behind his house, finally settling on a compound of putty, window caulking, plastic wood, and joint coupling. Molding and painting the face required twelve days. He felt a responsibility to get everything exactly right—features not glowing, hair short and curly black, a roly-poly face, the great hooked nose, and a grin. Only the eyes commanded, not dark like the rest of him, but a deep blue glimmer, a gambler's eyes. Harmon found the color in a fifty-cent bag of marbles he bought at Big Coal's Dollar General.

With the help of Glenna Anne and a wooden extension ladder, he set the head, which weighed thirty-eight pounds. He lowered it onto an eyebolt so mortared not even a gale off the Ram's Horn would disturb the mounting. Glenna Anne held the ladder, and when he climbed down, she shaded her eyes to look up at Him.

"Ain't the prettiest face I ever saw," she said.

"Looked beautiful to me when I smelt that death dog's foul breath," Harmon said.

He had other chores. He spoke to Hackett, the section chief at the Mud River Power Co-op, who agreed to install a meter and connect juice if Harmon set a post and box near their line. Harmon placed eight floodlights around the base of Him and tested them at high noon. He would keep it secret long as he could. There was talk along the valley. People could see Him soon as the sun burned off the milky morning mists. When they questioned Harmon, he kept moving. He wasn't impolite, just close-mouthed.

He'd have the switch thrown the last evening of Krogh Week, a time people born and raised in the valley returned for seven days of religious and social activities centered around their churches. Older folks called it Big Preaching. All denominations joined a final service at Glen Laurel, where Bitter Creek pooled before a fall. The dropping water spread a rainbow haze over grasses and wild flowers of the cove. Visitors arrived in cars, trucks, and campers. Some erected tents.

He arranged with his nephew Billy Ray Jeffers to cut on the floods. Billy Ray wanted to be at preaching, but Harmon bribed him. Billy Ray'd tickle a bobcat's belly for the five dollars he got to do the job.

"Wait till you hear them singing 'Bathed in Blood of the Lamb,'" Harmon instructed the boy, a wiry teenager who appeared mostly legs and could run faster than anybody in the valley. "Then scramble on down here."

That night after the feed under drooping locust trees, they listened to the Reverend Jimmy Johnson, who was seven feet tall and drove all the way from Chattanooga. When Jimmy got going good up on the wagon bed where the pulpit set, he'd cause children to cower, women to weep, and sinners to fall out begging mercy. "Put the fires of hell out with the Jesus hose!" Jimmy shouted so loud the frogs quit croaking. He spread scrawny upreared arms. "Everybody sing! Let's hear it for the Lord!"

Harmon lifted his face to the knob. As Miss Lucy Jessup at the upright piano on the back of a Dodge truck plunked out the first notes and voices rose, Billy Ray threw the switch. Him lit up like he'd been sent from Heaven. He seemed suspended in the high darkness. People were so surprised they broke off singing. Gasps sounded like wind rising. For once Jimmy Johnson didn't have words. He stared goggle-eyed, his jaw gone slack.

Folks gathered around Harmon, not only kin and friends, but also near strangers from the lower end of the valley. They shook his hand, touched his shoulder, slapped his back. Two ladies offered their cheeks, though doing so was not a way common even during Krogh Week. That was city, and those ladies had picked it up from TV. Still, he'd never minded delivering a kiss.

After the meeting, he stood on his porch smoking his pipe and gazing at Him ablaze. I kept my word, he thought. I always been proud of doing that.

The first trouble he didn't suspect was trouble at all. It arrived in the person of the Reverend Amos Stillwater, pastor of the Willow Springs Baptist Church, of which Harmon and Glenna Anne were tithing members. All the country ham, fried chicken, and 'tater salad women had piled onto Reverend Amos' plate over the years had put a rich sheen on his white flesh. He was so heavy that when he walked you felt his weight through the floor. Wayne Pritchett down at the post office had joked, "If Reverend Amos was a hog, we'd had him 'fore now."

He wore his black preaching suit and a pearl-colored Stetson. When he sat beside Harmon in the Chevy pickup, it squeaked and rocked. Reverend Amos fanned his face with the Stetson.

"'Preciate your hauling me up 'er," he said. "I been wanting to see close."

Harmon drove the trail to Mad Sheep Knob. He stopped at the switch to cut the lights. He opened the door for Reverend Amos, who moved slow as lard flowing across a hot skillet. The reverend had to set his feet under himself good to stay balanced.

Reverend Amos, needing to brace his shoulders to support his belly, circled Him. He walked around Him twice, fingered his double chin, and pondered ground before his slewed feet.

"I see you done a world of work up here," Reverend Amos said. "Lordy, yes. But who's it supposed to represent?"

"Him."

"Who him?"

"Just Him. Came to me in the hospital."

"Surely it don't look like our Lord and Savior," Reverend Amos said.

Harmon knew that. Since a boy he'd inspected the Jesus fans, furnished by the Woodfin Funeral Home—Big Coal's finest—in pew racks of the Willow Springs Baptist Church, the Savior with long shining blond hair, a shy kindly face, and girlish hands reached to the draped head of the robed, frightened woman who clutched at his garments. That Jesus was always aglow and spit-clean. No dirt would stick.

"Looks like what I saw," Harmon insisted.

"You was recovering from an operation and anesthesia."

"That's true, but I made a real promise."

"Ah, brother, brother," Reverend Amos said in his graveside voice. His mournful jowls quaked with each flowing step.

Harmon drove him back down off the knob to where the reverend had parked his Plymouth at the side of the house. Though they shook hands, Reverend Amos' sun-speckled plum-colored eyes shifted sideways. He drove off without another word.

"Probably piqued 'cause you didn't feed him," Glenna Anne said. "That man could eat the legs off an elephant and ask for the ears."

Each night at dusk Harmon drove up and switched on the floods. Others also climbed Mad Sheep Knob. What had been a trail was becoming rutted tracks. Gawkers walked around and studied Him. A few touched the stone base as if scared of being shocked. A young hellion tried to carve his initials using his buck knife. Harmon slapped it from the boy's hand and ordered him off the property.

"Ain't yours!" the boy said—lean, rangy, his towhair straggly. He looked like a Beasley from the county's lower end.

"This fist in your face will be if you don't hightail it!" Harmon said.

That night the phone rang. He and Glenna Anne shared a party line with three other valley families. Harmon didn't recognize the voice, which was deep and nigh to a growl.

"You best watch it," it said.

"Watch what?"

"Don't want no blue-eyed Eye-talians 'round here."

"Who said He was a blue-eyed Eye-talian?"

"He dark, ain't he?"

"Dark don't make Eye-talian."

"Whatever he be, we don't want 'em."

Harmon had difficulty sleeping after the call. He kept running the voice through his mind trying to identify it. Any of the other families on the line might've listened. The story would spread.

Who had to be contended with next was Hector Breathett, Krogh County building inspector. Hector drove a black government Ford which had a whip antenna clamped to the rear bumper. He'd been born cockeyed and was so trifling that if the politicians hadn't hired him because of his many voting kin he would've starved to death trying to figure how to raise food to his mouth and not burn energy.

"You got no permit," Hector said, a man who never in his life had hurried. He'd even been hatched late. He snoozed through preaching, and when he fished, he slept on the riverbank. Unless a sucker or bass jumped right on top of him, it never got caught. "It's how the statute reads. 'Any structure, dwelling, outbuilding, or edifice.' What you have up there comes under edifice."

"Not what I call an edifice."

"My opinion it is, and you need a permit."

"My opinion is you should've stayed in the bed."

"You don't get a legal permit, it's my opinion you'll be seeing an invite for a court appearance tacked to your door."

"How much a permit cost?"

"How much it cost you to put up that edifice?"

"I maintain it's not an edifice, and maybe fifty dollars."

"That's materials, not time, and what about the lights?"

"Time's my own."

"Time's the cost of labor. How long you work in hours?"

"I never counted."

"You gonna get that invite all right."

"How much you and the rest of the thieves down at the courthouse want to rob me of?"

"Twenty-five dollars. Cheaper than court."

"I look to the day they run you out of office," Harmon said but reached for his wallet.

"Not likely you'll live that long," Hector said and wrote a receipt, yet stuck the money in his own pocket.

Late that afternoon a reporter arrived from the Pikeville *Democrat*. He carried a camera and interviewed Harmon on his porch. The young man was fidgety. Acted like he had a lot more important things to do. Kept sticking a tape recorder in Harmon's face.

"What statement you trying to make with that effigy up there?" he asked, toeing the swing so hard it swung forward and almost banged Glenna Anne's potted geraniums.

"He's no dang effigy, and I don't know beans about a statement," Harmon said. "I kept a promise is all."

"Some claim it's a religion," the reporter said, looking at his watch and poking the recorder at Harmon.

"Mister, I want to be polite, but you making it tough. I was born Baptist, am Baptist, and mean to be Baptist the rest of my life."

"Is that effigy Baptist?"

"He's no effigy, damn it. He's what He is and that's all."

The story in the Pikeville *Democrat* was headed: CONTROVERSIAL EFFIGY IN HIGH PLACE. A picture of Him and Harmon appeared smack-dab in the center of the page.

Harmon worked to keep Mad Sheep Knob clean. More visitors were hiking up there. A few carried picnic baskets and spread blankets. At night rowdies began gathering. They played music and drank beer. Somebody, maybe it was the Beasley boy, cut initials into the stone base. Harmon filed them off.

The ministerial delegation arrived Monday. Harmon had just driven down from switching off the floods. Reverend Amos had with him a Methodist and a Church of the Nazarene. All three wore their serious preaching suits. They wouldn't come into the house but stood by Reverend Amos' Plymouth and glanced at Mad Sheep Knob, where mist drifted past Him. Only the base showed.

"Harmon, we know you a good man, yet believe you wandered off the path," Reverend Amos said.

"What you want me to do?" Harmon asked.

"Take it down," Reverend Witcher Hensley said. He was the Church of the Nazarene, a pinched-up man whose skin puckered like a June apple left too long to ripen. He had a deep voice for such a small person. If he was big as his voice, he'd have been a giant.

"Not wanting to do that," Harmon said, rubbing his neck.

"It's a blasphemy," Reverend Sam Belcher said. He'd lost his right arm in the hopper of a hay baler. For a time fingers of the detached arm sticking out an alfalfa bale opened and closed as if feeling after the body they'd been part of.

"To me He ain't," Harmon said.

"Ugly thing," Reverend Witcher Hensley said.

"Seen with my eyes, you wouldn't think ugly," Harmon said.

"People are laughing," Reverend Amos said. "Up and down the valley they are."

"Glad I'm providing entertainment," Harmon said. "I like making everybody happy."

"They not happy," Reverend Sam Belcher said. "They think you mocking Jesus."

"You believe God's Son looks like that?" Reverend Amos asked.

"Could for all I know," Harmon said, immediately realizing he'd spoken too quickly. But he'd seen plain as day, and it wasn't no hospital ether either.

They stepped back from him. Reverend Witcher Hensley's mouth flapped like he'd tasted sheep-dip. Reverend Sam Belcher's stump jerked in his folded coat sleeve. Reverend Amos raised and lowered his eyebrows as if he meant to agitate them off his face.

"You been deceived," he said.

"You have been tripped," Reverend Witcher Hensley said.

"You have been snared," Reverend Sam Belcher said.

"Take it down, take it down," they chanted. They laid their hands on him, and he felt they'd strip the clothes off his back.

"I ain't taking Him down," Harmon said. "I don't mean disrespect, but I been brought up to keep my word. I couldn't sleep nights if I didn't."

They released him, their faces mournful and accusing, like he was a

sinner sinking into the fire. Truth was they scared him. He sure feared
the eternal flames of Hell. Yet he was afraid of breaking his word too.

The three reverends bounced down the road in the old Plymouth,
which needed new shocks. Grayish dust followed them. Glenna Anne,
her arms crossed, had been watching from the porch.

"You kept your promise," she argued. "You put it up. That don't
mean you can't take it down."

"You crazy, woman? Don't put a thing up to take it down."

"I do," she said. "Every day. My wash."

Rowdies caroused weekends on Mad Sheep Knob. Ike Mac-
Dermott talked to Harmon about it when they met at the Willow
Springs Post Office, a white cinder-block building which had a flagpole slanted upwards above the doorway. Chirping sparrows perched
along it.

"You know it ain't me," Ike said, a lumpy man, the left side of his
face hanging lower than the right so it seemed he always stood on uneven ground. 'Course, lots of times he did. "Personally I been glad to
oblige you."

"I'm thinking of a fence," Harmon said.

"Something ought to be done. They not only leaving trash over all
God's green earth, they chasing my sheep."

"You don't mean—?"

"I not actually caught anybody, but those wild boys get to drinking, and my ewes has been acting peculiar. Used to they'd lick salt out
of my palm and now won't come near."

Despite Glenna Anne's fussing about the cost, Harmon started the
fence. He bought locust posts, planted them around Him, and strung
barbed wire. The steel gate he fastened with a chain and padlock. He
hammered up No Trespassing signs and paid for an ad in the Pikeville *Democrat* notifying the public Mad Sheep Knob wasn't to be set
foot on.

Early in October a funny little man knocked at the door. He was short, bearded, and wore thick black-rimmed glasses. The crown of his black hat looked like a sawed-off stovepipe. His black overcoat reached to his ankles. He talked like a foreigner—not just somebody from outside Krogh County, but a foreign foreigner.

"Be so kind to show me your erection," he said, bowing, his tiny white hands folded over his stomach.

Harmon stared a moment before he understood. "Take you up myself," he said. He had to switch off the floods anyhow.

"You are being very hospitable to me, a stranger," the little man said.

A shower had made the tracks miry. Harmon gunned the Chevy. The man held to his hat. His socks were black, as were his shoes, pants, and everything except his white shirt. He had it buttoned at the neck but wore no tie.

When they reached Mad Sheep, Harmon unlocked the gate. More trash lay scattered over the pasture. Signs and fences didn't stop rowdies. They'd crossed under the wire. A brassiere hung from a post.

Harmon cut the lights. The little man gazed at Him. Rocking backward and forward, he stroked his beard. He talked to himself, a singsong muttering. When he turned to Harmon, his dark magnified eyes seemed too large for the rest of his face, and the face did not appear friendly.

"What haf you got against Chews?" he asked.

"Got nothing against chews," Harmon said. "I chew myself and am carrying a plug of Brown's Mule in my shirt pocket right this minute." He patted the pocket.

"Not chews. Chews!"

"Ah," Harmon said, getting the drift. "Don't know any Jews. Got none in Krogh County."

"But as a matter of principle you do not care for them. They killed your savior. You make fun of them here with this."

"Sure as hell don't care for those who did that, though of course I never ran across any of them. And I don't mean to make fun of anybody, just keep a promise."

"He was a Chew!" the little man said, wagging a tiny finger at Harmon. "You should remember that without Chews you would have no savior!"

"It's a fact," Harmon said and got shut of the little man by driving him fast to the Willow Springs Post Office and leaving him twitching under the flagpole and fussing sparrows.

Something had to be done about the rowdies. Nights Harmon lay abed hearing shouts, music, laughter. He stood on his porch and saw figures cross in front of the floodlights—fleeting, flinging shapes, dancing or worse. Dirt bikes snarled and popped.

"They not our'n," he told Willie Blevens, the Krogh County sheriff. Willie had his basement office in the Big Coal courthouse, a concrete WPA building where wind flapped legal papers tacked on the gnawed bulletin board. Two tan-and-brown police cruisers were parked along the curb. Flags of the United States and Kentucky flew over a pigeon-splattered World War I cannon. Trooper chatter squawked from the radio behind Willie's desk.

"I heard," Willie said, fingering the collar of his brown uniform shirt. A muscular blond and pride of the large Blevins clan, his Sam Browne belt, badge, whistle, nametag, and nickel-plated Colt .38 Police Special gleamed. Polly Jo, his wife, shined them nightly. Talk was he might be running for the legislature. "I been hearing. Saturday nights some drive from Corbin and Sandgap."

"Don't I have a right to protection?" Harmon asked.

"Tricky question," Willie said and tipped to the side to dribble spit into a five-gallon lard can filled with backyard loam. "That edifice up on Mad Sheep Knob stands out a long ways. People see it from the interstate."

"I don't call Him no edifice."

"Particularly at night vehicles slow to look, and it could cause accidents. You're liable to be sued for creating an attractive nuisance."

"You telling me the law ain't helping?"

"I'm telling you there's a good chance the State Highway Department might be seeking an order to close that thing down because it threatens the public weal. My advice is shut off the floods. Daytime folks'll still be able to see, and the pressure eases on you and us doing our job here in the courthouse."

Harmon hated cutting juice to the lights, though it wasn't going back on his promise as he'd never guaranteed floods in the first place. They had been extra. Yet it still hurt. Nights when he gazed toward the knob, he pictured Him standing alone in the blowing darkness. Being alone in darkness was no fun.

Nor did lack of lights stop the rowdies. They carried lanterns and built fires that glowed around Mad Sheep. They chopped fenceposts to feed the flames. Mornings the fires smoldered, the bluish smoke mixing with mists. A charred stink lay over the land.

Late in October when locust trees yellowed and birds flew south, Harmon tried to run the rowdies off. He charged among them threatening arrest and stumbled over a naked couple. They yelped, scampered up, and hopped off pulling at clothes. Somebody threw an unopened can of Budweiser from the darkness and hit Harmon on the mouth. He staggered and tasted blood. Back at the house, Glenna Anne painted his split lip with iodine. An incisor in his false teeth was cracked.

"It's not worth it," Glenna Anne said.

"Never been a question of worth but of word," Harmon said.

Tuesday noon he rose from lunch at the sound of a vehicle stopping before the house—a long, gray Cadillac car. He believed it must be Clarence Woodfin, who owned the funeral home, but a thin waxy man sat behind the wheel. He rolled down the window to ask Harmon if he was Harmon.

"Name's Cadwallader," the man said and didn't offer to shake hands. "If you permit, I'd like to examine the figure on the mountain."

"Help your damn self," Harmon said. "Everybody else does."

"Rather hoped you'd direct me. I'll pay ten dollars for your time."

"You don't want to make the trip in that car. We'll use my pickup."

The man was tall and limber. He seemed to glide rather than walk. With his handkerchief he dusted off the pickup's seat before sitting. Like an undertaker, he wore a gray suit, a black overcoat, leather gloves, and gray felt hat. He held to the dashboard as the rutted tracks wrenched the pickup.

"I'm told you're a native of this region," he said, having to speak loud to make himself heard.

"Hell, yes, I'm a Shawnee Indian," Harmon shouted, gave a rebel yell, and was surprised when after a moment's hesitation the man smiled and nodded.

"Very good," he said. "Very good indeed."

He set on a pair of gold-rimmed spectacles to inspect Him. He strolled around the base to check every angle. Using a slim silver pencil, he made notes in a small leather notebook drawn from an inner coat pocket. Wind bent his hat brim.

"Remarkable your using chair-and-deck enamel for your paint," he said. "Would you consider parting with your work for a money settlement? The head, I mean. The rest isn't intrinsic."

"Nope, it's stone," Harmon said, and hope surged. He hadn't promised not to sell, and if Him left, problems would follow along. But just the head? "What you want it for?"

"I'm a private collector and believe your creation, at least the head, might find a nook in my museum."

"What kind of museum?"

"An establishment devoted to folk art. Chiefly American primitives."

"Meaning I'm primitive, huh?"

"The term isn't intended to be pejorative, merely descriptive."

"I don't know what it's meant to be, but it sounds like a damn insult. Besides, the head's part of the whole. You couldn't get it off without damage."

"I'm offering fifteen hundred dollars, and my men will assume the cost and responsibility of detaching the head and transferring it to Philadelphia."

Again Harmon was mightily tempted. At the same time he feared selling would be betrayal. God knew how people in a city might treat Him. Suppose they didn't understand and laughed the wrong way?

"Just dust off the seat 'cause we going back down the mountain," Harmon said. He highballed the pickup and bounced the prissy man so high his head banged the roof and flattened the hat. Harmon didn't tell Glenna Anne about the money offer.

He quit attending services. His own people were turning against him, not only the reverends and deacons, but also folks he'd been knowing most his life. They shied as if he carried a dread disease. He heard that the preacher at the Church of the True Gospel bad-mouthed him from the pulpit, proclaiming, "Beware of false prophets! The Devil is always amongst us!"

The note stuffed under his windshield-wiper blade was printed in crooked letters. You Are Making Us All Look Like Fools Around Here! So many calls came to the house he had his phone disconnected. He stopped going daily to the post office because his box held nothing except bills and mean mail.

Worst of all, Glenna Anne let out a war whoop Thanksgiving eve. She'd been watching the six o'clock Pikeville TV. There before Him stood an announcer, a slim black-haired gal wearing a white hardhat and holding a microphone.

"Hasn't been so much excitement down Krogh County way since

the bull got let loose in the courthouse," she said. "A hornet's nest has been stirred up by what some consider a shrine, others a joke. Local kids are calling the figure St. Banana because of it's big nose. Other observers think it resembles a stand-up comedian or used-car dealer.

"It's causing controversy outside Krogh County too. SLAP, a University of Kentucky feminist organization, objects to deities being projected as male. Rumor has it both the NAACP and the Jewish Defense League are disturbed by what they perceive to be a racial slur. Louisville's Westminster Canterbury Alliance is investigating. Father Anthony P. Withers of Holy Trinity by the Waters has been asked for clarification by his diocesan bishop. Reportedly the ACLU might research the legality of a sect inflicting its religious views on others by means of an effigy seen from a highway built with federal funds. Wow! Only Jimmy Swaggart and Jerry Falwell haven't been heard from. This is Jenette Jenkins, Action News, on Mad Sheep Knob in Krogh County."

"Sonsofbitches!" Harmon shouted. "Went up there without permission."

"Who don't?" Glenna Anne asked.

Late Saturday night as he lay in the bed, he heard snatches of music from rowdies. Indian summer had brought them out. More fires burned on the knob. He slipped from beside Glenna Anne, drew his shotgun from the closet, and let off the pickup's brake so it'd coast away from the house and not rouse her.

He stopped short of the knob and snuck to the broken fence. Rowdies were drinking, playing the Devil's music, and frolicking around fires. Cans and bottles glinted. Couples squirmed on blankets. As friends cheered, a youth spray-painted a great red sex organ on Him's soapstone base.

Harmon didn't actually shoot at the boy. He just fanned him and others with No. 8 birdshot. The rowdies ran so hard they fell over themselves. Girls hollered and screamed. Cars and dirt bikes raced down the mountain. A jeep smashed a sycamore, spun into Bitter Creek, and blew steam. Only the fires and smoke were left on Mad Sheep, which looked as if the German army had marched through.

Harmon tried to wipe the red sex organ off Him's base, but paint had smeared and soaked in. He covered his eyes and bowed his head.

His work wasn't finished for the night. He had no powder, yet knew there'd be a reinforced wooden box of dynamite in the state trailer where the highway crew had been repairing the bridge over Wilderness Gap. No watchman paced on duty. Using a wrecking bar he carried in the pickup, Harmon pried loose the door's hasp.

He slipped back to the house and out again. By dawn he'd dug a deep hole, worked the head free, and after wrapping it in one of Glenna Anne's clean sheets, buried Him. He augered the stone base, tamped the charge, lit the fuse. He crouched below the knob thinking, I kept my promise. This won't no part of it, and what I'm doing now's for You, not me.

The blast caused a smoky column to spiral high. Anybody down in the valley or on the interstate could see. Bits of stone sprinkled the trampled grass and smoldering fires. A dark dust revolved slowly and settled.

When he drove to the house, Glenna Anne met and hugged him. She'd been crying. She didn't ask about the sheet. He washed, shaved, and was ready and waiting by the time Willie Blevens and his deputies arrived in the police cruiser.

"We best go to town," Willie said. "You might want your toothbrush."

"I just run my choppers under the faucet," Harmon said as a deputy held open the car door for him. "Thing is I always believed it about the most important thing in the world for a man to keep his word."

NIGHT SPORT

The sixth night, and Chip continued waiting. The grooved pneumatic tires of his Electroped rolled like whispers over his bare floor. A levered rheostat, a throttle, controlled speed, and his right hand nudged it to the quadrant's limit. The steering gear was a joystick with which he held the tubular stainless-steel vehicle in tight curves as he wheeled through the darkness of his isolated cottage.

Because during the week he switched on no lights, he quickly re-developed a sense of darkness left behind across an Asian sea. He knew what fronted him the way a blind man feels a wall before stepping into it or a bat sends out unearthly beepings to alert itself to obstruction or prey.

Chip's feelers quivered toward windows and doors. The blinds, from Woolworth's, were drawn to sills of his cottage, a square frame tepee with a brick flue at the center into which his cast-iron stove was piped. The dwelling had been lived in by farm tenants, but the city of Richmond oozed westward along secondary roads, and that ooze de-voured field and forest. All the day long Chip heard bulldozers rooting. Aroused dust reddened the waning October air. Within sight grew a trailer park, where sheets popped on lines. They were ghosts, fleeing.

He'd recently been visited by neighbors from a double-wide, a truck driver and his wife, Fred and Maybelle, benevolent grits who'd attempted to customize their mobile home by planting shrubs and con-structing a salt-treated deck. Set on the deck were painted fruit cans from which flowers dangled till the first kill frost—early, this year, the middle of the month instead of toward the end.

Fred and Maybelle had tapped at his door while he sat facing it in the latest-model Electroped, a gleaming, rustproof wonder provided by the nation's taxpayers. It was the second Chip had owned, an improved machine, intricately evolved. He could gather so much speed that he had to lean in on corners. At the foot of his bed waited a small electric compressor he used to keep the tires pumped to 30 psi. Nights he plugged a thick black umbilical into a socket to recharge his batteries.

When he didn't answer their knock, Fred and Maybelle talked on the porch. They were worried about mail and newspapers piling up in Chip's rural boxes beside the road in front of the house. He'd just subscribed to a Richmond paper. He received lots of mail but no personal letters—mainly colorful flyers and shimmering catalogs useful for starting fires. He was on lists, the government's among others, and besides the monthly checks he got notices that he rarely opened, causing Gregory displeasure down at the VA.

"Gone," Fred said on the porch. "No car."

"We might should carry his mail over to our place," Maybelle said.

Chip felt their weight on his porch, the floorboards of his cottage transmitting it. Between them Fred and Maybelle weighed four hundred pounds.

"He don't like people fooling with his stuff," Fred said.

"Threw half a chocolate cake I took him out the door to the dogs," Maybelle said. "Knew I saw it too."

The boards were relieved of weight, and Chip's neighbors walked the road's weedy shoulder back to the trailer park and their double-wide. Mail and papers now lay on Chip's porch. He fumed but didn't leave the cottage. Mail and papers could be seen from the road, meaning things might yet work out.

The Electroped hummed and hissed through the house. During the day he expected nothing, though eyes might be observing. Clamped by metal bands to his chimney was an antenna from which dropped a lead-in wire. He owned no TV, but a person appraising his place from outside couldn't know. He lit no fires in his stove, despite the frosted nights. He kept away from windows, not cracking the blinds. He took no baths. He answered no calls.

Gregory had insisted on the phone, had sent the man from Chesapeake & Potomac. The Dingo-shod installer asked Chip where he wanted the instrument.

"Like how about up your ass?" Chip answered, and the rangy young man, who wore a leather jacket and a yellow hardhat, glanced again at Chip's legs and quietly connected the phone close to the bed. Chip had no table or other furniture, so the young man left the instrument on the floor—a pink model, a Princess designed for delicate, pampered fingers. Maybe a mistake, or Gregory's little joke.

One of Chip's first calls came from Barbara—Babs, his name for her way back. Nice cultured voice, soft, suggestive, vaginal. He pictured her dressed in a sleeveless white blouse and checkered summer skirt, standing before fluted columns of a white clubhouse, with perhaps a driver or sand wedge held in gloved ladylike fingers. Her arms were tanned, and she pushed a crescent of glossy black hair aside from her long, lovely face.

"I'm coming over anyhow," she said.

"Only if you wear heels, garter belt, ruby lipstick, your pearl earrings, and promise to blow me," he said.

"I won't let you disgust me, so just stop."

"What I'm doing," he said and hung up his simply precious phone.

At nights he listened. He understood his tepee, its vibrations. He'd been living in it nearly a year. Gregory at the VA objected and wouldn't help with the loan. The VA and Chip's family preferred to hold him in the city. They wanted possession. But he had his own money building up at the bank, the United Dominion, one of the many white towers along the James, and he signed the papers without requiring advice or authorization.

While Chip was still in rehab, he liked to sit by a window and watch gulls dip over the river, the birds a dazzling white above the greenish water breaking against flood-crusted rocks. "What's out there?" Gilchrist, the psychiatrist, asked.

"All fall down," Chip answered and made a cascading tumbling motion using his fingers.

At his cottage close to the piney woods he rested in the Electroped. He could doze in any position, silently, yet set himself on automatic alert. He'd developed that particular talent neither in Richmond nor in the hospital but in darkness as thick and raw as sewage, from which strands of himself unraveled to the foulness of decay and little men in black pajamas. The passage of a dung beetle through humid leaf mold sounded loud as a scream.

He ate from cans and munched his apples. Grimes Golden. He'd laid in a supply from the Winn-Dixie at the shopping center where his secondary road joined four lanes of the new highway. He owned two sets of legs, prosthetic miracles of American ingenuity, the latest pair electrically commanded, both equipped with smoothly working joints and gears, each fitted to him as carefully as handcrafted boots.

"You'll love these," the white-smocked technician said, his calipers, wrenches, and voltage meter carried in a fastidious red toolbox. As he knelt to make adjustments, Chip tightened a thigh muscle, causing a Fiberglas leg with its pink flesh tones and artificial veins and arteries to kick, its foot striking the bespectacled technician in his stomach and sprawling him backward. He heaved for breath. The fall smudged his nattily starched smock.

The hospital was glad to be rid of Chip. They couldn't wait to shove him out the door. This time he wouldn't go home. He'd been through that. His father, once Hellcat ace, was now the comptroller/

vice-president at a firm that manufactured line robots for the tobacco industry. He shot down inflated invoices, inventory leaks, and padded expense accounts with the same deliberate sense of attack that had earned him the Navy Cross, a medal displayed on framed blue velvet in the library.

For weeks Chip's parents allowed him to sit by the window, looking at the spangled flights of ruby-throated hummingbirds to blooming mimosas. Their house, built after the Federal style, was located in the city's west end, set on a bluegrass plot, and shaded by pruned white oaks. His mother tended a flower garden at the rear. His was still partially a boy's room, containing trophies, summer snapshots, a fraternity mug, and a charcoal drawing of Feather, a Llewellin setter so gentle of mouth when retrieving birds that he laid them like fine silk gloves in one's fingers.

The time to hunt birds was in advance of snow, because bobwhite quail sensed weather and were anxious to feed before the ground became covered. On a November afternoon Chip's father phoned Mr. Lamp, the headmaster, springing Chip from school. Chip hurried home, loaded Feather and the guns in the Jeepster, and met his father at the company's plant near Henrico.

They drove southwest to somber farmlands of Chesterfield County, where his father had hunting permits. As the first flakes slanted down, they stepped into an incredible streak of shooting. Feather squatted, seized by a trembling, tail-lifted point at the edge of a lespedeza field not a dozen yards beyond the Jeepster, and from that moment on they couldn't avoid birds.

The father carried his Parker twelve-gauge, Chip an L. C. Smith sixteen side-by-side, and they shot bird for bird the rest of the afternoon, each exceeding the limit of eight quail apiece, snow twisting into their faces, laughing, amazed at the ease and sureness of their shooting. Feather was delirious with the rapture of work, his tail slightly bloodied from whipping against briars. The game pouches of their hunting jackets became softly heavy at their butts.

They laid the warm bronze birds on the hood of the Jeepster. Feather stood on his hind legs to observe, actually grinning, fluffs of feathers hanging from his wet black lips, his amber eyes agleam. Chip and his father did a little dance and hugged each other, and Feather would've hugged too had he known how, as the snow fell on the birds so prettily arranged on the Jeepster's green hood.

It was a memory Chip nurtured during the blackness, the whimpering, shit-in-the-pants days that came before the light, the absolute brilliance which exploded not from outside but within—a white fire so searing and almighty it cauterized him clean. Afterward, when he drifted up to pain, he sought a different blackness, a friendly one. He begged for it.

"We understand," his mother said. "Don't think we're being critical or impatient."

She was a woman of breeding, in her background both a Virginia governor and an Episcopal bishop. Loving and kindly, she brought food up to Chip's room, though his father had carpenters install a one-passenger elevator that slid along the side of the front staircase. She served Chip hot bread, country ham, and buttered roasting ears. As soon as she left, he, like a child, hid most of the food and sneaked it to the trash. When she discovered his deception, she cried—not in his presence, but in her perfumed, rose-tinted bedroom.

His mother and father drank civilized highballs each night before dinner, two bourbons with branch water during the week, perhaps a third on weekends and holidays. By then Chip had his first set of new legs, clicking along on greased ball-and-socket joints and lubricated bearings. He rode the elevator down and ambled to the dining-room sideboard, where he lifted out a bottle of Virginia Gentleman to carry back to his room.

He drank looking from his window toward the precise weedless garden and became so bombed he fell from the chair. They heard his body's thump and hurried up the steps to find him bucking and vomiting on the Navaho carpet. His father undressed him. Using a wet, warm towel, Chip's mother washed him. Her wiping strokes made him think of being erased by the fiery, omnipotent power of the great light.

Daily he journeyed down for his bottle, starting his drinking early. His parents became so disturbed they stopped buying liquor for themselves, allowing him to empty the sideboard, including finally the wine, B & B, and crème de menthe. By then he owned a car, paid for and specially modified by the good old U.S. of A., and he left the house and drove to the ABC store in Midlothian, where he bought the one-gallon limit, four quarts of Ancient Age. He locked what he wasn't drinking in the Oldsmobile's trunk.

"Is it the terror of memory?" his father asked, a tall, graying man with a clipped moustache and outswept chin. His red-and-black tie loose, his pinstriped vest hanging open, he stood helpless and sorrowing before the first Electroped. Even during his Pacific killing forays he'd never seen the light but had remained clean and elite in the mothering quarters of an immaculate carrier.

"I don't remember much," Chip said. "Mostly one big thing."

"You're destroying yourself."

"Never felt better."

"And us who love you."

Chip's mother called in the Reverend James M. Dunne—Jimmy, to his adoring congregation and friends. Everybody liked Jimmy. Once an Olympic swimmer, he was built along the lissome lines of water athletes, and when he uncovered his pearly whites or touched his chaste fingers to his wavy blond locks, the ladies became excited, as if he were a golden stallion coursing among mares.

"There's One to lean on," Jimmy said. He'd first chatted Chip up about the Redskins beating the Cowboys. "God loves us. We can't fathom His ways, but He cares deeply, and you must understand no pain is random, no loss accidental. All life is part of a purpose to be made known in the fullness of time."

"I do have a theological question," Chip said, and Jimmy, wearing Docksiders, a glazed tan corduroy suit, and an open-at-the-throat chamois shirt, leaned closer to smile encouragement. "Did you pretty boys queer each other in the seminary?"

Chip had to leave home. That's when he drove out in the Olds to search for a house. He thought of shaking Virginia's dust from his feet, even of deserting the land of the free and home of the brave, but doing so would only cause his parents further distress, and it wasn't their fault, or pretty Jimmy Dunne's, that they'd never lived in shit or glimpsed their legs lying like slashed and bloody meat apart from the rest of them. They'd never learned the absolute truth contained in the light.

He located his ratty little frame tepee out in the western boonies of the county, a cardboard For Sale sign tacked to a tilted wooden stake pounded in a yard of crabgrass. The place was far enough away that his parents weren't all over him, yet close enough to allow a visit now and again. They could keep in touch.

"You like everything so clean you might wash the windows or let somebody do it," Gregory said.

"What do I need with washed windows?"

"You're always looking out."

"What I see is dirt either way," Chip said.

He used to park his car in the sandy circle at the front of the house, but ten nights ago, while he lay sloshed and unhearing, some bastard stole his hubcaps, CB, and custom cushions. Chip didn't call the sheriff or insurance company. He brooded a few days and then in the darkness hid his car off a fire trail through the piney woods. He hiked back using a cane. If questioning required it, he could say the Olds was stolen. He'd wiped the wheel and gearshift.

No colorful flyers or shimmering catalogs burned in his stove, no smoke rose from his chimney, and the night coldness seeped into the house. When he opened cans of beans or munched apples, he caressed silence. He could've been snaking through the elephant grass of a putrid savanna. In the living room he set beers on his Maytag. The worst part of waiting was he'd had to give up the bathtub. He always felt the need of baths.

Tied by three leather thongs to the rear of the Electroped was the canvas scabbard made for his L. C. Smith, the Crown-grade double given him at fourteen by his father, who taught him to shoot with both eyes open.

On a hot, still September afternoon, Chip had attached his newest legs, driven to a picked cornfield lying in a spongy bottom alongside the Appomattox River, and, walking with a rolling gait, positioned himself under a dead sycamore tree.

When a gang of doves circled above the flowing shadowed water and swooped in to the field, he poleaxed the leader with a clean head shot that spun the bird limply to a crash. Pinkish gray feathers erupted and spiraled. He hadn't lost his shooting eye. Gunning was what he'd done best. He held the dove's puny softness and watched a single drop of scarlet blood slide from its beak onto his palm's lifeline.

He hadn't asked for permission to hunt the field, and the bearded farmer came running and shouting from the high ground. He flailed his cap. His pounding clodhoppers raised puffs of red dust. He threatened Chip with the game warden and arrest until he saw the peculiar gait of Chip's legs.

"Go ahead," the farmer told him, spitting to the side and leveling the International Harvester cap. "Shoot all you want."

Chip left. It'd been dumb to come out, a vestige reflex from another time and place. He tossed the stiffening dove into a thorny ditch at the side of the road.

"I don't believe you," Gilchrist, the psychiatrist, said. Though his name sounded English, Gilchrist looked Italian—plump, olive-oily, his dark eyes seemingly without pupils. "Everybody dreams."

It wasn't so. Chip never had nightmares, hadn't wakened sweating, yelling, and shaking, as it happened in the movies. The light had cleaned him out.

He chewed a slice of white bread. His mother bought him a bread box, painted yellow and patterned with two entwined red roses. She wanted to furnish the house, but he hadn't allowed the men to carry in the table and chairs she'd ordered trucked from the city. Once she slipped into his house, her ladylike fingers would attempt to close lovingly about his life. To grant her something, he kept the bread box.

"Doing all right," he told his father. "Got shelter, a new Electroped, and Uncle Sammy craps over me every month. High life."

In murkiness he stared at the top of a bean can and contemplated the beauty of 0. He saw zeroes everywhere—wheels, a hubcap, the toilet bowl, his bathtub, a rat's eye. The perfect symbol zero, round or egg-shaped, no entrances, no exits. 0 times 0 equals 0. 0 plus or minus or divided by 0 equals 0. Profound mathematics. Zero was the slate wiped clean.

From the Maytag he lifted the knife he'd finished at rehab, the handle alternate layers of filed red, yellow, and translucent Plexiglass salvaged from a smashed helicopter, the blade a VC bayonet shaped on an electric grinder. He opened cans with it, honed it patiently along his whetstone. The knife had the good feel of a balanced heft.

He couldn't allow mail and newspapers to pile up much longer. Fred and Maybelle might call the sheriff or rescue squad, and if Chip didn't open his door, they would force entry. It was crazy anyhow, growing from the theft of his hubcaps, CB, and custom cushions—a sporting idea hatched in beer. He'd once been a sport, a gun his third arm. Sport for a sport over a baited field.

He half slept, passively contemplating 0, yet listening. His bed tempted him. His method was to swing to it, legless, by using the trapeze bolted to a ceiling joist. He yawned, unfastened his legs, and stacked them against the Maytag. He'd have a bath first.

As his fingers closed around the Electroped's joystick, somebody touched the cottage. The cottage was his skin. He subdued his breathing in the way he'd learned and sped his senses into darkness. The night was quiet except for a plane flying over high, a hound barking from the direction of the trailer park, and an occasional shrill of wind.

Maybe Fred and Maybelle were again checking on him. Or a sheriff's deputy. Slowly he turned his head from side to side, like a cat hunting. Somebody was moving around the cottage. At the north side he—they?—touched it a second time. Chip pushed out farther, his feelers threading through walls and beyond. He'd once heard a black-pajamaed Charley swallow spit on the other side of an earthen dike and had hosed him in midleap. Charley pinwheeled into a rice paddy that smelled like hot piss.

A knock on the front door—not bold, but tentative, unsure. A pause, a shift of weight, another knock, louder.

"Anybody home?" the male voice called. "Had a flat down the road and need to make a phone call."

Like hell! Whoever stood at the door had to see lights at the trailer park. In the other direction was an all-night Amoco station where an illuminated sign revolved. Chip waited.

The person on the porch tried the door. The knob turned and rattled. The door was pushed. The person released the knob and stepped off the porch. He walked not away but to the rear of the cottage.

The person tried two windows and the rear door, which had a diamond-shaped pane of glass in it. Nothing. Chip tasted the night, licked it like a snake. He'd been able to direct his senses through the shadows of tree canopies, among detritus, and beneath the ground into holes. It was like turning into smoke and drifting to where shapes waited among fronds. He'd smelled death on air so thin that it wouldn't disturb the fall of a sparrow's feather.

A quick hard tap, the tinkle of glass breaking and spilling across the kitchen floor. Chip reached over his shoulder to unsheathe the L. C. Smith. He settled it atop the Electroped's metal arms, index finger on the trigger commanding the right barrel. His thumb hardened against the safety. The person would next fit his hand through the broken pane to the key inside the door. Chip had foreseen how it would be done.

Quietly the door unlocked. Another pause. A hinge squeaked.

Someone took a slow step inside. A foot gently crunched glass. Breathing. Hesitation. Chip's left hand tightened around the checkered forearm of the shotgun, the oiled walnut friendly to his fingers. He thought of the birds he and his father had placed on the Jeepster's green hood.

A soft click, a concentrated beam, perhaps a pencil flashlight or a larger one choked down. Steps crossing the kitchen. The light sweeping about and for an instant outlining the doorway. The person bumped a pyramid of Bud cans Chip had built on the floor. They clattered.

Silence, breathing, shifting, saliva. A figure sidled into the bedroom. Floorboards gave, a shoe sibilance—rubber soles—the sound loud in stays of inhalations. A muffled word. Nothing to take. What? Canes, legs, ashtrays, the Princess phone faintly aglow by the bed.

A shape, formed behind a slash of light, approached the front room. Chip bent forward to the Maytag. He allowed the person to reach the doorway before lifting his hand to the wall switch. As the beam whitened his face, he knuckled the switch and raised the L. C. Smith.

Shocked and blinking before him, caught in midstep, stood a white youth wearing a dark blue turtleneck sweater, rock-washed jeans, and grimy running shoes. Fright bugged his eyes and gapped his mouth to a silent outcry. On his hands were white cotton gloves, the kind Chip's mother wore to her garden. Both those hands were lifted. He held a key-ring flashlight. His silky brown hair was perfectly groomed.

"No, don't, please!" he said, the gloved hands pushed forward as if they could stop lead shot.

"Give a good reason why the hell not," Chip said.

"I knocked and everything. I have a flat down the road—"

"Spare me the crap and empty your pockets on my faithful Maytag."

The youth set the flashlight on the washer, peeled off the gloves, and laid out change, a broken roll of cherry Life Savers, and his wallet, real pigskin with elaborate black stitching. He glanced at Chip's empty khakis, the stacked legs, and the antenna wire that fed no TV. He looked at the knife on the Maytag.

"Turn them inside out," Chip said.

"I just need a phone to call—"

"Raise your sweater. Higher. Now do a three-sixty slow."

The youth obeyed, his sweater and white T-shirt held under his armpits. A pretty boy, tender, nice skin, like a girl's, a trace of tan, hardly any hair on his body, a little blondish fuzz. He had clean hands and wore a Seiko with an alligator band. Looped through his jeans was an alligator belt. Apparently these were his designer stealing clothes. No weapon. On a finger a crested gold ring.

"Toss your wallet," Chip said.

He one-handed the L. C. Smith aimed at the youth while with

the other he leafed through the wallet's vinyl windows. Thomas Berry Walker. Address: Richmond's Windsor Road, a classy drive that skirted the Country Club of Virginia.

The wallet held an operator's license, Visa card, the vehicle registration for a Honda, and color snapshots, one of a derbied girl astride a bay horse, another of a nicely dressed middle-aged couple standing beside a stone birdbath among crimson azaleas. Money: a Jackson, a Hamilton, a Lincoln, and two George Washingtons—thirty-seven dollars.

Christ, no trash off the street, no lush, freak, jiving spade, or even rowdy-dowdy country jake—but a rich kid! Definitely not the type to steal hubcaps. Hooked on highs maybe, yet needed no money for a buy. He reeked of green.

"This'll kill my parents," he said.

"Before I call the sheriff, you get a minute to explain. Keep your own time on the Seiko."

The kid was still half crouched, his fingers twitching as if turning knobs, his legs shaky, and he jerked his head sideways to keep his pretty hair from falling across his brow. Good-looking all right, handsome one day when the angles rounded, slick with girls.

"It's this club I want in out at St. John's," the boy said. "God, I'm sorry!"

St. John's was a private Episcopal academy housed in Georgian buildings and surrounded by grassy playing fields. Life was patterned after English schools, with emphasis on classics and sports. Students wore blazers and ties to class. They dated at St. Martha's, a sister institution. Young southern gentility being formed.

"Initiation requires you have to do something daring," the boy said.

"Stealing hubcaps, a CB, and custom cushions is daring, huh?"

"I didn't do those. Honest. One member hopped a freight train and rode it to Norfolk. Another climbed a TV tower and hung his girl's brassiere from a red light. I meant to take your TV set, show it to the club, and slip it back after a couple of days. Putting it back would be the daring part. I've been driving around most of the week looking for a house, nothing too close home. Don't call the police. Please, I'm begging."

The kid was so afraid. Oh, fear had a real glitter to it.

"Sit down," Chip said.

In the room was only the one straight chair, bought at Kmart. It had an orange plastic seat. As Tommy lowered himself to it, he glanced about, still eyeing the Maytag, the stacked legs, and the lead-in wire curled across the floor. He looked again at Chip's khakis—the windless windsocks.

"You probably never saw a washing machine in the living room before," Chip said. "It's top of the line and'll do everything except put out the dog and love you up."

"You can have the money in my wallet," Tommy said.

"I know that. Most people don't have proper appreciation for a good washing machine. She keeps me clean. That's important, so I give her respect and don't stick her back in some dark place."

The boy sat erect at the front edge of the chair, his maidenly hands clamped hard over his knees. His honey brown eyes were lustrous with fright, yet had no pain, no loss in them. They were unsullied by loss. Again they flicked at Chip's empty khakis.

"You ever been dirty, Tommy?"

"Yes, sir. Sure, I have."

"Probably a scrimmage on St. John's Commons."

"You know about St. John's Commons?"

"Would you believe I went to school there?"

Hell no, the kid couldn't believe that but was too scared to say it.

"I been dirty, Tommy. Had shit all over me, not only my own. I take lots of baths, sometimes three or four a day, and keep my clothes washed. Cleanliness is important to me. It's why I shave my head. You see any dirt under my fingernails?"

"No, sir," Tommy answered, peering at Chip's extended right hand.

"All the crevices of my body are clean, though this last week has been an exception."

"I'll have the glass fixed," Tommy said.

"Nice of you to offer."

"I honest-to-God meant to bring the TV back. Let me go."

"You did a dumb thing, Tommy, and we always pay for dumbness. What's the name of your club?"

"John's Jesters."

"When I was there, we had the Brawnies."

"Still do," Tommy said, for the first time believing a little. "Students who earn three or more letters." The honey brown eyes flicked at the windless windsocks. "You were a Brawny?"

"I ran the middle distances. Hard to believe now, huh? Guess you'll be graduating soon."

"Early June, and then on to the University next fall, if I get in. Otherwise, Washington and Lee, where my father went."

"Amazing how much we have in common. I attended Wahooland. One year on the lawns of Mr. Jefferson's university. Before my quest. I carried a pretty girl's picture in my billfold, like your equestrienne. She went to St. Martha's over Rappahannock way, and on to Sweet Briar. Had beautiful legs. Still does. And you're dying to know about mine. You keep trying not to look at them."

"I know girls at St. Martha's," Tommy said, averting his eyes.

"I was certain you did. Maybe you been to the tea dances."

"Sure, all the time."

"The Christmas one's the best, the ball with candles and holly. Girls go out and pick the holly. Get time off from classes. They wear shiny white gowns and come down the grand staircase singing and carrying white candles."

"Right!" Tommy said, believing now. He believed altogether.

"It was snowing," Chip said. "All the fires in Astor House were lit, and snow fell on the river, gulls flying through the flakes. They were gliding through snow. Girls carried the candles and were singing."

"I'm supposed to be back at school," Tommy said, raising the wrist with the Seiko.

"Ten demerits if you miss check-in."

"It's five now."

"Deflation in d's. I'm going to let you leave, but go ahead and ask about my legs."

"I didn't mean to look at them."

"It's okay. Want to see the stumps."

"No thanks!" Tommy said when Chip made as if to uncover them.

"Don't blame you. Ug-lee! Hate to look myself. What I got for being dumb. Had this crazy idea I could fly. Drove to the mountains, an October morning, out past Roanoke, almost to West Virginia. Thousands of hawks sail past a place up there, on their migration south, and you can stand on this cliff and watch them at eye level or lower."

Tommy was again wary and worried.

"Know what I did? I stripped off my clothes, stepped from the cliff, and joined them. Spread my arms and flew. I was up there soaring along over winter wheat and green rivers, everything pure, feeling thermals on my belly, and some of the hawks turned their heads and looked at me out of golden eyes. They smiled at me. Yeah, they can smile. I thought I'd never come down, would coast on forever, till this big bastard of a black eagle dropped on me. He was a sonofabitch. His beak hacked off my legs. Hell of a thing for an eagle to do midair and all."

Tommy was nervous. His hands moved to the seat of the chair, which he gripped as if it might eject him.

"The war you mean?" he asked. "Nam?"

"Got patriotic," Chip said. "Wasn't much older than you, and practically the first kook to stand in line at the recruiting office."

"It should never have been," Tommy said. "We talked about it at school. A bad war."

"You know about good and bad wars, do you?"

"The Virginia Diocese sponsored a three-day symposium at St. John's. Posters, speakers, films. All those civilians killed, babies even, on fire. The students voted two to one to designate it a national tragedy. We agreed never to let a government do that to us. You soldiers were used. We agreed we wouldn't kill anybody ever. We couldn't live with it, we decided. Sickening. I'm really sorry about your legs. I wish I could give you mine."

Chip stared. The little prick felt not only sorry for but also superior to him. The new breed, chosen, anointed, the slickies he saw tooling around the shopping center with blue-lidded piglets in rock-pounding Corvettes and TransAms. Righteous little farts. He stiffened as if about to be scorched again by the great exploding truth. Goddamn it, they ought to have to learn. They needed to know.

"You okay?" Tommy asked, scared.

"Everything's lovely," Chip said, squirming free of it. "Where was I? Yeah, so I fell to the ground and got legs back from another fucking eagle, not a blackie this time, a baldy. You can't fly without legs. A matter of balance."

"May I go, please?"

"Right. Wouldn't want them to gig you. Happy to know you'll never be as stupid as I was. Hope for the future and all. I want you to have something. A memento. Take the knife. Show it to the Jesters."

"You're giving it to me?" Tommy asked, rising from the chair. He pushed in his emptied pockets and reached for the knife on the Maytag.

"Housewarming gift. Made it myself. Don't forget your other stuff."

"Let me pay," Tommy said when Chip handed back the wallet. Tommy slid it into the left hip pocket, the cotton gloves in the right.

"No deal. I enjoyed your visit."

"I promise I'll reimburse you for the broken glass. Have it fixed, and I'll send the money."

"No sweat. I'll tack cardboard over the hole and sweep up."

"I'd like to say you're one fine gentleman," Tommy said but didn't offer to shake hands. He started for the kitchen and the door he'd come through. He held the knife by its hilt.

"Take care now," Chip said. "Uh, Tommy?"

As Tommy turned back politely, Chip thumbed the L. C. Smith's safety forward. He pulled each trigger, firing the right barrel for Tommy's left calf, the left barrel for the right—the shells No. 8 dove load. Tommy's legs were slammed back beneath him. The front length of his body pounded the floor. That silky hair covered his brow now. Dazed and astonished, he lifted his head, and the terrible knowledge, the deepest knowledge of all, flowed into those honey brown eyes. He struggled to right himself, howled, and now sobbing on his side, hinged forward as if exercising to touch his toes.

Chip sheathed the L. C. Smith. He left the knife where it'd bounced on the kitchen floor. He guided the Electroped to the dainty little Princess phone glowing pinkly. He called the sheriff's office and told the dispatcher his house had been broken into and that he'd been attacked by a youth holding a knife. They should send a doctor and an ambulance.

Before steering around the mess, he tossed a bath towel to the keening, terrified Tommy. Chip would raise some blinds, switch on a few more lights, and bring in the mail and papers from the porch.

POINTS

When Beau woke during the night, he believed he heard sleet rapping the roof. The sound turned out to be a thrashing mulberry limb striking siding of the frame colonial house, where once British officers had billeted as the redcoats campaigned westward through Virginia. The dwelling was no longer part of Charlottesville's most preferred residential area, but its historicity provided authority, allowing him to entertain at small parties friends who lived in the hunt country north of the city. He rented the second story and had his own side entrance.

Actually, he'd hoped for rain. The past week had been shrieking cold, the ground freezing, the farm ponds filming over with brownish ice so thick it easily supported the weight of fat, waddling Canada honkers. He'd suffered pain too from his leg, the left knee surgeons had carved upon and reknitted. The ligaments hadn't been the same since his fall at Jumping Ridge. Lately there'd been moments in the saddle he felt he was merely holding onto a vehicle careening out of control.

He snoozed till the alarm buzzed at seven. His tea water heated automatically in the kitchen he'd decorated by hanging pewter tankards from oak ceiling beams, a collection begun when antiques were still not beyond the reach of his pocketbook. He'd not recently considered a purchase. Prices were mad. His consolation was the hefty lump of money offered for his tankards. He thought of them as a flourishing investment—certainly better than stock-market values. Several times a year he lifted and dusted them. Earlier during the winter he'd found a dead mouse curled at the bottom of one.

He had no hunger for breakfast before a chase. A drink, yes, though that avenue was closed. Despite radiators, the apartment felt chilled, and he switched on the bathroom's portable heater. He'd had words with Mrs. Winston, widowed proprietor of the house, who lived below. She insisted his lease permitted neither heater nor air conditioner, that such appliances placed too great a load on the old wiring. Only after he agreed to pay a higher share of the electric bill were her feathers smoothed.

Ice swirls coated the inside of the bathroom windowpanes, the glass still dark at this hour. Using a fingernail file, he scraped a peephole. He saw his own light on the barren frozen garden. If not rain, he thought, let us have snow, just enough to keep people snug between their flannel sheets. Little chance now, though the sky appeared empty of stars.

He shaved, leveled his silvered sideburns, and tended his mustache—careful as always not to trim it so precisely it looked dwelt upon. His was a small face, narrow at the chin, and Ellen, his first wife, had told him that helmeted he resembled a fox peering from a burrow. She claimed he lacked only whiskers poking horizontally under his nose.

She'd said that endearingly when they married, yet toward the end, after she began slipping around with the Irishman, she'd spoken the words to make sport of Beau. She called his foxiness to the attention of guests. He might carry her a drink and she'd shout "Tallyho!" causing laughter. He surprised her and the Irishman in the upstairs Victorian tub, suds and water sloshed all over the tile floor. "Tallyho!" she called again. The same afternoon Beau packed and left. The house belonged to her.

He stepped quickly from his pajama bottoms and pulled on a pair of panty hose split at the crotch. During the coldest days the panty hose were more practical than long johns. Long johns plus high wool socks bound his boots too tightly around his calves. He had trouble enough tugging them on using talcum and hooks, the old Dehners he'd kept oiled and repaired for years past adding. He suspected other men wore panty hose. Of course they wouldn't speak of it. He tossed those he purchased into a cart while grocery shopping at Food Lion.

He buttoned his oxford-cloth shirt over his underwear, drew on his freshly washed white breeches, and sat for the boots. He loved the Dehners' feel, the elegant dash they gave his legs. Lightly built, he had just the body for hunt attire. He maintained his weight at approximately 145, gaining a pound or two winters when less able to exercise, losing them summers on the tennis court.

He drank his mug of tea and smoked a Camel. He honestly preferred tea, and it had nothing to do with his being an Anglophile. He did admire the English, especially their riders. No bolder race of men ever threw a leg over a horse, not Mongol, Scythian, or Cossack. Flying Spitfires had been simply a change of mounts. He and Ashley, his third wife, had hunted a winter in Dorsetshire, and he'd witnessed pale, languid English ladies put their equines to ditches so wide that jumping them seemed insane. Ashley, young and unprepared, had screamed at the immense terror of soaring over them and the exhilaration of remaining alive.

Friends considered Beau a master cook and made over the Creole dishes he prepared in this kitchen. He'd cut back not because of money—mere dollars never subverted a good table—but his blood pressure; it reared high on the diastolic. He'd bought a sphygmomanometer he kept out of sight in his walnut secretary.

He walked quietly across the floor. He used few rugs because the house had its original broad pine boards worthy of display. He didn't want to disturb quarrelsome Mrs. Winston. Between sips at a second cup of tea, he tied his stock before the bureau mirror and pushed the golden pin through laps of the immaculate linen. The pierced dandyish knot would hold high all day.

He buttoned on his canary yellow vest. Vests would be in order this morning. Let there, he thought, be no wind. Let the sun warm the earth, yet not so faintly that the ground thaws only on top and remains frozen inches beneath. Allow footing to be safe. Permit no jump approaches to become icy bogs horses slide and crash into. Let the fox run straight and true. Let, permit, allow—his litany, like a Catholic saying his beads, though he was Episcopalian and had served twice as a warden at St. John's.

He rechecked his fixture card, certain the meet was to leave from Two Rivers Farm, home of Bettina and Clive Rankin. He winced. No invitation yet for the February Frolic. He blocked the anxiety. His club, the Blue Mountain, met thrice a week, weather permitting—Mondays, Wednesdays, Saturdays. Januaries they gathered at ten.

He pushed arms into his Pinks, the scarlet coat bought in England, wool twice the weight of anything found in the States. The material was so stiff when first worn that as he took jumps the collar jammed his ears and nudged off his topper. Some eighteen years later it'd become completely fitted to his body's bends, a suit of armor he felt comfortable in, protected, even transformed. Cerulean blue, the club's color, decorated the collar. It'd faded to Confederate gray.

Over the Pinks he zipped up a sheepskin jacket. He set on a corduroy cap and stuck fingers into fur-lined gloves. He collected his Steuben, saddle pad, bridle, and whip, it ancient. He'd broken the stag handle during a spill and had a jeweler repair it at a cost that would've bought half a dozen new ones.

Newness he suspected. Plastic lurked everywhere. He loved hunting's encrusted traditions, the connections with a grand past. For him the chase was choosing to reach back into the best epochs the centuries had to offer, as well as a statement of where one stood in respect to a world becoming increasingly common, disordered, and hateful.

He'd whipped a number of years while William Garrison served as master. Now William lay in the grave, had died pulling a New York strip from his freezer. A wiring defect had electrocuted him. At the funeral Beau himself sounded "Gone to Ground" on the horn. Non-hunters found that amusing, even ridiculous. The worst part of being an American was the reverse snobbery—as if it were somehow commendable to be ordinary.

When Warren Burns became the new master, he didn't ask Beau to continue on the staff. Warren wanted Vicky, his wife, to ride whip. Beau understood. Warren contributed significantly to the keep and training of hounds. He footed the bill for a whelping kennel. He had a perfect right to choose his people.

Beau never spoke his disappointment, though during early days of the new order he received looks of both sympathy and disgust when Vicky did her job in amateurish fashion. That was okay. She learned, had even asked Beau's advice, attempting to make the severance easier for him. She needn't have bothered. He knew his place—at the head of few tables, often not his own.

He switched out lamps, lugged his tack down the side steps, and walked into the shocking cold of early morning. Ice coated concrete where a downspout had discharged, reflecting the streetlight under which he'd parked his gray Mercedes. The car was so ancient it'd again become respectable. "Charlottesville Chevys" the university students called Mercedeses. Beau had no gift for mechanics and was given a grand welcome at the garage, which specialized in imported cars. The owner made out like a bandit.

He laid his tack on the rear seat, folded himself under the steering wheel, and felt relieved when the engine caught on the second try. He sat a moment allowing it to warm. He squinted at the sky and spotted a single star—Venus, he guessed. The cloud cover might be breaking. A gaggle of silent crows flew over the dark trees, the elms some of the last in the city. The mayor had shepherded through council an appropriation to pay an arborist to inject the trunks with antibiotics, just as a doctor might treat diseased patients. Deformed and tortured those elms being administered to appeared in ghoulish light.

Before gearing his car, he shivered and allowed himself a second Camel. He tried to follow rules about smoking, never a cigarette before tea, not more than three between breakfast and lunch, half a pack the entire day. Doctors automatically told you to stop. The hue and cry against tobacco, the very foundation of Virginia's wealth! His son, Alfred, had been at him too, on the last visit when he drove down from Washington to stay the weekend. Alfred had never been tempted by cigarettes and drank each evening no more than two ounces of liquor.

How could youth be so controlled? Beau remembered the glorious excesses of earlier years when he and Ellen stayed smashed for days and floated about in a warm, rosy bubble encompassing lots of both loving and laughter. Neither smoking nor drinking was intelligent, but weren't they human? A young man's reach should exceed his grasp, or what was a martini for?

No heat yet as he chugged through the deserted glittering city of ice. Much too early for students. Not a single moving vehicle along Rugby Road. He'd studied at the university, Alfred too—Beau history, his son a business curriculum. The choices explained much about the differences between them.

Alfred was a child of Beau's second marriage. Ginger, his mother, despite her inheritance, turned out to be so penurious she wouldn't buy a decent horse. She didn't really believe in horses. She played the stock market, phoning her broker daily and earning serious money. She also bought cheap cuts of meat and once asked Beau not to flush the johns in her Georgian mansion so often unless he'd seriously used them. Using a john seriously! Well, Alfred had her nose for money and self-denial.

Beau crossed out Jockey Road past new orange and yellow brick apartment buildings. They had names like Foxhill, Hunting Acres, and Reynard's Repose, though no club members rented there. They were mostly lived in by university people. Even here one saw Mercedeses as well as BMWs, Saabs, and of course Volvos. All sham. Once when the chase charged through the area in pursuit of a cunning gray, young mothers snatched up their children, glared, and even booed. Hounds put the vixen to ground in a culvert behind Safeway.

He kept Windlord at Fox Haven Stables, which he reached by a gravel road through a stand of hardwoods stripped bare by winter winds. He'd once owned a stable, well, his and Ellen's, as well as paddocks and a show ring. Fox Haven wasn't in the same class, yet Polly Wentworth, who owned the place, saw to it her boarders were well tended. She had a way with black help that won their loyalty. Familiarity of persons was essential to the care and comfort of horses. The tab paid for services Polly provided was high, though as good as might be expected around Albemarle.

She sat in her small office at one end of the stable, a desk light on, a fire crackling, the iron stove throwing out solid heat. Coffee was brewing, and country music played from the radio. She set her five-string guitar against a sack of Purina sweet feed. She wore Wellington boots, black jeans, and a black turtleneck sweater covered by a chamois jacket. Nearing sixty, she'd remained slim and fit. Weather had bronzed and rutted her face. Her hair was short and white. She offered him a mug of coffee. They spoke of scenting conditions. She had his penciled monthly bill ready.

"I thought I'd mailed a check," he said, startled because he honestly did believe it.

"We both need secretaries," she said. "Among other things."

Polly was a random victim of bad dice. She'd ridden show circuit till she broke her back in the Upperville Grand Prix, a wreck on a green horse over a triple. Her husband, an actor and director, had cast her aside. She now stayed one jump ahead of a sheriff's sale, yet her courage and stoic style never faltered.

He thanked her for the coffee and crossed from her office toward Windlord's stall. Though doors were closed at each end of the stable, cold found passage. Beau stuck the bill into a jacket pocket. At one time he'd employed a secretary, no, twice, the first when he peddled equine insurance and the second during the year he sold prefabricated barns. He'd also tried to make a market in antique carriages. Though the money looked good on paper, hardly any stuck to his fingers. Epperson, his banker, had despaired.

"There are times you have to tighten the belt," Epperson said, a big man soft in body, hard in mind, who despite his fleshiness and benign expression played deadly poker. He could've taken a riverboat gambler to the cleaners. Beau's mother had left him a small trust fund. Epperson did all he could to defend against invasion of the corpus. He was Horatius at the bridge till the sickness that brought Beau down and sent him away. Only a few lonely dollars now remained in the account.

Beau hung his bridle and saddle over the rack. Windlord knew it to be a hunt day. The big chestnut stretched his neck across the stall's gate. He snorted twice and walled his bright purplish eyes. He was an intelligent animal who possessed an abounding will to hunt. Never did he willingly quit the field, even when sweat scudded his flanks and his breathing sounded like wheezing agricultural machinery. Because of his age, Windlord could not safely endure a long chase, yet gave unsparingly of his spirit. He provided living definition of the word *nobility*.

Epperson had moaned when Beau bought the gelding. The price back then seemed high and was to be met by borrowing. Beau attempted to make Epperson understand.

"You see, hunting's what I live for," he said as the two ate crab salad in the basement grill at Farmington. "Even out of season I'm thinking about it. Buying a good horse isn't a luxury for me. It's a necessity. I could no more do without than relinquish my eyes or use of my limbs. And is it truly that expensive? Ten thousand for a hunter is only a thousand a year if he lasts ten. I spend nearly that on tobacco."

"Suppose he lasts only a year, a month, a day?" Epperson asked, always the skeptic. He was a good man, honest, yet never in his life had he known the thrill of giving himself fully to anything except the successful handling of money.

In former days Ashley had seen to it that Windlord was groomed. She braided mane and tail as Beau instructed her. Now he did the tail twice a season: at opening meet when hounds were blessed and at Thanksgiving. The rest of the time the mane alone sufficed. After Ashley left for Europe with the renowned lesbian playwright, he discovered his fingers had lost much of their nimbleness. Still, he taught the French weave to a number of ladies and their daughters.

He attached the shank to Windlord's leather halter and led him out. Windlord pranced in a circle. His shod feet struck sparks on the concrete alleyway. Beau had never liked pavement in a stable. True, it was easily hosed down and kept clean, but an excited horse could slip and fall. Concrete had no sympathy for hooves.

Polly walked from her office to hold the shank while he saddled Windlord. The animal was lean, the summer's fat run off, a glint of ribs showing. His neck had thickened, natural with age, and when in the company of strange horses he arched it as if a stallion and seemed to float in a high, springing step. Beau kept him clipped during the season. Worked to a fine sweat, he gleamed like a new penny.

"Want him wormed this month?" Polly asked as Beau fitted the broken-bit Kimberwicke into Windlord's mouth.

He told her he did, this being the third month, and his schedule called for it each quarter, just as Johnny Whitt, his farrier, would shoe the horse every seventh week. Doc Broaddus, the vet, did the worming, pushed a tube through the animal's nostril to the esophagus. He pumped the anthelmintic from a stainless-steel bucket.

Beau exchanged the corduroy cap for his topper and removed his sheepskin jacket. The sky shone a pale sun, yet he felt little warmth and shuddered in the gusting north wind. Knives in the blast. He pulled on thin Italian leather gloves which allowed his fingers sensitivity to the feel of the reins. Once in the saddle, he'd be all right except for his feet. These days they grew cold despite the panty hose and heavy socks.

He used the mounting block just beyond the stable's door. Polly handed him his whip, and he touched it to the topper's brim. She crossed back toward the office, absolutely erect because of her spinal trouble. She could no longer hunt, and when she saw others leave for a meet, her expression became a person's looking into a promised land, entry denied. Beau always sent her a sugar-cured ham for Christmas.

He walked Windlord through the paddock to a gate. Two Rivers Farm was a twenty-minute hack along the trail. Windlord wanted to move out, but Beau reined him. The old warrior should limber up slowly as well as conserve energy for the runs. Hills particularly drew Windlord down. His flanks heaved, his head lowered, and he lunged impatiently against inclines.

Ground-ice, shaded by pines, cracked underfoot. Frosted boughs drooped. Quail on their way to feed in a lespedeza patch flushed noisily. Windlord shied, but Beau sat him effortlessly. If nothing else, his seat and balance remained. He looked good mounted, a classic rider, and during the chase the less-experienced riders liked to follow him because he knew the terrain and best approach to fences. Occasionally he glimpsed his own shadow, the form of his jumping silhouetted against the rushing ground, and its dashing stylishness made him proud. One more thing Epperson would never discover or understand.

He skirted Whitetop Farm, where he and Ellen had lived. After he left, she stayed a time with the Irishman. She easily grew weary of people and places. Like a child she needed new toys. She bred, raised, and trained Arabians and sold them at a profit, though money mattered nothing. Now the farm belonged to a man who owned carpet mills. He didn't hunt and was rumored to have Jewish blood—as if that counted any longer.

Alfred had dated a daughter, dark-haired and lively, very athletic, a member of her college's skeet team. She courted Alfred more than he her. She'd phone or drive by in her silver Jaguar. Alfred was essentially bookish. He did swim and dance well, taught the latter by Beau. A Saturday night in June he returned home early, his dinner jacket unbuttoned, his tie hanging loose. He'd taken Rachel to a club dance.

"Trouble?" Beau asked, Wearing his madras bathrobe, he had been reading a Dick Francis thriller. He was still living in his own house then, a small but comfortable two-bedroom stone cottage on a fringe of the hunt country. Epperson had helped negotiate the purchase.

"Dad, if she raised her face and opened her mouth and you dropped in a pebble, it would fall all the way to her feet and resound like an empty metal barrel. She's hollow. Know what she said? She said we should post troops at this country's borders because foreigners were ruining it. Hell, she was a foreigner not long ago, her grandfather was. She really believes rich people are better."

"Often they are," Beau said. Of course Alfred couldn't understand that. He thought of money only in terms of dollars, not the grace attached, the concomitant manners. Granted, riches in the wrong hands were ugly, but rightly used they might produce great beauty—a gracious lawn party under lanterns at twilight, the fireflies glowing among oak shadows, the scent of perfume, a whisper of silk, the art of life. Alfred failed to grasp that living could be a portrait in which a person was both subject and artist.

"Doesn't say much for you then, does it?" Alfred asked, a vicious remark and reference to the state of Beau's bank account. Beau didn't answer. He walked to his bedroom, closed the door, and paced till his anger cooled. Alfred never apologized. He believed apology posturing. He considered civility a nuisance.

The trail broke from spruce pines on high ground overlooking the back side of Two Rivers Farm—a patchwork of pastures, frozen ponds, and dark creosoted plank fences. Geese rose gabbling, their shadows skimming the land. Atop a southern ridge, Beau spotted riders hacking toward the house, which couldn't be seen in its grove of tulip poplars.

He unhooked a gate, passed through, and refastened it. Windlord was a prime gate horse. No matter how anxious to keep up with the field, the animal understood his responsibility to fenced stock. A gust shrilled down from distant bluish mountains. Peaks wore shawls of snow. Beau turned up his collar and hunched his shoulders. Windlord's nostrils steamed.

Beau and Alfred had their fight toward the end of summer when his son drove from Washington on his monthly visit. Alfred believed himself doing well working for the Department of Commerce, some project involving statistics to track the flow and multiplier effect of Japanese investment, all esoteric stuff. Beau made the mistake of taking him to dine at Rinaldo's atop Afton Mountain with its view over a valley fit for a calendar picture—quaint farms, unspoiled woodland, sheep grazing, golden grainfield ripely awaiting harvest. Rinaldo reportedly had cooked for Jackie Onassis, and his modern redwood-and-glass restaurant, first considered by old hands an eyesore, not only provided excellent Continental cuisine, but also projected patrons into clouds, furnishing the sensation of flight.

Rinaldo's became fashionable, reservations required as well as evening wear on weekends. A lot of the hunt crowd were dining. Beau stood repeatedly to greet friends. He caught Alfred eyeing him with a wry expression.

"What?" Beau asked, rearranging his napkin.

"Brownie points," Alfred said. "You've been hopping around like a maître d'. You're so anxious to please."

"Meaning?" Beau asked, though he had a dread inkling.

"Dad, you owe these people nothing. They've never done anything for you. Why kiss their asses?"

Slowly Beau laid down his fork. He came very near to reaching across the table and slapping his son.

"I wouldn't expect you to recognize the difference between syco-phancy and good manners," he said, his voice muted but intense. "Now I'll sit here and pretend to enjoy your company while I finish my veal, and we'll walk out together, but you may then get your royal red ass back to the trashy world where you belong!"

Alfred left that same night. Beau hadn't heard from him again till Christmas, when he arrived bearing a VCR Beau never used and picked up the two tankards, authenticated by stamped London benchmarks, Beau'd wrapped for him. They'd not written or talked since.

What bothered Beau most was the mite of truth in his son's accu-sation. He did try to please those whom he no longer had a right to consider his equals. He felt his smile was too quick, his wish to find favor too strong. But what Alfred never understood was that these people's world provided the element Beau lived in. He could exist in no other without suffocating—a poor fish left high and dry on the beach.

He let himself through the last gate and glimpsed the sprawling manor house with its many chimneys, scattered dependencies, and steepled stables. In fenced pastures horses ran about, bloodstock, year-lings, and though too young to race or hunt, they sensed excitement, spun, kicked, reared.

Riders moved toward the house from all directions. They gathered on the front lawn. The view was down over the junction of two small rivers for which the farm had been named. The rivers were partially frozen. Clive and Bettina Rankin had set up a hunt board and bar on a hay wagon covered by linen tablecloths. Gusts flapped drapes of the cloths. A leather-jacketed black moved about carrying a tray of hot ham biscuits. He wore gloves and earmuffs. Another servant offered the silver stirrup cup, fashioned like the inverted head of a fox. Colorful liquor bottles lined the board. Fried sausages on a silver platter steamed. Bettina in her shadbelly directed a dispensing of tods.

Beau doffed his topper to her, and she knew him well enough to serve him hot cider rather than sherry or whisky. Everyone remembered his absence after the collapse of his third marriage. His leaving wasn't greatly unusual. Among the hunt crowd a brotherhood existed of those who'd disappeared for an interval. They could've organized a society. Absence and recovery were battle scars honorably laid on.

Next Beau spoke pleasantries to Warren Burns, the master, who rode a clipped bay and was impatient to confer with his whips. Vicky Burns returned Beau's greeting. He realized he'd been possibly overly effusive to Bettina. There was the matter of the February Frolic. Inside the house the Rankins used a dining table that seated thirty, and they confined the invitation list for the annual event to that number.

Beau had made the cut since the inception of the party some five years previously. The problem was the influx of moneyed newcomers to the county. He couldn't provide elaborate entertainments as he once had. A quiet dinner, good wine, conversation before a log fire, yes, but little else. Moreover, to Clive Rankin tradition meant nothing. CEO of a motel chain, he was strong-willed, his certainty undergirded by enormous financial success. He flew his own plane, gunned grouse in Scotland, and played hard, bruising polo.

Clive stood jerking at billet straps of his saddle, a large towheaded man, not tall, but broadly and powerfully built. He rode thoroughbreds, this one a dappled gray. Clive needed mounts heavy of bone to carry him. He hunted boldly, though his hands remained insensitive to an animal's mouth.

"Stand still, you bastard!" Clive commanded the gray and merely nodded to Beau. Immediately Beau felt defensive. Was he not worth a word, a tip of the hat? What did Clive's indifference indicate about the February Frolic? Perhaps invitations had already been mailed out. He'd not question anybody. To do so might be an admission of a fall from grace.

He finished the cider, carried the cup back to the hunt board, and handed it down to a servant. Bettina was now mounted. She rode a glossy black gelding, which her groom had braided using white yarn. The effect was eye-catching, though not, Beau believed, in the best of taste. The hunt field was no place for faddishness.

McCargo, the professional huntsman, arrived driving the van carrying the hounds—twenty couples, all white except for masked tan faces. The hounds spilled out to the ground and flowed like a tide around his boots. McCargo slouched till in the saddle. Then everything about him firmed up, and he appeared composed and in touch with his roots. He joined Warren and the rest of the staff to make final decisions concerning the country to be drawn.

Beau counted twenty-two members of the field, as well as a few hilltoppers. Occasionally hounds growled or snapped at each other. McCargo cracked his whip over them, not actually striking any, but the report was loud enough to cause cowering and tail tucking.

Warren wheeled to make his announcements—where they'd meet on Monday, warnings about the footing and need to stay off seeded land, a breakfast at the Rankins after the chase. He wished everyone a good hunting. He'd been a military man, a colonel.

McCargo lifted his face to sound his copper horn. Hounds clotted behind him as he led them down from the house. Staff and field followed. Sunshine laid a sheen on the frosted grass. Beau loved this procession. To him nothing was more moving than this display of steaming horses, coats glistening, men ablaze in scarlet, brass buttons gleaming, the beauty of derbied well-turned-out women on spirited mounts, the juxtaposing of femininity and strength. Those who'd never been a part of the cortege could not fathom it. Hunting, in addition to being a harkening back to the best of the past, was a declaration that elegance still existed in a world addicted to proletarian sports.

A hedgerow at the slope's bottom bordered a small winding branch. Whips took their posts to the flanks as McCargo cast his hounds. They bounded forward, heads low, tails circling. McCargo hied them on, his manly voice rising to the falsetto and sounding like a maiden in distress. Jezebel, the pack's best strike bitch, gave cry. Other hounds rushed to her. From his days as whip Beau had learned the names—Maggie, Gump, Moon, Ruby, Queen—and could recognize from their plaints who led and what scent was being worked.

McCargo let out his wail—"Ah-ee! Ah-ee! Ah-ee!"—to urge them on. He and Warren galloped forward. The field followed. McCargo sounded the horn. Beau didn't have to touch his heels to Windlord. The old warrior surged, pride of strength in the fullness of his stride. Beau fell in behind Alex Chappel on a liver chestnut and Lady Walton riding her young Trakehner. Hooves pounded and hurled clods. Soil struck Beau and stung, yet a good pain. He bent low over Windlord, who at the gallop was as smooth as smoke.

The fox had to be a red. Beau knew from the hounds' frenzied voices and the straightness of the run. The fox made for the Rivanna River. At the end of the hedgerow the first jump, a coop, and Beau drew Windlord down to take his place in line. Alex and Lady Walton curved away. Beau turned Windlord to the fence. Along charged Clive Rankin, who cut in front and crossed over.

Windlord still made it, through he got in under and had to hump the coop. A rear hoof banged it. They galloped on. Clive's big gray threw more clods. Beau ducked. Clive dug spurs at his horse. He generally overpowered his mounts, rarely patient enough to learn one's feel and personality. Through his legs Beau felt himself joined to Windlord in heart and mind. He had but to think and Windlord understood and obeyed.

They reached the boundary of a field planted with winter wheat, took another fence, and Windlord gave Beau a jump so strong it seemed they'd never again touch the earth. Then an abrupt turn into the pine woods. Windlord was gaining. He became leaping speed. To give yourself fully to a galloping horse was placing yourself in Dame Fortune's palm for a tossing up of your life. Ahead waited groundhog holes, loose gravel, patches of ice. Cannon bones might fracture, horses pitch head over heels. The exhilaration surpassed liquor and women, attained a headiness that must be, Beau thought, much like experiencing the near presence of God.

The frozen trail snaked downward. Trees broken under recent ice storms lay smashed across paths. Windlord jumped at full gallop without missing a stride. They reached the frothing river. Ice fringed its edge. The hounds had already swum across except for Hooper, an old tracker who hated cold water. McCargo leaned from his saddle, caught Hooper by the scruff, and carried him over. All during the passage Hooper bayed.

Lady Walton's mare stumbled in the fording. The rocky way was narrow, the footing treacherous. Current washed strongly against horses' hocks. Downstream lay a drop-off. Her Trakehner went to its knees. Water buffeted them. The horse struggled, tried to set its legs, but fell and sank. Lady Walton too. She came up spitting, water coursing from her attire, her derby floating away. The Trakehner swam to shore and fled up the bank. Lady Walton trudged to shallows. Sportingly she waved them on. As long as she wasn't hurt, nobody would turn back from a run. She'd have to hike home unless hilltoppers caught her mount for her.

Windlord made it across. Ice shattered under hoof. The bottoms of Beau's boots were wet, and he felt the river's coldness through the leather. Climbing now, still in woods, the trail slick, Windlord slipped despite corks on his shoes. At the front galloped Clive and Alex. Alex's liver chestnut got turned sideways on the incline, skewed, and tumbled. Alex kicked free, yet held his reins. He and the horse slid down together. Alex too signaled them on.

Only Clive, Warren, and McCargo raced ahead of Beau now. Windlord was breathing hard. He hated hills. They and his years drew him down. He'd be good for just a short distance more unless the hounds checked. McCargo sounded his horn and urged them on. They ran in full cry among the pines. At the top of the slope a fence. Beau followed Clive over. Windlord, definitely weakening, grunted.

A pasture in which Angus cattle stood astonished. They scattered before horses, some lowering their heads to hook. Smart fox. He'd led the hounds through cow scent to lose them. A check at last as they worked it out. Beau talked to and patted Windlord, who heaved and tossed his head. The hounds nosed circling. Tails were bloodied from beating hawthorn. Beau stroked Windlord's neck. Flushed from the chase, Clive tugged at the gray's mouth and grinned.

"Let's catch that red sonofabitch!" he called.

Beau nodded and smiled agreement, though he never desired a kill. His feelings had nothing to do with the usual cruelty-to-animals sentiment. Rather, he hoped to have the fox back for another day's sport and loved its gameness and cunning. Foxes were themselves killers. They in turn accepted death as they gave it, in the natural way of all wild creatures. But, oh, the spirit, the life lived to the edge!

Buster, a serious young hound, picked up the line along barbed wire, lifted his head to utter a wavering ecstatic wail, and stretched running across the pasture. The pack rallied to him. McCargo hied them on. Warren, Clive, and Beau followed the huntsman. They'd lost the rest of the field in the woods or back at the river. Somebody could've taken a wrong turn or caused a crack-up. One thing, in this heyday of rich physicians, plenty of doctors belonged to the club and followed the chase.

A stiff fence at the south end of the pasture. Clive's gray took it long. Through Beau's legs he felt Windlord's strength waning. The horse would gallop till his heart exploded. They swerved into woods. Go to ground, Beau pleaded. He wanted Windlord to finish this run. As if sensing the thought, Windlord found reserves of staying puissance and drew abreast of Clive. Startled, he glanced at Beau. Clive wasn't accustomed to being overtaken or challenged. Moreover, if there were a kill, he wanted the brush. He preserved them in Lucite and mounted them as trophies on lacquered plaques of his cherry-paneled den, the breed of fox, sex, as well as date and place of demise inscribed upon brass.

Beau now desired it too. It'd been a while since he and Windlord had retired from the field displaying a brush carried across the pommel. The old warrior deserved it. Despite the horse's labored breathing, Beau allowed him to plunge on. Don't die on me, he prayed. Don't kill yourself for me.

Ahead waited a fence made strong by topping it with a chain-sawed section of a thick, splintered power pole. The trail itself narrowed. Beau and Clive still galloped abreast. Only one should take the jump at a time. Beau's first instinct was to pull Windlord in, allow Clive to go on after Warren, but Windlord resisted responding to the bit. Furthermore, he was perhaps a nod ahead, and Beau thought of Alfred, of toadying and brownie points. Side by side they charged the fence. Clive's boot rubbed and rasped Beau's. "Give way!" Clive shouted, and together they arched over the jump, the two of them joined at the knee, their horses squeezed shoulder to hip, the animals synchronized as if trained and performing.

Hooves struck the frozen ground hard. The horses bumped, and Clive's gray stumbled. Clive was thrown forward onto its neck. The gray didn't crash, yet Clive lost reins and a stirrup. He fought to stay mounted.

"You little fart, you rode me off!" Clive raged as Beau galloped on.

When Beau broke from woods into the wan, picked cornfield, hounds swarmed around a dead locust tree wind had toppled across a ditch. The fox had attempted to reach a burrow beneath. Hounds tossed his carcass among themselves. They rolled in blood. At Warren's assent, McCargo dismounted, horned the long mournful notes of death, and spoke lovingly to his hounds. He took the fox from them, all the while praising their skills and goodness. From his breeches pocket he unclasped a Buck knife, cut the brush, and handed it up to Warren.

"Not bad for starters, eh?" Warren asked, elated with the hounds' work. The staff and field approached. Hounds rushed about deliriously proud, their instincts fulfilled. Warren used the raw end of the brush to blood the foreheads of two wide-eyed juniors who'd never before been in on a kill. He then rode to Beau and presented him the brush.

"Request permission to retire from the field," Beau said. "Old fellow carrying me's a bit undone."

"Granted," Warren said, wiping face sweat. "We got us one hell of a pack."

Beau tipped his hat. He reined Windlord among other horses. Riders called congratulations and raised their flasks. Clive stared. Bettina, beside her husband, looked puzzled and disturbed. Beau lifted his topper to the field and started back toward the river. Gently he used spurless heels on Windlord. The old boy still wanted to hunt.

They'd talk about Beau's taking the brush, particularly at the Rankins' breakfast, which he'd forgo. He'd hose and scrape Windlord, stable, water, and bed him down with an extra ration of hay and sweet feed. As to the brush Beau dangled across his aching knee, his impulse was to stuff it into a manila envelope and mail it first class to Alfred, no message enclosed. Let Alfred form his own conclusions.

But, no, a gentleman would never do that. He'd wrap and place the brush with others dried to desiccation in the old hatbox on his closet shelf. Perhaps someday Alfred would learn.

BUSINESS TRIP

"We don't mix one with the other," Harrison said, an accusation.

Business and our mountain cabin he was talking about. In days of our having little money and great prospects, Harrison and I'd purchased fifty acres of land on a steeply wooded slope of West Virginia's Big Allegheny. We'd borrowed the dollars, foolishly we were told. Later, as the economics of our lives improved, we bought building materials and hauled them up a switchback road we'd cleared by chainsawing a way through wild cherry, red oak, and hemlock. We snaked the oak to a sawmill and used planks for floors and siding.

Harrison, an architect, drew the cabin plans as carefully as he would've for his corporate or government clients. We wanted everything simple and tight. Strength, not frills. For our chimney we mortared stones lifted and rolled from the stream's edge. It ran so fast beside the cabin that water spilled from its coursing and froze lacelike on bordering laurel.

We made a pact. No gambling, no carousing, no women. Neither of us ever brought our wives. No indoor john, just a privy down the path. An underground half-inch PVC pipe ran water from the stream to the top of our steel sink. Kerosene lanterns provided light. The cabin and our conduct in it was our shrine to the ruffed grouse. We demanded it and ourselves remain as unencumbered and untainted as possible by lowland civilization.

We were damn particular whom we invited each season. First, a guest had to be serious in his pursuit of grouse. Second, he had to see hardship as homage to the king of birds. Third, the guest needed to find joy in adversity. Last, in the high country truth prevailed.

Typically we prepared for the hunt in late August. We knocked down dirt-dauber nests, swept up the accumulated dust of summer, and stocked our shelves with canned goods. During the season, which started in September, we slipped away from work at every opportunity and drove hell-bent for the cabin. Despite our wives' grumbling, we saved vacation time for the hunt. Each kill was recorded in a ledger—hour, place, sex, craw content, and man whose gun had brought the bird to earth. We reverently tacked spread tail fans to walls.

We instructed guests if they became lost to follow water downward. Water always led somewhere. We kept our boots oiled and wore long johns, multiple layers of clothing, and heavy wool jackets because a deadly cold in the high country dropped with darkness and reached for the heat of life at the center of man. We allowed ourselves a small battery-operated radio to listen to weather reports. The weather changed as quickly as at sea. If we met a stranger during a day's shoot, we felt intruded upon.

Before each season we sat on either side of Harrison's desk in the gleaming concrete building by the Potomac and decided who would be issued invitations. We huddled like members considering the extending of bids to an exclusive society. Crew-cut Harrison was short, husky, and suffered no fools. We thought alike and rarely disagreed till Clarence Toller.

My wife, Trixie, put me up to it. She worked for Clarence. Divorced, he'd come to the District from north Georgia. His store specialized in early American antiques, particularly pine furniture fashioned in southern Appalachia. Trixie had never held a job till our son graduated from college and joined the State Department. She was high style—tall, eyes dark, her stride sure. She carried a gloss. She liked the money Clarence paid, and so did I. I wasn't against money. Only at the cabin.

Lately our marriage had drifted close to the rocks. She'd become restless, edgy. When we were alone, a vacuum formed. Open the door of our house in Falls Church and air would've hissed in. We'd had a couple of bad fights. I'd driven her to Kiawah for a week, and it rained. We never settled in. The last night we again shouted at each other.

She felt sorry for Clarence. The IRS had been waltzing him around. She'd come upon him at his desk holding his face in his hands. She believed a change might help.

"Not our type," I told her, the understatement of the decade.

"He's been good to me," she said, pausing before our bedroom mirror to examine her sharp slender features. She used a fingertip to draw a strand of straight black hair off powdered cheek.

"Bake him a cake, he's no grouse hunter," I said.

"But he told me he hunted with his father down in Georgia."

"Is he in shape?" I asked. Clarence was a large man tending to softness. I'd never seen him on the links.

"He swims regularly at a spa and besides might sell me his business."

"What?" I asked and lowered the cleaning rod I'd been using to stroke my Parker's glistening barrels. "Where would you get money for a buyout?"

"You have those stocks," she said. "He wants to take a long trip to Italy and Greece. Well-disposed, he might turn the store loose at a very good price."

"I'm not borrowing on my stocks, which are for our retirement, and we don't tolerate business talk at the cabin."

"Wouldn't kill you to accommodate a person who's been nice to me. If he sells to someone else, I'll be left jobless, and we've gotten used to two incomes."

A backhanded reference to my work at Treasury. I'd been coming along in high gear till I backed Contrell for division head. Politics aside, he was the best man but made the error of speaking out against a cabinet appointment. Denby, whom I beat regularly at racquetball, received the promotion. Denby now had a special sad smile for me.

I made respectable money, was awarded the usual government perks, yet hadn't attained what Trixie and I'd envisioned. We owned the house in Falls Church but no cottage at Jekyll Island or yawl to cruise the Chesapeake. We'd sent our son Lee to Woodberry Forest and Princeton and were still paying in blood. Moreover, she'd always resented the cabin.

"I want to be nice to everybody," I told her. We no longer slept in the same bed. Humoring her was better than further connubial warfare.

I picked up Clarence the last week of the season in February. I checked his gear: the twelve-gauge Browning automatic that looked as if it'd never been fired, a pale blue outsized suitcase, tweed jacket and dark flannel slacks covered by a transparent vinyl bag—the stylish clothes protected, yet no case for his shotgun. He wore suede loafers, fawn corduroys, and a white turtleneck sweater.

"You won't need these," I said of the clothes in the vinyl bag.

"Thought we might be dining out," he said.

"The nearest restaurant's twenty-five miles and has a sawdust floor," I said. It was in a town named Bear Paw.

"Better safe than sorry," Clarence said.

I worried Harrison might sulk. He waited with his liver-and-white pointer Zack in the Jeepster at the bottom of the switchback trail. Like me, Harrison wore boots, hunting pants briarproofed by leather facing, a chamois shirt, and a down jacket that had shell pockets and a game pouch. He reset his long-billed blaze-orange cap.

"You come to shoot grouse or dance?" he asked Clarence but shook his hand. They looked each other over. Clarence's straw-colored hair was too long and curled upward on his neck.

It'd rained earlier, and the stream ran fiercely. Red-oak leaves plastered the ground, causing the Jeepster's tires to slip even in four-wheel.

Clarence expected something grander. He normally took vacations to Cancún and Steamboat Springs. He always sported a tan, though I suspected it was preserved by lamp. I'd been to his apartment at a Christmas party—no pine items, but lots of glittery wire sculpture and basalt chunks illuminated from spotlights located among ferns and tropical plants. The audio system played banjo music.

When we reached the cabin, Clarence glanced at me. Possibly he believed it servants' quarters. The interior was dim and cold. Harrison opened shutters, and I built a fire using kindling and hickory logs stacked under the overhang at the rear. Harrison and I'd sawed and split wood during the fall.

Clarence searched for the john. The cabin had only two rooms, one for bunks, the other a combination kitchen-eating-sitting area. I explained about the privy down the slope.

"How quaint," Clarence said.

"Ain't it?" Harrison asked as he carried in gear from the Jeepster. "Get my best thoughts there."

Routine called for each man to take his turn cooking evening meals. That night it was me, and I baked potatoes in the fireplace, laid buttered T-bones on the iron grill, and tossed a salad. Angie, Harrison's wife, had sent along a German chocolate cake. We ate off paper plates and drank everything except our whiskey out of Dixie cups. We honored good liquor with glasses. Clarence asked about wine and Russian dressing. We'd never stocked either.

Those who hadn't cooked cleaned up after meals. Paper plates and cups were burned. We ran water from the stream into a large pan, heated it on the cookstove, and dipped the glasses and stainless-steel cutlery.

I was relieved Clarence didn't quite pick at the plain food, yet when we finished eating, instead of following Harrison to the sink, he strolled to the fire and rubbed his hands over the flames. Harrison gave me a look. I explained to Clarence.

"Sorry," he said and joined Harrison. "You've had this water tested, I'm certain."

"No need to test," Harrison said. "Nobody lives above us up the mountain. This water beats itself pure against rocks. Bacteria can't stand the bashing."

"Couldn't somebody camp up there?" Clarence asked.

"We would've seen signs," I said.

"Climb the other side of the mountain," Clarence insisted.

"It's possible," I said, aware of Harrison standing rigidly at the sink. "But about as likely as Martians on our roof."

"What about animals?" Clarence asked, refusing to let go. "Their waste."

"Nobody yet has ever died from trout crap," Harrison said.

The tone of his voice stopped Clarence. He dried the glasses and set them on the shelf. Harrison gave Zack a steak bone. He'd ration them to the pointer.

Harrison and I sat in front of the fire to light our pipes. Clarence didn't smoke. He moved restlessly and asked about a deck of cards. We had none. He crossed to the table, switched on the radio, and located faint classical music from Roanoke Public Broadcasting. Again I got the look from Harrison.

"We don't play it for amusement," I explained. "We save the batteries. The radio's our weather arm."

"What do you do nights in camp?" he asked, cutting off the radio. His violet eyes caught a gleam from the fire.

"Hit the bunks early," Harrison said.

But Clarence wasn't ready to settle. He opened the door and looked into the dark. Cold air seeped past him. He examined every item in the room—cans on shelves, gear hanging from wooden pegs, dried grouse fans tacked to walls. He leafed through the grouse book. He spotted Zack and knelt to the pointer.

"Him's a good boy," Clarence said and would've fondled him except Zack was an old dog treated fairly by Harrison but never babied. Zack didn't understand. He still gnawed a sliver of bone. He growled. Clarence stood quickly and backed off.

"Let's turn in," Harrison said, smiling.

"It's not eight-thirty," Clarence said. "Never do I go to bed this early. Usually I'm just starting out."

"Tomorrow you'll be glad," I said.

There were four bunks. Harrison gave Clarence his choice of the double-decker at one side of the room. Harrison and I shared the other, he the top, me the bottom. We unrolled our sleeping bags. Clarence's not only had the sheen of newness, but was also decorated with prancing reindeer.

"I've never used it," he explained. "Bought it solely for this trip. Tried it in my apartment, and it fits."

Harrison looked away and closed his eyes. I felt around in my duffel bag for my flashlight. Privy time. I left the cabin first. Harrison went next. Clarence, who hadn't thought to bring a flashlight, borrowed mine. Leaving, he again allowed the cold wind to blow through the doorway.

"Very dainty fellow," Harrison said. "He a fag?"

"Whatever makes you ask?"

"Manicured nails, silver cuff links, cologne, and way he sits with his knees together. Bet he has pajamas."

Before I could answer, Clarence returned out of breath. He slammed the door and stood against it.

"A thing out there!" he said. "It moved in the dark!"

"Coon or fox," I said.

"Bear," Harrison said. He pried the door open against Clarence's body to let Zack out for a run.

"Bear?" Clarence asked, a hand raised to his throat.

"Big male uses our privy," Harrison said. "Has bladder trouble."

"You're telling me I might've bumped into a bear?" Clarence asked, sidling away from the door.

"He's kidding," I said, and Harrison laughed.

Clarence shivered, crossed to his suitcase, and opened it on his bunk. He began to undress. Around his neck he wore a golden chain and silver St. Christopher medal, the latter lodged in curly blond hair of his chest. He did have pajamas, white with red horizontal stripes, and a bathrobe and slippers.

"Don't suppose there's chance of a bath?" Clarence asked. He'd turned in maidenly fashion to step into his pajamas.

"Only if you brought a tub," Harrison said.

Clarence brushed his teeth at the sink. Harrison let Zack in and blew out the lanterns.

Clarence couldn't get comfortable on his spartan bunk. The mattresses, bought from army surplus, were thin and hard. Harrison and I'd become accustomed to them. They were part of the joy-through-adversity factor. Clarence wiggled from his bag and pulled on his bathrobe and slippers to cross to the sink for a drink of water. He stumbled over a wooden ammo box. As he hopped about on one foot, Zack again growled.

Listening to wind, the crackling fire, and the rushing of the stream, I sank to sleep. When I woke, Clarence's face shone above the glare of my flashlight.

"I need to go to the johnny house," he said.

"Go, for God's sake!" Harrison said.

"You were really kidding about the bear?" Clarence asked.

"No bears," I said. "Winters they hibernate."

"What I thought," Clarence said.

He took my flashlight, laced up his new boots, and tightened the belt of his bathrobe before opening the door and leaving.

"Definitely sweet," Harrison said. "Feeling around on me in the dark."

"Confused without a light," I said, no longer certain. Why had his marriage come apart? And he and Trixie had met through her theatrical group. Wasn't it a way of life among actors?

"I should never have allowed you to talk me into this," Harrison said.

Clarence returned quickly. He couldn't have gone as far as the privy. Harrison wouldn't like that either because his respect for the wilderness forbade even taking leaks except within defined territories. Clarence washed at the sink, hung his bathrobe on a peg, and worked into his bag.

"Myriads of stars," he said, squirming.

We didn't answer. A second time I slept. When I woke, Harrison was snoring, and a shape stood in front of the fire's glow. Clarence's silhouetted shape held a shotgun, raised it, and swung as if tracking a bird. He fitted the gun back into the wall rack made of antlers. He tiptoed to his bunk. For a while I listened to his breathing and sighs.

Harrison needed no alarm clock. His feet hit the floor at exactly 0500. He lit lamps, and I built a fire in the cookstove. Harrison boiled coffee hobo-style, no filter, no percolation. When the water roiled black, a shot of cold water settled grounds. I cooked link sausage and scrambled eggs in a skillet seasoned by years of use. He baked the biscuits.

Clarence still lay in his bag. Not sleeping. I saw his eyes' glitter. When he stood, he shuddered, pulled on hunting breeches so new they creaked, and hurried to the stove. He rubbed his long hands over the heat. He finished dressing beside it. I asked what he'd been doing up during the night.

"I'd forgotten my vitamin pill," he said.

"You were fooling with a gun," I said.

"Couldn't sleep," he said.

Harrison fed Zack. We listened to the weather report: a cold windy day promised. When we finished breakfast, I cleaned up at the sink. Harrison fixed ham-and-cheese sandwiches he wrapped in wax paper. Each of us would carry an apple. Drinks were no problem. We'd never be far from streams and could drop to our knees anywhere and suck up water so cold it stabbed pain from the teeth to the skull.

Our plan was to hunt the spine of Blind Sheep Ridge till we reached the head of Slash Lick Hollow. We'd drop down the hollow to Burnt Cabin Creek, follow it to Sugar Camp, and climb toward the Pig's Ear. Harrison and I worked out routes on our topos.

We had to wait for Clarence to visit the privy, wash, brush his teeth, and use his battery-powered electric shaver. We had no mirror in the cabin. He'd brought one and set it before himself on the table. He combed his hair. Fussily he adjusted his cap and gloves.

"You sure you're ready?" Harrison asked, yanking the door open. "Maybe clip your nails, pull hairs from your nose?"

"Old habits die hard," Clarence said.

Outside the cabin, the light was just murky enough to see the wet path. Around us dark hemlocks dripped, and the mists were clouds. We loaded our guns. Zack coursed ahead. Harrison had fastened a small bell and blaze-orange jacket on the dog. The bell sounded faint in the wind.

The climb to Blind Sheep was less than a quarter of a mile, yet before we topped it, Clarence was lagging and had slipped several times.

"What sort of hunting you do with your father down Georgia way?" Harrison asked. He'd eyed Clarence's ventilated-ribbed Browning. Harrison and I used doubles, another part of the sporting code we followed in pursuit of grouse.

"Frogs mostly," Clarence said. "Lots of farm ponds around."

"You mean you gigged, not hunted them," Harrison said.

"Didn't carry gigs. So bloody removing them from the barbs. Ugh! We had nets."

"Like for butterflies," Harrison said, and I knew he was looking at me. I didn't look back.

"Kind of. We carried the frogs in buckets back to the house, where Mamma prepared the legs. A favorite with the family."

"Jesus," Harrison said and led us the rest of the way to the ridge, where feeble sunlight penetrated clouds. Down the slope a turkey gobbled. Somewhere in mist ravens lamented raucously—agonized voices crying from the depths. Harrison remained nervous about Clarence's careless handling of the Browning.

"Throw a good pattern?" he asked Clarence.

"Don't really know. I've never fired this exact gun, but I do know how to use one. On my last cruise aboard the *Mermaid* we shot clay pigeons off the boat deck."

"But never at game?" I asked.

"Believe I'm up to it," Clarence said. "The instructor aboard ship told me I had quite an eye."

We reached Slash Lick and started our descent. Jagged ground-ice made footing treacherous. Clarence's feet skidded. He dropped the Browning to reach out and soften his fall. He stood brushing mud and leaf mold from his tawny hunting breeches.

"Nasty," he said and made a face.

We continued down the hollow, and the trickle of water widened into a run which swirled among rocks. Dark green moss grew along the banks. Though sun had burned through mist, the mountain still shaded us, and only the hemlock tops caught the golden light.

Zack made game. His tail wagged in short, rapid, erratic strokes. From a laurel thicket a grouse boiled up. Its wings battled laurel.

"Take it!" both Harrison and I told Clarence, the first shot a courtesy afforded guests.

Clarence awkwardly shouldered the Browning, and we heard the click of his safety, but as the bird banked down the mountain he didn't shoot. He tried. He tugged the trigger. The grouse swerved into hemlock gloom.

"What happened?" Harrison asked, eyeing the Browning.

"Don't know," Clarence said. He examined the gun. "Oh my!" he said and laughed. "Safety's on. Must've done it backwards."

"All this time you been walking around with the safety off?" Harrison asked. His voice had become gravel.

"Dumb me. I have it set right now, don't I?"

He held the Browning to Harrison. Harrison stared at it, at me, spat to the side, and continued down the hollow.

Laurel whacked our legs. Clarence again slipped. Harrison grabbed the Browning and checked the safety before handing it back. Clarence's smile was apologetic.

Zack's bell quieted. We found him on point among a stand of thorn apples. A grouse flushed. Instead of flying ahead it winged toward us. Rarely could you hit a bird speeding at you. The thing to do was wait and take it going away. When Harrison and I fired, the bird's neck bent under, and it tumbled, bounced hard, and lay still. Feathers slowly settled after it.

Zack retrieved, his mouth gentle, never breaking the skin and leaving just a little spit. He presented the grouse to Harrison. He and I stroked the bronze feathers, both of us displaying the peculiar loving bond between hunter and kill. For Harrison and me the feeling amounted to ritual and communion. The bird's intricate coloring and design drew from us a feeling which was as close as we came to religion.

Clarence stood beside us, his shotgun half raised, his expression confused. Our shooting had bewildered him. When Harrison showed him the red-ruffed male, Clarence moaned.

"Such a beautiful creature!" he exclaimed and cradled his gun to take the warm bird in cupped palms. "Oh, you lovely, lovely creature!"

"Think you hit him?" Harrison asked, turning to me. Grouse were to be honored but not emoted over.

"Felt I had the gun on him," I said.

"Was good shooting and goes in the book a double," he said.

"Such an exquisite living being!" Clarence said. "What will you do with him?"

"Lick his bones clean tonight at the cabin," I said. We further celebrated every grouse killed by not wasting it. Eating too could be a worshipful act.

"How can you!" Clarence asked. "Oh, I wish I were able to breathe life back into him."

Neither Harrison nor I replied. Harrison took the grouse and slid it into the slit of his game pouch. Abruptly he continued down toward the valley.

Zack criss-crossed in front of us. At the hollow's mouth, he pointed. We moved alongside his body's rigid trembling. A grouse rocketed up far ahead. We glimpsed the bird, a glint of feathers, curve into a stand of ironwoods. Harrison and I reset our safeties. Clarence hadn't lifted his gun.

"Thank goodness!" he said, happy the bird had gotten away. Then he realized Harrison and I faced him.

"This is a hunt," Harrison said. "The purpose is to sportingly kill game. It's the reason we built the cabin and bust our asses running ridges."

"Maybe I could go back," Clarence said meekly. "I did bring a book."

Harrison couldn't wait to lead him, though doing so meant abandoning the day's plans. Wordlessly we circled to and climbed a logging road overgrown with clawing hawthorn.

"Don't wander off," I told Clarence at the cabin. Harrison had hung the bird on a nail driven into a wall stud.

"Don't worry," Clarence said and held up his book. The title was *Early American Silversmiths*.

Harrison and I again set out. We'd hunt beech flats along the south slope of Blind Sheep.

"Hope you learned your lesson good," he said.

"I been thinking of shooting the sonofabitch and then myself," I said.

Sidehilling it, we raised two more birds that afternoon. Zack nosed up the first by pushing too hard, and the second flew from a white pine. Harrison and I missed. We weren't pleased, not only over Clarence, but also about the dog and our shooting. Zack sensed it and acted as if he'd been caught sucking eggs.

When we reached the cabin at dark, the mountain cold searched for our warmth. We found the door locked and banged to bring Clarence. He'd been sleeping, for his eyelids were heavy and his hair tousled. He wore the white turtleneck sweater, plaid slacks, and bedroom slippers. No fire burned.

"I was beginning to fret," he said. He shivered.

Harrison brought in wood for the fire. I carried the grouse to the stream, where I plucked and gutted it. I beheaded the bird, severed its feet, and shoved it under rushing water. I stuck fingers into the body cavity. The stream's hard flow washed it clean.

I tossed the head to Zack. Harrison roasted the grouse on the fireplace spit. He fried potatoes, baked a pan of cornbread, and heated stewed tomatoes. Clarence watched—smiling, affable, of no use. He meant it about not eating grouse. He asked permission to boil an egg.

He did help rinse and dry at the sink. Harrison ledgered in data on the single bird killed. We hit the bunks. Clarence had slept most of the afternoon and moved about restlessly. He read his silversmith book by lantern light before the fire. Harrison would be thinking about the waste of kerosene, which had to be bought and toted to the cabin.

That night when I woke, Clarence still sat in front of the fire. He wasn't reading but looking through the doorway at me. Burning logs kindled his eyes. For an instant I felt alarm. Was he attracted to me sexually or what? Then he turned his face away, sighed, and gazed at his book.

Next morning Clarence twisted from his bag when we did. Without being asked, he carried in an armful of wood. He'd not split any, however, a thing he could've done yesterday instead of sleeping. We spooned hot milk-gravy over cornbread. He swallowed a vitamin pill.

"You reading today?" Harrison asked, the question a wish.

"Actually, the book doesn't hold my interest," Clarence said. "Dated and rather uninspired. Hoped I might be allowed to tag along with you fellows."

Expression unchanged, Harrison unrolled our topos. We'd hunt fringes of the national forest, cover terrain where flocks had once been herded, grassy knobs of windy high country.

"I do want to take part," Clarence said, surprising us by bringing his Browning. Wordlessly, Harrison reached for it and checked the safety. He worried not only about accidents, but also that in a short while Clarence would need to be escorted back to the cabin.

The country was rugged and rocky, steep slopes, swift streams to ford. We flushed no birds, received not even a false point from Zack, which further annoyed Harrison. A lack of grouse wasn't Clarence's fault, yet because of Harrison's and my mood, it seemed to be. At least Clarence kept the pace without complaint.

We ate our apples as we rested on bone-colored boulders beside noisy Rattlers' Creek. I bellied down to drink. Clarence produced a collapsible aluminum cup he dipped underwater. He didn't offer the cup to us—not that we'd have used it.

We hiked upstream till we reached a confluence of waters. Our routine was to split because the branches rejoined half a mile higher. Harrison took Zack along the left fork. I had Clarence with me on the right. The way steepened, the footing trappy, causing ankles to wobble.

"Has it entered your mind Trixie's so downright unhappy she's thinking of leaving you?" Clarence asked as we climbed.

I stopped and faced him, for a moment unable to speak.

"She told you that?"

"Not directly," he said. "Lately she's been troubled. I'm hardly her confessor but rather good at surmising. When she suffers, I do. We're extremely close."

"Our problems are none of your business," I said.

"I've seen tears," he said.

"What the hell am I doing talking to you?" I said and continued climbing beside the stream. My feet dislodged rounded rocks, which clattered aside.

"It might be well for you to see the light," Clarence said behind me.

"How do you define 'the light'?" I asked, again stopping.

"As being loving and generous. You should particularly understand taking a hard line's a mistake in domestic matters."

"What I understand is you sticking your nose where it shouldn't be," I said and climbed on.

We heard a distant shot. I wheeled toward the sound in case a grouse might come batting across the leafless gray alders along the creek. Seconds later I spotted the bird, its wings set, canting downward toward a cluster of ragged spruce pines.

As I waited for the grouse to sweep within range, Clarence blasted away beside me. The bird folded, and the high impetus of flight carried it fifty feet before it thumped to the ground. Feathers spread over running cedar sparkling from thawed frost. I turned in wonder.

"Picked him right off your gun barrel," Clarence said.

That had been a hell of a shot. He thumbed another shell into the Browning, crossed to the bird, and lifted it.

"Cock," he said. "Young and dumb. Yours to keep."

Now ordinary people can't determine the sex of a grouse. You have to be able to read the black band of feathers along the tail. As for age, size and weight are the main factors. I hefted the bird and stroked feathers against the grain. Clarence was correct.

"Where'd you learn to make the distinction?" I asked.

"In those Georgia hills called home. Daddy had all us redneck boys out hunting soon as we could carry guns. When you killed your first buck deer, they made you cut its throat, gut it, and drink a cup of hot blood. I puked and shamed Daddy."

"You told Harrison all you did was frog hunt," I said.

"I like kidding old Harrison," he said and picked up his ejected shell. He slipped it into a pocket of his jacket.

"You claiming that shot wasn't luck?" I asked.

"Shooting's like screwing," he said and winked. "You don't forget."

We moved on up beside the stream. He had me thinking and glancing back.

"You're such a gunner, how come you stayed in the cabin yesterday?" I asked.

"Hunting's ridiculous macho madness," he said. "A Daniel Boone charade. Rather read a book anytime. I came on this jaunt to talk about

Trixie. Just waiting a chance to get you alone. She needs tender loving care, which you're not providing. So I've been hoping to help."

As I faced him, we again heard Harrison shoot. I turned to the alders. No bird this time. He'd probably bagged it.

"We'll meet him soon, won't we?" Clarence asked.

"Another couple of hundred yards," I said and, burning anger, hiked on fast.

"You could work this out if you put your mind to it," Clarence said. "You owe Trixie. She's given you the best of her youth. Let her have the store."

When I faced him to tell him go fuck himself, he'd raised the Browning. It pointed at my stomach. I was more astonished than frightened.

"You thinking of using that gun on me?" I asked.

"Heavens no!" he said and smiled as he lowered the Browning.

Again we climbed. Trixie had mentioned his having trouble with the IRS. Was he using her to get money? I slowed to allow him to draw even, but he hung back. I looked ahead for Harrison. When I again glanced at Clarence, he was watching me intently. With his every other step the Browning swung toward me.

"You carry life insurance?" Clarence asked. "Man who hunts ought to. Likely pay double indemnity for accidents up here. Those dollars could be important to Trixie."

He couldn't be meaning to do it. He'd need to shoot Harrison too. Yet each step jarred me, and my fingers began to sweat gripping the Parker. You're being stupid, I told myself. Afraid of a damn queer. He was playing with me. I could duck back, grab the Browning, and eject the shells. And explain how? Harrison would fall out laughing. I'd be ashamed to tell him.

"Old Harrison," Clarence said. "Believes I want to blow him. Actually I don't much care for men. Still, in my business a certain innate limp-wristed demeanor has been useful. Associated with sensitivity. Women trust me and feel I'm no threat whatsoever till they realize I've slicked the silk panties right off their tender lily-white bottoms."

Was he telling he'd bedded Trixie? She'd asked about my stocks. I remembered those nights she was supposed to be at the store or play rehearsals. They could've worked this out.

"You read about hunting accidents," he said. "Harrison would be an expert witness. He'd honestly testify what a booby I am in the woods. What jury would convict a sweetie like me?"

At the shot, I felt heat of the blast's shock wave, threw myself down, and moaned. I thought I'd been hit. When I rolled sideways, he was smiling over me. My Parker had been flung to the rocks.

"That darn safety again," he said. "See how easily accidents happen? Believe I hear Harrison coming. Give me your hand and let's help you up."

I scrambled to climb fleeing to Harrison. I'd wet my pants and bloodied my forehead where I'd sprawled. "Hell's happening?" Harrison kept asking. We stared downstream to see Clarence laughing and holding my Parker above his head.

"Look what I found!" he called. "Look what I discovered!"

THE SECRET GARDEN

I am a flower—sometimes a tea rose, occasionally a purple iris, often a long-stem tiger lily.

Mostly we discovered her moods by what she played on the piano. She'd carry a vase of freshly cut yellow asters and a glass ashtray to the Baldwin in our music room. Typically she napped and lighted a cigarette before walking down the wine-carpeted steps. She remained careful of her cigarettes despite seeming to be always a little off course, gently bumping tables and wainscoting or tipping on Oriental rugs. Often we noticed faint blue bruises on the elbows and forearms she used as fenders.

Though able to, she never performed classical selections. She preferred the old romantic ballads like "Smoke Gets in Your Eyes" and "Deep Purple," the sort of tunes popular during the era before World War II. She still visited Pastor's, Richmond's antiquated music store, where clerks wore ties and starched smocks, the listening booths were dusted daily, and a person could buy a golden harp whose strings children loved to sneak to and twang.

I, her son, watched. We all did—my grandmother, my sister, and our maid, Viola, who crossed town each morning on the city bus. Viola and Mother sometimes smoked together at the kitchen table on which biscuit dough was rolled. My grandmother purchased Gold Medal flour in fifty-pound bags. They were stored in a wooden barrel beneath a trapdoor of the long stainless-steel counter. Viola dipped from it, her blackness powdered when she rose holding the sifter.

Mother no longer drove. If the weather was wet or cold, she called a taxi. She liked to walk, especially spring and summer. She gazed at flowers and plantings along the brick street. Frequently she brought home bouquets purchased from the colored women who sold them on the corner of Strawberry and Grace. Whenever she left our stone Victorian house, she wore a large garden-party hat as well as gloves, hose, and heels. She'd been sent to a horsey Warrenton girls' school run by a severe French headmistress who drilled into her charges that a lady unless properly attired never allowed herself to be touched by the light of day.

Mother had her hair dyed black and wore it longer than the current fashion. She was conscious of her posture, yet her body became askew like a person who feels the ground under him tilt or meets an obstacle in the road. Perhaps in her mind memory was a rock that had to be stepped around, a puddle avoided, a ravine leaped. We'd all in our various rooms listen to her play—my grandmother upstairs by her window, Viola in the kitchen, my sister and I wherever we happened to be around the place.

If it was one of Mother's better days, she'd play everything allegro, hitting the notes correctly from the first try. She liked to sing, her voice girlish, though she often stopped in the middle of phrases to reach for cigarettes. She never let a cigarette dangle as popular pianists do in the movies. She considered that common. Her favorite brand was unfiltered Lucky Strikes.

When the tempo of her music slowed and became confused, we quit whatever we were doing to look at each other through walls. She might touch her temple and transform "Blue Orchids" into a wandering, chaotic dirge. If we peeked through a gap of the mahogany sliding doors that had brass latches, she didn't seem unhappy or distressed, yet her fingers clawed keys, causing dissonances she apparently didn't hear. Her voice changed, no longer innocently girl-like but more the throaty chanteuse, husky and lots of vibrato. She knew French, had been trained to speak it as if her natural tongue.

We waited for packages. She carried many home herself. Delivery trucks arrived, a few at first, then some days half a dozen—from department stores, gift shops, bakeries. At Sears she ordered a set of tools she had no use for we could divine. She did keep the canaries she purchased for her bedroom—the same in which she'd grown up, it still maidenly, though smelling of Lucky Strikes. Recently, pastels drawn by my sister of blooms from our garden had been framed and hung on the walls: sweet william, Shasta daisies, white, rose, and crimson peonies.

"I've made up a new list," said my sister, three years older than I and an art teacher at William and Mary. Slim and blond, her actions quick and precise, she didn't favor Mother. Mother was dark-eyed, flowing, languorous. She couldn't draw a line, while my sister as a child had been able to take a piece of yellow chalk and scratch out horses, giraffes, and elephants on the concrete driveway. Now my sister had a particularly fine hand with pond scenes, the willows drooping boughs into greenish benign waters and leaving shadowed furrows.

The list she spoke of lay in the drawer of a small cherry table by our house's front entrance. The table held a rectangular silver tray used in days when people still presented social calling cards, my grandmother's day, who sat most of the time in her upstairs den. She suffered rheumatoid arthritis and positioned her rocking chair by the window so she could look down to the lawn, birdbath, and street beyond the red oaks. She needed a cane to move about. Whenever my mother left the house, my grandmother leaned to the window and peered as intently as if searching for a long-sought shore.

Grandmother too had been a pretty woman. A closeted album held snapshots of her during a European tour. Flanked by costumed guards holding halberds, she stood before the Tower of London, gloved fingers at her throat, a hand steadying a great round yellow hat. Her hair then had been coppery. Now it was thin and gray, almost a skullcap. Her pale blue eyes were still good, and she liked to read all the newspapers, including the *Wall Street Journal*. She'd gotten in the habit through my grandfather, who'd been a partner in a Richmond investment house that dealt primarily in trading municipal bonds.

"How many today?" Grandmother asked. She still wore stylish clothes, and rings on crooked, hurting fingers. Alma, her dressmaker, came to the house. Through the window Grandmother looked to the street to see my mother returning from downtown carrying packages. Once when I entered the den so softly Grandmother didn't hear, I found her weeping quietly, crippled fingers touched to her powdered brow. Becoming aware of me, she straightened and said nothing but turned away her face.

"Only three," I answered. I'd already entered deliveries on the list.

"Ten days more or less," Grandmother said. "Perhaps two weeks."

My sister and I returned packages, those my mother hadn't already given as gifts. She loved giving. We'd wait till she was out and slip into her bedroom to remove them. She never noticed. My sister drove Grandmother's Lincoln downtown. The mission was no longer embarrassing. Clerks at the stores knew and made no fuss about exchanges for credit. Kindly people after the southern fashion. They loved my mother, smiled fondly at sight of her, sent cards on her birthday.

My sister alerted Dr. Richard Winston. He'd danced with Mother during his courting days. He told me he'd never seen a lovelier woman. She'd been standing, he said, in a field of daffodils, the sun beaming on her and acres of blinding yellow blooms. He said it was as if she'd grown among them, been one of the flowers, out of the earth, her face itself a bloom, bees buzzing around her, the sun golden on her laughing face.

I've always loved gardens. Times I've knelt among forget-me-nots, collected their fragrance, felt we've sprung from the same black rich loam. I've been fed upon by bees. I've lain in soothing grass and become part of it. I welcomed ants who crossed my breasts. I placed them gently upon the ivy-covered sundial. My bare arms wave in the sultry wind like weeping willow boughs. I am the vine, the rose, the nectar.

"Rachel, no!" they call to me.

Even later they scold, after they've no right, seizing me from the succulence of daphne, the hummingbird's visit. Always calling. I stop my ears. I drip my fingers onto piano keys and ride bursts of color. Voices always nibbling at me. I make a garden of quarter notes. I climb music as if it is a rose trellis reaching the sky.

"You are indeed something," Richard Winston says, he too lying in the sun, a pliant male flower on a white blanket, perhaps monkshood. I spread my petals and see him feed from me. His skin is slightly salty, and I love salt. I do not understand how salt harms growing things. Mother pours it to kill grass edging the walks, but Richard's salt is sugar on my tongue.

"You may not!" my father tells me, his refrain. He is tall, courtly, his face long, and he wears a Phi Beta Kappa key across his vest. As a child I reach to it when he dangles it over my eyes. I grasp too tightly and tear loose a black button. He is disturbed and pushes at the fabric as if it will join and heal itself.

"You must never!" Mademoiselle says to me, a lady of burnished ivory, spectacles, a gray shirtwaist closed at the collar, her raisinlike eyes rarely blinking. Her permed darkish hair has been set so hard it might chip. "We've grounds for dismissing you. Climbing from a window! It is only out of respect for your family that we do not!"

Flowers sheening in sunlight. There are always gardens. Up and down every street, on windowsills, in narrow alleyways. If you look carefully when people gather, they are also blooms among the box bushes. Women given off nectar to the bees. It is so obviously a part of nature's plan you wonder why everyone doesn't see we are all gardens. I am the mimosa, and hummingbirds dart to me.

I cover my eyes. Winter howls and ice cracks. I hate the redness of eyelids. I do not like blood. Screams, shouting, the sounds of hate. I have told them I possess rights. I am an adult. I make my own decisions. They examine me. People forever have their hands on me.

Deep purple falls. Sleepy garden walls. The best time, best place. I know deep purple. I am Spanish iris. My body scarcely touches sheets before blazing yellow butterflies light on me. Music starts in my breasts and lives in my fingers, though I sit not at the piano. Even in darkness I feel sunshine as if I'm an opening Oriental poppy. You must not! they say.

The first piano lesson. Mrs. Bennett Flournoy is my teacher. She drives to our house and sits beside me on the bench. She has been touched by winter and lost her full flower, a wilting hyacinth. "Think of your fingers as rain upon the keys," she says. I picture a summer shower in the garden.

No! people call. What does a garden understand about no?

I love rain. I grow in rain. I luxuriate. I lie eyes open and offer my tongue to the darling drops. I am a living tree. I think of my roots drinking rain. I imagine fruit growing along my arms, and men picking from me. I am a pear, a plum, a Georgia peach. Men feed off me.

But always the winter, the ice, the red shrieking wind which rends the blooms, dashes them into swirling night. Words are often wind.

Pleas and threats. The first rule is never trust any wind. Voices speak of God. God is the sweet morning mist and summer sun.

I build a high wall around my perfect little garden. It is deep within me where wind cannot enter, my private place. Only a riot of blooms, the bees, the music. We twine as the deep purple falls.

They don't know what I've learned about my mother, Rachel. More than my brother, kind and smart for a boy, smart and dumb. I've been hateful to him. I shoved him off his roller skates as we played in the garage during a thunderstorm. I realized early I was more devious. He accepted everything he'd been told. I once explained that the reason we have rain is that clouds weep for the pain we caused God. He looked up at the sky and cried. Nobody could ever fool me that way.

So many times I watched my mother touch a finger to her temple, the tiny new moon hidden by the curl of her dyed hair. Grandmother never told us. My brother and I'd lived with her since a time she won't speak of. I asked, and Grandmother stared as if my voice hadn't reached her ears. She slept rarely and never switched off the Tiffany lamp of her bedroom.

What and who were we? Unlike my good little brother, I questioned. I wanted to know about my father. Grandmother told us the war killed him. Where was his grave? I asked. I told her I'd picked mums to lay by his headstone. He never came back, Grandmother said. He was a naval commander whose submarine plunged to the sea's bottom and never rose. He rested in an unreachable dark canyon of the Pacific.

Yet where were his pictures? Why was there no photograph around the house or in the album? We are not people who put stock in pictures, Grandmother said. I'll ask Mother, I said. You must never cause her pain, Grandmother said, feet drawing together and hands tightening on her chair arms. But I do. I found vacant patches on album pages. I sat beside Mother as she played "Blue Orchids." She told me to drip my fingers like rain upon the keys.

"Did they try to find the submarine?" I asked. She drew her hands from keys and let them fall to her lap. Her dark eyes became moist and luminous. Mother? I asked. Mother? She lifted a pink dahlia from the Chinese vase and offered it to me on her palm. That night Grandmother had to phone Dr. Winston.

My cousin Wendy and I attended Camp Sail each summer, the green cottages located on bluffs above the Rappahannock. She was prettier but I the stronger swimmer and won the racing trophy. I knocked her off the dock and ducked her till wailing and choking she told me what she'd heard from her mother. He was never that, she said. I held her under, and she became limp in the strong tidal flow. That same night she called her parents to come fetch and drive her home.

I barely remember moving to Grandmother's, a rainy day which had a chauffeur named Hubert carrying in baggage. Mother wasn't with us. She came and left, came and left. I began to sense a rhythm to it. Grandmother provided the money. Once a quarter an elderly man from the bank sat with her in the parlor to go over finances. Grandfather, a faceless shadow from my child's mind, had left her rich.

During my fourteenth year Grandmother sent me away to school, not the fashionable place my mother went, but St. Helen's in South Carolina. I knew none of the girls. I asked why I didn't go where Mother had gone. Grandmother told me that Mademoiselle had died and the school's standards had slipped.

I learned the terrible things from Alfred, a second cousin once removed. We hated each other. He had red hair and a prissy mouth. When canoeing on the lake, he used his paddle to splash my new sunsuit. I stuck a yellow-eyed puff adder in his bed. He screamed like a girl.

For what he told me his father spanked him hard, but I heard the words. I found out.

❋

I could very nearly set my watch by the regularity of their calls. We had a procedure, a routine to deceive, if in truth that's what we did. I thought of Rachel browsing among the arbor, blue juice on her scarlet lips. Bees attempted to drink from them. She wore black hair to her hips, and grape bursts had stained her white pinafore.

I dated her before med school, that wonderful Christmas of my senior year at Hampden-Sydney when invitations gathered along the mantel. She was the first girl to bare her breasts to me. She unbuttoned a ruffled blouse, jerked up her brassiere, and took my head between her palms. She laughed when I proclaimed my love for her.

"You love Rachel's ripe apples," she said and became shockingly ardent. I didn't know till then girls could be.

I rarely saw her after I entered Duke. I phoned several times, but she was usually away on trips with her mother—to the Homestead, Italy, west to New Mexico and a dude ranch. I saw a photograph of them in the society section of the Richmond *Times-Dispatch*. They wore sombreros and sat astride sad-looking burros. Cactuses bloomed around them.

I made a last date with her during a steamy summer break. I believed then she was considering me, thinking of casting her net for me, as my mother put it, the future doctor who would earn an income allowing Rachel to continue living the graceful life. That idea turned out wrong. She had no understanding of how to use people. She simply gave herself to those she liked.

Her mother watched as we left the house. We drove to the bay, where I'd borrowed the use of my uncle's Cal 30 sloop. No wind crossed the water, and we weltered becalmed in the lower Chesapeake. Rachel lounged under shade of the listlessly flapping mainsail, her long, tan body oiled and voluptuous, water beading her skin, her black hair shiny wet from a dip.

"I hate clothes," she said and stretched toward the sun. "I hate being bound. Clothes are a sham. They are trickery. Would you love me naked?"

"I'd love you anyway anyhow," I told her and meant it.

"Poor Richard," she said. "I do cause him terrible yearnings."

And she removed her black-and-red striped bathing suit, a slow sexual ballet, and we settled to the blanket on the cabin, all the while the sail swinging and snapping above us, bay water splashing against the white hull. She was soon married, and I now believe that last afternoon a gift to me, her way of saying farewell and thanks for my admiration, presenting me the best of what she had, and what she had more than anything was the gift of love.

I never done nothing to cause it. I had my job gunning the backhoe when we laid the new water mains down the old brick street lined with three-story mansions. They was dog days, the August sun blood red and out to blister the sweating working man.

Those awninged houses made me think of fussy old women who sniffed at you when you was dirty. I walked to a corner pile of stone big as church to fill my water jug, knocked at the back door, and asked permission to use a yard spigot. The yard had a fountain, a pond with goldfish, and a million white lilies. Water dripped from the mouth of a green iron frog. Sprinklers whirled above grass as level and trim as a pool table. I never saw her beside the iris. She'd been sunning among purple blooms, and when I walked past I didn't know she was lying there till she sat up and stared. She had on a yellow halter and shorts. Her dark eyes ate me up.

"Take all the water you want," she said. "We have our own deep well. Wait! You've hurt yourself!"

It won't no hurt, just a scratch from a lug wrench which slipped while I was tightening the blade. She come toward me, this tall woman who set on a yellow straw hat. She was barefoot and bare-legged. She laid fingers on my arm. I never felt volts travel so hot from a woman.

"Anytime you need water," she said, and those fingers with red-painted nails slid along my skin, leaving rows in the sweat. "I know what it is to be thirsty."

I filled my jug and got the hell out of there. Sometimes when I was gunning the backhoe, she'd step out among columns of the house porch and stand holding her hands behind her back. A black maid cared for a couple of kids. As we worked on down the street, I never believed I'd see her again even from a mile off till just at dark when we quit early on Friday before Labor Day. As I swatted gnats, flies, and skeeters and climbed into my Ford pickup, the big Chrysler drove up beside me and stopped. A light clicked on when she opened the door.

"Just as you are," she said. We'd parked out west of Richmond on a country road among loblollies. She licked my sweat. She called me earthy. I'd been among women, but none like her. I was a big man, strong, yet she wore me down. She took to driving to my rented room south of the river, always at night. I asked about her husband. She said he'd gone to war. In a crazy way I guess I kind of loved her till her father come charging in the door. She screamed, and her father just collapsed like a rag without me hitting him. I never touched him. Blood shot from his nose and mouth. They threw me in jail, and I had to prove to the police I never hit him. The old lady's lawyer brought money for me to leave town. I come down to Carolina, hell yes, where I got me a good woman and a boy. But I remember Rachel laying her fingers on my arm. I don't know. I've never been able to figure things out, yet I know it was a kindly act.

She said love can't be contained. "Can foxglove or hibiscus?" she asked. I told her anything can be contained except death and even that held in abeyance awhile. I fled. I became certain of nothing. Who did I see when I looked at the children? She didn't act guilty. There was no shame. Rueful, yes, slyly saddened, but no remorse that led to repentance. I had a name, a position in the community, and she treated me as if those attainments were trifles.

She caused me to doubt my own manliness. I worried I might be homosexual, though I'd experienced no desire for male flesh at Woodberry Forest when some of that ignobility made the rounds. I kept an appointment with a Charlottesville doctor. I'd arranged for it secretly.

"You're dwelling on it too much," he said, tapping a Cross pen against his golden watchband.

"I have to think about it. She's beautiful and makes me think about it."

She seemed always to be eyeing me. A terrible thing to be constantly under the gaze of judgment. I was a normal male. Tests proved that. Yet she devoured me with her dark eyes. Nights I'd wake to find her lying with them open and staring. Dim light from the bathroom aroused smudged embers in her irises.

I moved to Florida. I'm an attorney, remarried, and the father of a daughter I can be sure of. I never understood Rachel. I think she loved love, or what she took it to be. When I discovered she'd been with Bobo Gaines, my old roommate from the university, at a Virginia Beach motel, I didn't confront him, but her.

"He was so nice to me," she said. She pulled strands of hair before her face and stroked them with a long-handled silver brush. "He'd just come from the ocean, water dripping from him, a leaf of sea lettuce on his tan shoulder. I found it difficult not to let him take my hand."

"Your hand, hell!" I said. "If you want to save this marriage, it has to stop!"

"Bobo looks so dashing in his hunt attire," she said. "No man in boots has better legs."

It did not stop. She was the wayward one, yet I experienced the guilt. I felt despair more than anger. How could such loveliness be so wanton? The children I've not seen since I left Virginia. When toward the end I became frantic, she gazed at me from those bottomless nocturnal eyes, shook her head, and lifted a palm as if to indicate who would know.

"We are all flowers, and they are beautiful children," she said maddeningly. "Who serves best, the bloom or the bee?"

Why should I continue to carry guilt?

God keeps score and never forgets. We do not escape. I saw that article of His justice when the perfidious part of me gave way only once in my life—a scratching at the door of my London hotel by the sleek sinuous Spanish pretender while Henry shot grouse in Scotland. I believed I'd buried the lie deep till I witnessed Rachel's openness, her trust, the innocent giving of herself. She loved every cur dog who strayed into the neighborhood. She never passed a panhandler she didn't wish to open her little pocketbook for. She dug a cemetery at the rear of the garden where she laid to rest a sparrow that flew into a broad parlor window. Grown, she had a heart too soon made glad. What is love if it doesn't seek the good of others? I've always sought the good for Rachel.

Joseph, the teenage boy from south of the river, his skin undoubtedly darkened by a strain of Negro blood. Summers he rode his bicycle to the house and cut the lawn. I missed her. When I quietly opened the door of the white shed where garden implements and the mowers were kept, a flash of flesh broke shadows. Their bodies slanted across stacked bags of bone meal used to nourish the box bushes.

I slashed Joseph with a trowel. Blood seeping among his fingers, he ran, never to return. Rachel rushed crying to her room. I followed and found her pressed back among fragrant dresses of her closet.

"Was he inside you?" I demanded. "Dr. Shokley will tell."

I drove the Packard. Dr. Shokley had been our family physician since I was a girl, an eminent, lumbering man whose skin was like fresh cream. His white hair straggled down over the rear of his high stiff collar.

"She has been penetrated," he told me, his voice little more than a whisper. "After such a short interval, a douche should suffice."

The douche did not. Rachel had to be sent to Chattanooga, where my sister Emily kept her till the thing was done. Henry, my good and trusting husband, who had no eye for suspicion or the delving of secrets, became half crazed. He didn't go to his office, and it was the only time during our marriage I saw him lose his dignity and become fallingdown drunk. Yet when Rachel returned, she was as lovely as ever, if anything more beautiful, stunning for a girl so young. She'd been in the house less than ten minutes before boys rang our bell. I sent them away. Father Alex, our pastor, counseled her. She simply smiled at him. God chastises us for our sins by letting us see their ugliness in those we hold dearer than life.

Henry and I watched. We hoped to save her from herself. Rachel attended private schools which provided discipline. She never traveled alone and was allowed to be escorted only by boys whose families we approved of. Still, as she grew older, we couldn't keep her caged. Gaps of time existed she wouldn't account for. When she came in late, she didn't answer our questions or heed our rebukes. She passed by us and glided up the steps to her room. We'd hear her singing to her canary. Henry lowered his face to his hands.

We wanted only a safe marriage for her, a loving protective husband, and when Charles Fontaine proposed, we believed our prayers answered. It wasn't she didn't love Charles. She loved everybody. She didn't know where to stop loving—as if there were no difference among people. Then the night of terror Henry surprised her in the arms of that brute of a common laborer. I had no choice. After the funeral, arrangements were made. I hated God for His using beauty to inflict the greatest punishments of all.

People are so foolish. I wipe the curl of hair from my temple and watch my fingers lower to the keys like a gentle spring rain. Often my fingers seem separate from me, to live their own lives—tiny people going about their business. They make the notes, little workers creating melodies for me. I have nothing to do with them, and music rises to form bouquets of the most amazing colors.

I never stop hearing music. Colors are music, the scent of lilacs. The music is a wall, though sometimes howls intrude like wild dogs in the night. She watches me. She is upstairs in her chair by the window but sees down through walls. My children eye me. They listen. When I kiss them, they stand stiffly and try not to show their wish to draw away. They've never cared for my embraces. She has told me my lips are too profuse.

Yet many have desired my kisses. I gave them away on grassy terraces, weltering boats, and darkened rooms above the Atlantic. I remember looking over a quivering muscled shoulder and seeing gulls soar at dawn. Dazzling white, they rode air currents and cried freedom. I sailed with them on the ocean wind.

I have been used. I am a tea rose, a purple iris, and often a long-stem tiger lily. I scare men. I see fright flare in their eyes. I try to explain the nature and completeness of my gift to them, but they do not want completeness. They expect possession, as if I could disassemble myself, present them a leg, a breast, a vagina. Occasionally my petals fall.

Mother watches. She has always watched. If I sunbathe in the garden, she peers from shadows behind the window. She does not allow me my own breath. Yet many times I've eluded her, drifted from the house like smoke in the night. My father too spied on me. When I attended dances, he followed in the Packard. I weep for my father and all flowers that have withered and died. Many, many flowers. My fingers are busy little people on the keys who play tunes which are wings and wines of color. I have been chiefly a flower. It is the great truth I've perceived.

I dressed in my summer dinner jacket and drove to the house, my medical bag in the trunk of the Buick. I hadn't understood till her mother came to the office, the chauffeur waiting at the front curb in a No Parking area.

"It's time again for her to leave," she said, her brittle body curved to the ebony cane. "Did not Dr. Shokley inform you?"

Dr. Shokley lay in his grave. He died while sitting in his backyard workshop repairing an antique clock. Old clocks were his hobby. I inherited his medical practice. Such was our understanding when I agreed to become his associate. After her visit I checked files. There were two sets—one on the ground floor, the other in a locked basement area. Dr. Shokley had left keys for me. I found them while going through his desk drawers. The embellished penmanship on the envelope read: Be above all discreet and forgiving.

I studied Rachel's files. At a time people believed her to be on an European tour, she was a patient in a Philadelphia clinic. The first time I examined her and fingered the rigid curl off her temple, there waited the scar hardly larger than a caraway seed. My hand flinched as if I'd touched fire. The operation, which had seemed to offer so much promise in those years, was now judged barbaric, a horror seized upon in panic. Then a second act of surgery which ended life's renewal.

At the house ancient, uniformed Viola opened the door. I sat in the dusky parlor, it's dimness hardly penetrated by light from the teardrop chandelier, till Rachel descended the steps, this time wearing a black silk gown and pearls. She would've appeared regal except she listed slightly and an arm bumped the carved oak railing. I offered my hand. She took it, righted herself, and kissed my cheek in lingering fashion. I pinned to the shoulder of her dress the orchid I'd brought. Her lipstick had not been precisely applied. We sat on the blue divan to smoke and drink exactly two manhattans each Viola served from a silver tray.

Her son and daughter approached to say good-bye. They spoke words and kissed her, but they'd be relieved when she left the house. Rachel gazed at them as if they were articles in a shop window. Viola opened the door for us. She and the children stood on the stone porch. As we walked to my car, I carried a covered canary and knew that if I looked back at the upstairs window Rachel's mother would be watching.

During the trip to Baltimore, Rachel smoked Luckies and chattered. Headlights reminded her of fireflies. She liked to remember the year she'd been a member of the Water Maidens, a swimming team at the Warrenton girls' school whose members formed floral patterns in the gym's turquoise pool. Her fingers moved as if a keyboard lay across her lap. She could become excited. She might suddenly cry or attempt to kiss my mouth. When her agitated hands fluttered, I'd capture her fingers and hold them till they quieted against my palm.

Entering between the ornate iron gates, she straightened, touched her hair, and smiled at floodlit flowers planted inside the concrete circle before the brick, partially dark Victorian main building.

"Coralbells," she said.

EXPIATION

Leland drove roads little changed from the time way back—more of them hard-surfaced now, yet still winding narrow strips between stands of shaggy pines which dropped a ragged shade. The pines smelled of hot resin, and some bled yellowish white sap from bark-beetle wounds. He steered the beige Sedan de Ville past fields grown wild with bull thistles, others sprouting a thin gray cover resembling an ancient's hair—red soil too worn to eke out any except a wan vegetation. Dark stalks formed jagged lines in rows where last year's tobacco had been pulled. Then the splintered desolation that timber companies left. Finally the remains of Ballard's Store, tumbledown, climbed over by creeper, honeysuckle, poison oak . . .

. . . *the boy stands in the yard beside the frame cabin set at the corners on fieldstones . . .*

. . . Anne, Leland's wife, seemed to be enjoying herself. They'd driven down to Virginia from Connecticut to bring their daughter Jennifer to Sweet Briar for her senior year. Usually they unpacked her things, kissed her good-bye, and returned to Interstate 95 after staying a night at the Richmond Marriott. Anne had been delighted to go along with his impulse, but as he stopped at a junction remembered as Jericho Crossroads, he again felt his stomach tighten and realized he gripped the wheel as if his car were trying to escape . . .

. . . *no grass, not attempts at it, the ground worn bare as bone by the trod of brothers, sisters, hounds, by hogs too that would be slaughtered at first kill frost. The scalded and scraped carcasses hung clean and bright as newborn flesh from limbs of the hackberry tree . . .*

. . . "We're close now," Leland told Anne. Eighteen miles back they'd turned off the dazzling new highway to gas up at a sun-speckled superette where a gristmill once stood. The mill had vanished, and an Amoco sign soared eighty feet above lines of red pumps and stainless-steel vending machines. No mules now, no wagons hauling wheat, barley, oats, but snarling trucks that had more power under the hood than half a dozen teams . . .

. . . *from the yard the boy looks across low ground of broad cultivated acres astride the river, this soil not red but black loam yearly enriched by flooding. No manure or fertilizer necessary. Corn, tobacco, and alfalfa nigh on to leap from this earth. During heat of summer, air above the bottom becomes wiggly, and the southwest breeze carries odors of sultrily growing crops and the river's mud . . .*

. . . *the boy hiked to the river after work in the fields. Ditches had to be cleared. Otherwise the low ground wouldn't drain, causing crops to shrink and drown. He carried his own hoe, the handle trimmed to his size by his father. All his brothers and sisters had their first hoes provided by the Ballards, but if you lost or broke yours, you had to do the repairing or pay for the replacing . . .*

. . . "I've always wanted to," Anne said. She was wearing a lemon-colored linen suit and a pink silk scarf. "You've talked about it so much I'm dying to see." He'd spoken about it, yet never accurately. This September afternoon was hazily dry . . .

. . . *a black shape moves at the edge of the hushed motionless corn . . .*

. . . *he chopped weeds and Johnson grass from the ditches, working beside his brothers. The oldest, Keith, had been hired for stable help and came home nights telling of the big house. "They feed hounds meat we'd put on our table," he said . . .*

. . . "No need to rush back," Anne said. "You can take an extra day without the world ending." The evening before they'd eaten Brie and boiled shrimp on Sweet Briar's emerald lawns. Candy-striped tents had been raised, and a string quartet played Mozart. Jennifer and the other seniors sang the college hymn. Never in Jennifer's life had she seen hogs butchered, heard their terrified squeals, felt the heat of spurting blood, or plopped stinking red innards into galvanized tubs . . .

. . . *a dog, the boy thinks* . . .

. . . *the big house, three quarters of a mile off, had its own private entrance and road. Mr. Ballard's road was paved while half those in Howell County were still dirt. Along the lane dogwood and magnolias had been planted. At Christmas, lights were strung out to the white Kentucky gate. The Ballards had been first in the entire district to have electricity, like seeing night come alive in a burst of fire* . . .

. . . "I wish I could've known them," Anne said, speaking of Leland's parents. "Your father must've been handsome if you got his looks. A shame the fire burned all those things." Leland didn't turn his head to answer her. When dealing with the past, he never spoke quickly, if at all. Bending the truth was like stepping on slippery rocks while crossing a stream. A careless step, and you could be swept away . . .

. . . *or a calf broke loose* . . .

. . . *the boy had never been down the private road to the Ballard house. After hearing his brother's stories about the peacocks, fountain, and piano, he snuck through woods of an evening. He kept to deer paths softened by dampness and pine tags. His breathing quiet, he stalked the house. The Ballards were hard on poachers. They stood them before the county judge or fired them off the place. The boy had seen wagons and Model A's leaving, mattresses and chairs twined to the roofs. He believed terrible things must be down the road, not the private one to the big house, but the county secondary which led to the outer world* . . .

. . . "We should've done this before," Anne said, a tall, trim woman, good posture, her features tending to sharpness, her hair still coppery. They'd married late, and she was ten years younger than he. When he met her, she'd been working for the Hartford School Board. He'd tried to sell his line of Royal typewriters, and she'd laughed behind her hand . . .

. . . no calf or dog either . . .

*. . . on his belly he pushed and squirmed among pines to the wall, it slick
and mossy on the north side where he lay listening for hounds, not watchdogs,
but the Triggs and Walkers. All the Ballards were hunters. It was told they
bought harriers from beyond the sea, though the boy had never seen the ocean
and could only picture it as river water stretching all the way to Tobaccoton,
Lynchburg, or Danville . . .*

. . . "Not exactly the way I've imagined it," Anne said, gazing at
cutover forest, fields grazing a few poor cows, land gone to broom-
straw. She'd been thinking fox-hunting country, white plank fences,
and manor houses on expanses of bluegrass. She made a face at sight of
a run-over blacksnake, a mashed and glistening spectrum in a patch of
sunlight . . .

. . . too large . . .

*. . . he shinnied up a pecan tree close to the wall, bent back limbs, and
peered across lawn greener than any pasture he'd ever seen. He saw the
splashing fountain, flower garden around it, and three stories of a brick house
that had chimneys everywhere. He heard a piano, a canary singing, and
caught the glimmer of a chandelier . . .*

. . . and fast . . .

*. . . "Got ya!" the nigger said, Black Amos, who wore clothes finer than
most whites, owned a Chevrolet car, and strung a gold watch-chain across his
vest. When Mr. Ballard and his guests shot birds, Black Amos took the wagon
reins and unleashed the English setters that jolted to quivering points in the
lespedeza. Black Amos had sneaked up under the pecan tree, grabbed the boy
by the ankles, and dragged him down. Bark skinned him like fire, and he
wet himself, causing Black Amos to hold his nose and say, "Who-wee, you
stinks worse than a hog in heat!" . . .*

. . . "You southerners are supposed to be crazy for cemeteries,"
Anne said, proud of his coming from Virginia, always letting it be
known when they met new people. He'd not denied being kin to a
cavalry officer by the same name who rode with Jeb Stuart during his

dash around McClellan's army midst the Peninsula campaign. At the Hartford Library she'd located an elaborate coat of arms and had it engraved on a gold ring she gave him the Christmas after they sent Jennifer to her first ballet lesson . . .

. . . *hide too dark for deer* . . .

. . . *Black Amos shook the boy and slapped him when he kicked. He jammed the boy against the wall and pushed a knee into his stomach. He leaned his shiny pocked face close, teeth big as dice, and breath sweet from the Ballard's fancy peppermints. "Don't you come here again, boy. You remember you don't snoop around peeping at people. You don't belong on high ground. Hear me?"* . . .

. . . "We kept the plot trimmed," Leland told Anne, remembering his mother and his brothers and sisters taking turns using the sickle at the cemetery. He pictured too how Jennifer had dreamed of becoming a ballet star. In a production of *Sleeping Beauty* she and other children whirled across the stage as silken snowflakes. Often she'd danced for him alone, and he'd thrilled at the wonder of anything so lovely and loving having a connection . . .

. . . *the shape growing* . . .

. . . *when Black Amos turned him loose, the boy ran through the woods. Limbs whipped his face, and he jumped the branch where he and his father seined shiners. He ran among tobacco plants drooping heavy and coarse under a hot moon. He crawled between rails of the cedar fence his father had split by pounding an iron wedge with a wooden maul. He was so scared he clawed himself under the cabin beside Buck, their redbone hound. He knew now what a treed animal felt like, a coon or bobcat spitting down at hunters raising their guns* . . .

. . . "So few houses," Anne said. Leland explained many farmers had given up and left. Others had not returned after wars. Youth had traveled to cities. Mostly the old remained. Stone chimneys stood where frame dwellings had burned—not from wrath or vengeance but the carelessness of the aged in tending fires . . .

. . . moving faster . . .

. . . he, who'd never thought to live in a dwelling other than a tenant cabin, left the county for the army, lied about his age at the Danville recruiting station, and was sent by sooty day coach to Georgia and infantry training. Nor had he seen a vessel larger than a johnboat used on the river for fishing till he hiked up the gangplank to the dark immensity of the Queen Mary. *The ship's great salons had been paneled with plywood, all the fine murals covered, the tapestries removed, and while enduring the vomit stink of seasick soldiers, his lieutenant told him of the rich and mighty who'd once promenaded on her polished decks. Perhaps Mr. and Mrs. Ballard were among them, bejeweled upon a dark white-capped ocean . . .*

. . . leaping . . .

. . . the boy saw Mr. Ballard close up on election day. The Ballards owned the store too, issued their own money, scrip, so that if you dealt there, you took your change in their paper and were bound by it. Mr. Ballard arrived in a gray LaSalle driven by Black Amos. He wasn't a big man, not as tall as the boy's father, yet believed himself large. When he walked among what he called "his" people, they shrunk and he grew. The boy would've never dared look directly into that round florid face. "You voting right, Henry?" Mr. Ballard asked the boy's father. "I'm with you, Mr. William," the father answered, the bobbing bend in his spine automatic . . .

. . . "And people don't seem to be doing much," Anne said. "Doesn't anybody work?" She didn't understand the call of seasons. Most had their tobacco pulled, were stripping or curing it in log sheds that fumed a slight blue smoke. Few other crops were grown now. The men that had local jobs cut pulpwood and saw timber or drove trucks to logging yards. They trooped from forests at twilight, their sweat powdered by yellow dust . . .

. . . the fear he'd felt when Black Amos seized him and another greater terror that shook him like a kicked hound, a hot shrieking force, his vision knocked cockeyed as he stumbled wet from assaulted waters onto a shell-torn landing ramp and ran through a slash of sandy headland, the earth rising

and spinning. He dug himself deep into a Norman orchard, throwing soil between his legs like a dog, screaming, weeping. He became a whimpering ball of flesh within the earth . . .

. . . the shape slides under sycamore shadows along the river . . .

. . . his father, holding the lantern, called him from under the cabin. The father smelled of soured sweat, his clodhoppers covered by bottom dust, his face darkened by beard stubble. Together they squatted in moon shade of the hackberry. "Reckon I could kill that nigger," the father said. "Thinks he's something 'cause they let him wear they old clothes. I'd a got out long ago if there'd been anyplace to get to. But you stay away from up 'er. I'll take care of things in time . . ."

. . . "More blacks, relatively speaking," Anne said. Leland had grubbed beside them during the summer as they labored to keep the ditches free. His blisters raised blisters. He fought a burrhead named Josephus over his drinking water from a white man's dipper. They hit, kicked, and butted till both lay heaving and sick in the ditch hearing hoots and laughter from the other hands. He and Josephus stumbled bloody to the river and washed together . . .

. . . out of sight . . .

. . . No blackness in her neat Yankee world, no stink, no dirt, no mess. She'd never understand shitted pants or a body burrowing into a hole . . .

. . . the lieutenant a captain now, who spoke French and bartered eggs from the wooden-shod Norman farmers. He coaxed Leland from the hole, quieted him as you might a runaway horse, and made him his Jeep driver. When the regiment was overrun by Panzers during the last German offensive through the Ardennes, it was Leland who knew how to hide himself and the captain under a mound of stable droppings as tanks and artillery clattered along the Belgian road, Leland too who at dark dragged the bleeding captain from beneath manure, shouldered him, and with a woodsman's sense of direction carried him to a nameless village. A nun at a church that had a

shattered steeple took them in. She was aged, bowed, and silent. She bound the captain's wounds and hid him and Leland in the sacristy till the British recaptured the town. The army considered Leland brave for not abandoning the captain, when all the while he'd believed he had a better chance of surviving capture in the company of an officer . . .

. . . the boy crosses to the well for a drink from a bucket drawn up on a wooden windlass carved by his father . . .

. . . his father drinking after losing half an arm in the baling machine, the first in Howell County, so new that farmers came and squatted to watch it plunge mowed alfalfa into a compactor. Leland heard screams on a muggy June afternoon as he bent among tobacco plants to pick the green worms so fat and soft they squashed of their own weight when thrown to the ground. Men rushed his father by truck to the Farmville hospital. Mr. Ballard himself cut the bale and found the arm. He threw it into the river, calling it catfish bait. Field hands laughed . . .

. . . "Did people tell you you resembled your father?" Anne asked. "I'd think somebody would have an old snapshot." He'd lied about the fire too. Who back then owned a camera or had money for film? Only the Ballards and their like. Anne probably envisioned his father wearing a white suit, string tie, and planter's hat. She'd never lifted poke salad, cracklings, and field cress to her mouth, or felt the fire white lightning burned in a belly. The father drinking alone in hackberry shade. No insurance for the loss of the arm, no workmen's compensation, though now and again the first Mrs. Ballard, driven by Black Amos in the LaSalle, stopped out front and honked for Leland's mother to walk to the car and accept a few dollars worth of store scrip from a gloved white hand . . .

. . . by a ferny spring deep in the woods the father cooked a little liquor, most of which he drank himself. He used corn and sorghum stolen nights from the Ballards' crops. The sheriff knew, yet took no action 'cause what good did it do to send a man to jail and the county have to feed his family? The

Ballards never missed their puny loss. The father had a cooling-out hideaway down by the river, a damp shade under the stringing willows, and enjoyed wetting a line in the flowing water, catching bluecats he'd carry home for the mother to fry. He didn't return to the cabin on a September evening or the next morning either, and when the boy climbed along the bank, the father was gone. How or why he'd slipped into the river nobody could figure for sure. Deputies found him floating facedown, his overalls snagged on a toppled birch. The father still wore his bandless felt hat. At the funeral the Ballards were nervous about muddying their shoes . . .

. . . the boy drinks, draining the dipper, and hangs it on the ten-penny nail . . .

. . . "You may not admit it, but you're proud of your Confederate forebears," Anne said, speaking in her preachy schoolteaching tones. "Despite their standing for the most abominable practice in our country's history, by which I mean slavery." Forebears he'd never learned much about. He remembered a grandfather whose yellowish white beard itched like dry straw and an old woman whose face was as lined as a rutted road. Her kiss stung of snuff. There was vague talk of cousins in the Tennessee mountains. No portraits such as hung at the Ballard house, none certainly of an officer wearing a butternut uniform and plumed hat, his hands cupped to a polished saber guard. Blacks and whites were all slaves to the land back then, rooted to it. The land owned them no matter the color, and the Ballards held title to that. White men stepped out of Black Amos' way. At settling-up time, when Mr. Ballard sat at his store desk with his ledger, black and white stood passively in line waiting together, their hats removed . . .

. . . the shape springs from shadows, passing the greener growth along the river, horse and rider, the animal's black flesh catching a shifting glint of sun . . .

. . . the sun browned Leland, and he'd quit school as had his brothers, already scattered. Two went to the navy, one to jail for cutting in a roadhouse

brawl. The sisters too left, joining men in other cabins or finding jobs at Tobaccoton's new shoe factory. Like chaff tossed into the air, they were blown by winds of hunger and need. Some reappeared for birthdays or Christmas. A parcel-post package might arrive at Jericho Crossroads holding a carton of Camels, socks, a box of chocolate-covered cherries. Occasionally a penciled letter he'd work out the words of for his mother. She'd gone to the big house, to the Ballards' kitchen to bake their bread and iron their linens. Nights she trudged home carrying her tote—pieces of clothing, leftover food, a heavy slice of angel cake, most of the white icing gone. She brought a tan coat, knee length, that had moth holes in the lining and ratty fox fur torn from the collar. She sewed the fur back and stood before her oval mirror straining to see herself as a fine rich lady . . .

. . . horse and rider gallop toward higher ground, along a wagon road . . .

. . . "Hot," Anne said, fanned her face, and reached to the air conditioning . . .

. . . the big snow and freeze while Leland snaked logs from the woods for the Ballard sawmill. Wind slashed in, the river iced, and trees cracked and crashed to the ground. Two days before he could get home. His mother had firewood. She was able to use an ax. When he hiked through drifts to the cabin, no smoke wisped from the chimney, no fire burned. The dishes were clean, her bed was made. He believed she must've gone to the big house, where he pushed to, knowing better than to knock at the front door. Black Amos did allow him to stand in the kitchen out of the cold. "She ain't here," Black Amos said. He wore his dark suit and vest with the gold chain across it. Leland thanked him, struggled to return to the cabin, and found her in the outhouse just sitting and looking off, wearing the coat as if she were on a bus traveling, her hands folded on her lap . . .

. . . disturbed crows fly from pines, their caws echoing across the river . . .

. . . "I remember first hearing you talk," Anne said, smiling. "I thought it was a joke, somebody in the office putting on an accent. You were trying to sell typewriters. You kept coming back and finally got an order. Everybody felt sorry for you, and I thought this is the funniest-talking man I've ever heard. When you asked to take me to a movie, the most surprised person in the world was me hearing myself agree to go . . ."

. . . *he didn't return to Howell County after the war. What was to go back to? The captain, already discharged, invited him to Connecticut. Leland rode the Greyhound, and the captain, learning to use his new leg, met him at the depot. They drove a Chrysler to the house, not big and fancy like the Ballards', no columns, formal gardens, or fountain, but trimly white and neat, no wall either or barking hounds, no strangling sweet wisteria hanging from the oaks. The wife hugged Leland and kissed his cheek. At the dinner table, the captain explained about the GI Bill. If Leland agreed, he would be hired to work in the office-supply store and nights attend a second-story business college that had no entrance requirements other than the where-withal to pay tuition . . .*

. . . "You've hardly any accent now," Anne said. "Though it occasionally comes through when you drop *r*'s and *g*'s and pronounce *fire* and *house* as if they had two syllables . . .

. . . *he sold typewriters on the road and drove small stick-shift cars to save mileage money. He stayed in cheap hotels, often fixing himself a meal of canned soup by using hot water from the bathroom faucet. He ironed his blue serge suit and kept account in a ledger of every penny he spent. He studied not only books from the business college, but also people around him, listening to how they talked, observing the way they dressed, used the right fork. He blew fuses in a motel where he sneaked in a hot plate and complained to the management about the lack of power . . .*

. . . *the horse and rider gone, only dust settling, the crows again circling to pine boughs . . .*

. . . *the captain stocked the most advanced electric typewriters, and Leland needed to be trained to service them. It was discovered he had a mind for understanding complex circuits. The captain took him off the road, made him a troubleshooter, and put him in charge of the new department. When calculators were introduced, Leland sat in a show window to answer questions and do demonstrations for people on the sidewalk. He figured compound interest, odds on the bowl games, and tax levies. He wore a Santa Claus suit . . .*

. . . the boy turns toward the cabin and chores. His mother is working at the big house. Bucket in hand, he passes the rail fence on his way to the garden to pick snaps and butterbeans. He drops the bucket, believing he sees God gigantic and climbing, black and soaring, and he throws up his hands as if he will be taken by the angel of death . . . !

. . . before turning in on a January night, the captain stepped out for a breath of air. His front stoop was iced. His feet flew from beneath him, and he sprawled helpless till his wife in her bathrobe opened the door searching for him. By the time Leland got word, the captain lay dead, his body already resting at the funeral home, the widow wearing a black dress. She and her lawyer met with Leland three weeks after the burial. She offered him the business through an installment buyout over a fifteen-year period. She asked no down payment, maintaining the captain had owed his life to Leland. He would want Leland to have it . . .

. . . "And your clothes during those early days," Anne said, laughing. "You looked as if you bought them down at the Salvation Army . . ."

. . . the great black horse and rider, a woman tall and white, a giantess she seems sitting calmly and gazing down at him as the horse arches past and lights in the yard. Chickens fly squawking and dropping feathers. Buck's so scared he yelps, tucks tail, and dives under the cabin. Hooves pound and spume dust, the horse heaves, and foam flings into sun shafting among hackberry limbs . . .

. . . "Your trousers were too short," Anne said. "You wore white socks and got all mixed up on your subjunctives . . ."

. . . being responsible for the entire business frightened Leland. He'd learned to hold onto money, grasp it tight, and now he had to part with amounts he'd never believed would pass through his fingers. He released it grudgingly, afraid of inventory buildup. He picked paper clips and rubber bands off the floor. He slept easy at night only when he saw he could meet payments to the widow out of cash flow. In little more than a year, he banked money and thought of marrying Anne. He bought her a small diamond. Her father, a college professor who'd disapproved of her keeping company with a southern-talking boy who'd been merely a road salesman, came around and gave his blessing. For the honeymoon Leland opened his wallet and took Anne to Bermuda, where they stayed in a white cottage above a blue sea and he drank wine as if used to it. He had read up on wines to make no mistake . . .

. . . "The first thing I thought was I'll have to help that poor rebel boy pick out his clothes," Anne said. "And get him a proper haircut . . ."

. . . the boy half lowers his arms to stare at the lady wearing a black derby, a white blouse, fawn breeches, and black boots with silver spurs. She pulls the lunging horse around and makes it stand. It paws dust and walls its eyes. The lady smiles and says, Little boy, do you know the way to the Ballards? I've lost the trail. Yes'm, he says, and she reaches down for him, her long white fingers fastening around his wrist and drawing him upwards . . .

. . . as profits rose, Leland opened a second store and a third. He'd made connections with bankers and Digital Sciences, a pioneer manufacturer of computers who helped financing in return for pushing company products. He had an eye for hungry men like himself, workers willing to forget the clock. He hired them, and when they did well, he rewarded them with praise and bonuses. He opened savings accounts in the names of their children . . .

. . . "You're certain this is the way, you're not lost?" Anne asked as the pavement ended, though the road continued, hard-packed red clay that left a rooster tail of dust behind the Caddy. The road sloped downward, trash lying in ditches—cans, a rubber tire, parts of an old sofa, a refrigerator. Ahead Leland spotted the iron bridge, a single span, the superstructure once painted black now rusting. The weight limit had been reduced to five tons. When his wheels rolled over planks laid across girders, the sound to him resembled a troop of galloping cavalrymen. That's what he'd last imagined sitting beside his father, who drove a Ballard truck to Tobaccoton to buy repair parts for the Oliver tractor . . .

. . . *her hand pulling him behind her to the saddle, his bare legs squeezing the hot sweaty horse, this white woman so beautiful he thinks she had to be fallen from Heaven, who smells like lilies, like paradise itself must. The horse rears and circles. The lady gathers the reins and says, Little boy, wrap your arms around me and hold tight . . .*

. . . *a fourth store, and the house he bought after studying the real estate market, picking the brains of brokers. He walked streets to look at lawns, check schools, taste water, sniff air. He settled on the white Cape Cod with a large yard and sugar maples down an incline to a cold, purely running what he now called creek instead of branch. The house had three bathrooms. He punched floor joints using his pocketknife before finally agreeing to a sales contract . . .*

. . . "Will it hold us?" Anne asked of the bridge, leaning away from the door and toward him because of the span's height, rattle, and sway. Below, the river ran muddy from a recent rain upstream. Willow limbs dangled into water, streaking the flow which broke around a single boulder crusted brown . . .

. . . *he holds on for life as they surge toward the fence. The lady seems to lift the horse using her long narrow hands as if the great animal is a puppet to her fingers, and they curve over the fence, soar, and gallop toward the bottom. He closes his eyes, clenches them, his cheek pressed to the sweet female silkiness of her back, till she slows the horse and asks the way to the house. The boy fears letting go and indicates with a stab of his hand, causing the lady to laugh. A hank of yellow hair falls from beneath her derby, her teeth the whitest he's ever seen, her tongue the reddest. I know now, the boy thinks, what flying is like . . .*

. . . *Leland stood on his darkening lawn before the Cape Cod house where*

Jennifer was conceived and carried home to, the windows lighted, the grass shining. Thoughts of his delicate unblemished daughter made him drunk. He remembered a sister born at the cabin after the black midwife named Aunt Lulu plodded humpbacked across the plowed field and the males waited outside under the hackberry listening for the cry of new life, that same baby sister so tiny when buried she hardly filled a shoe box, the Baptist preacher offering her to the Lord, his hands raised as if she rested on his palms, the women's keening like wind. I will love and protect you, he spoke into the night, promising Jennifer. My house is strong, the roof tight, the many windows stars . . .

. . . "It was here?" Anne asked as they left the bridge and continued along the lowland road. Greenbrier, scrub pine, and kudzu had claimed the fields. Leland passed the place the cabin had stood, relieved it was no longer there. Not even a trace. He pulled to the ditch, cut his engine, and opened the door for Anne. Part of the hackberry remained, through broken and split, colored patches of lichen on dead limbs. He kicked among tangles of honeysuckle and found not a rotted plank, broken rail, or rusted plow point. "This doesn't appear like much of a spot for a house," Anne said. He knelt and crumbled a clod of hard dry soil between his shaky fingers . . .

. . . galloping toward the river, the speed bending trees, the corn, the land. Then another fence. The boy feels the horse gather. He ducks to protection of the lady's back. They shoot into the air, the horse stumbles on landing, and levels. A second time the lady laughs. I have my arms, he thinks, around a being I've never been near before and surely will never be near again . . .

. . . "And the cemetery?" Anne asked. There was none now, no slabs of rocks set up, no names and dates lettered on in white house paint. It had gone, either plowed under or swept away by gully washers. He tromped among wild growth, and his foot hit not a single stone. He thought of his mother, who'd at last stopped leaning on a hoe and had pulled on the coat with the torn fur collar to sit down at rest one final time . . .

. . . the big house on the highest ground, suspended above the river. The lady now knows the way, spurs the horse, who needs no urging. Sweating men picking field corn rise to wipe and watch. The boy peeps over her shoulder as the house grows larger and larger till it becomes the whole world. Black Amos hurries from a door to catch the reins of the blowing excited horse . . .

. . . "There was another house," Leland told Anne as he held her elbow to help her over the uneven ground to the car. He drove them down the road once forbidden, still magnolia-bordered, to the Kentucky gate, its posts in place. Wisteria snaked over walls and entwined pecan trees. The big house wasn't in disrepair, had no gutters hanging loose or broken windows, yet there was an air of loneliness. The formal gardens had grown up, the fountain was dry, and grapevines had become so heavy the bower sagged under their weight . . .

. . . the lady reaches around to the boy as he loosens his grasp of her. She swings him down to the cobblestones where Black Amos holds the horse. Then she too is off and brushes at her breeches. She removes her derby and lets the rest of her yellow hair fall free. You wait, little boy, she says, this fair kindly smiling lady who he later learns is Mr. Ballard's new wife from up north. She strides into the shadowy house where silver glistens. Her boots strike hard on polished floors. She comes back and presents it to him. Awed, his fingers close over it and clench so tightly they hurt . . .

. . . Leland's reaction when Jennifer told him she wanted to come south to college had been to deny her. On reflection he realized nothing could hurt her now, not after all these years, and Sweet Briar wasn't located in southside Virginia but not too far from Charlottesville, where money hummed almost as loudly and sped as fast as it did in Connecticut. No way could his daughter be wounded . . .

. . . "This was the family place?" Anne asked, thrilled by visions of past status and grandeur. From behind the house strode a man wearing brown laced boots and a blaze-orange hunting cap. He scowled, authority in his gait. "Private property," he called. "Didn't you see the signs?" Leland explained he'd once lived nearby, asked about the Ballards and Black Amos. The man's weathered, fretted face smoothed, and he spat. "I don't know," he said. "A timber company owns the property now." He was the caretaker. During fall and winter, men drove from cities to hunt doves, quail, deer, and ducks along the river. They used the house as a club. "The lady, the second wife?" Leland asked. "Never seen her," the caretaker said. "All the people who was around here is gone. They all gone . . ."

. . . *he runs from the big house down over the fields and jumps ditches, never opening his hand, squeezing the treasure it held. He runs faster and springs farther than ever in his life till he nears the cabin and stops panting in shade of a red oak. He has to pry his own fingers. They do not want him to see the sheen of a pure silver dollar, a coin he's never looked upon till this time, hardly known existed, like a magic ember placed into his palm . . .*

. . . "None of this was ever mine," he said to Anne, no longer fearing or able to profane what had vanished here, his blood, his bone. "I never liked the lying." Shocked, she stared as he told her about his mother's coat, the winters they'd eaten what whites called nigger food—chitlins, possum, groundhog he'd trapped. He voiced memory he'd hardly dared think before: his first day in school when the prim young female teacher from Lynchburg found lice in his hair and sent him home. As his father clipped his head using sheep shears, the girls' laughter rang off chimes of the blades . . .

. . . *ten months he keeps the silver dollar wrapped in a Bull Durham sack and buried in a Clabber Girl Baking Soda can under a Judas tree. At dusk he often slips to his cache to unwrap the treasure, just hold and feel it, let it catch a last light. He breathes on it and wipes it tenderly with the sleeve of a clean work shirt. But during the dry year when he sees his mother on her knees clawing the hard soil to dig a few misshapen rutabagas, guilt shames him. He carries the silver dollar to her, presents it on his washed palm, and she stands gawking as if witnessing the dead rising from their graves . . .*

. . . "All these years you've lied?" Anne asked, gazing at him like a woman who'd come across a stranger, or a lover who'd betrayed. He drove them away from the house. "It was a good lie well intended," he told her. "It worked for us. You ought to be able to live by it as I have . . ."

. . . *the silver dollar they spend for dried beans, a slab of fatback, flour, cornmeal, and a penny bag of horehounds, the mother's thanks given not in words but a trembling hesitant touch of those leached and scarred fingers through brown paper of the sack. They both watch Mr. Blackburn take the dollar, he also surprised, his arthritic hands tender upon it. He places it in the crank cash register, which has a bell that sounds like a prizefight gong. The boy and his mother walk the dusty road home, and he wakes during the night to see her standing at the window looking into flickers of lightning, her shoulders humping as she weeps among chirring pulses of crickets, katydids, and tree toads. Thunder and the drum of rain along the river. He'd never heard anybody cry like the lapping of water . . .*

. . . Ahead Leland saw a car at the side of the road, a four-door Dodge, reddish paint flaking from a rear fender, a red taillight smashed, the radio antenna bent. A youth gazed furiously into the engine well before ducking forward so far his feet lifted from the ground.

"You're not picking him up?" Anne asked, alarmed as Leland slowed. "He's black!"

"This is the South, not Yankeeland," he said, the words out before thought.

"I wouldn't brag too much on the South if I were you," she said, erect and distant from him. Her hand rose to lock her door. "Don't!"

But Leland stopped, put the Caddy in park, and stepped to the weed-fringed asphalt. The youth rocked from the engine well. He had a long intelligent face, corn-rowed hair, and wore harness-strap boots, jeans, and a midnight blue shirt that wound curlicues of golden thread across his chest, shoulders, and collar. He cursed because he'd smeared grease on a cuff. Steam hissed not from the radiator but the block itself.

"Can give you a lift if there's a garage around," Leland offered.

"Oh, they's garages," the youth said and kicked a fender. Caked red mud fell to the pavement and broke. "They's garages everywhere, prob'ly even in Hell, but they don't always help. Sometimes nothing helps when you got yourself a cracked fucking cylinder."

Anne had swiveled her body to look back at them. Leland lifted a hand to let her know everything was all right. Still she appeared anxious. He glanced at the Dodge's interior. It was packed for a trip, with clothes piled on seats, a boom box, sombrero, iron skillet, and a red-white-and-blue five-string guitar. There was also a handle of some sort, perhaps a rake or hoe.

"Tripping are you?" Leland asked.

"I was leaving I was. You know how far I got down this damn road? I got less than two miles down this damn road is how far I got. Once you in Howell County, you never gets out!"

He again kicked the fender. He wore a pearl-colored cowboy hat and a black belt that had a large Mexican silver buckle with a round artificial turquoise at its center. He cursed, punched the air, and turned away.

Why, Leland perceived, he's about to break. He will hunch, weep, and sob. The sight caused Leland's heart to squeeze, and he pictured youths leaving, all over the world, hundreds, thousands headed down alien roads to find what waited at the end. He saw himself. He reached into the jacket pocket of his light gray suit and drew from it the book of traveler's checks. He unclipped his pen. He walked to the Caddy's trunk, leaned over it, and signed a check. He crossed back to the youth.

"Any bank will cash it," he said. "Not silver dollars but almost as good."

"Silver who?" the youth asked, his plum-colored eyes staring at the check, gaping. "You bullshitting me, letting me have money not knowing I'll ever pay back?"

"Here's my address if you're flush one day," Leland said and gave the youth a card from his wallet. He returned to the Caddy, folded himself inside, and drove away. He glimpsed the youth in a rearview mirror looking after him and still holding the traveler's check with both hands, as if it might fly off.

"How much did you give him?" Anne asked, intense, squirming, fuming.

"Not enough to hurt us," Leland said.

She started to speak, closed her mouth firmly, and gripped her fingers on her lap. He steered listening to the sticky whine of tires rolling over and crackling on hot asphalt. He wondered how long she'd punish him, make him pay. Surely the bonds of their long marriage and Jennifer were strong enough to hold them together through this. He spied the junction where the four-lane route would lead them to tidewater Virginia and north to the other life.

At the stop sign, he gazed behind him, a last long look along the shimmering twisted road before entering traffic. His eye paused a moment on a tangled expanse of wildly flourishing trumpet vines dangling fiery orange blooms from askew locust posts and strands of rusted, broken barbed wire.